the
further
adventures of

SHERLOCK
HOLMES
THE GREAT WAR

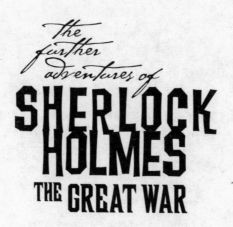

the further adventures of

SHERLOCK HOLMES
THE GREAT WAR

SIMON GUERRIER

TITAN BOOKS

THE FURTHER ADVENTURES OF SHERLOCK HOLMES:
THE GREAT WAR
Print edition ISBN: 9781789096941
E-book edition ISBN: 9781789096972

Published by Titan Books
A division of Titan Publishing Group Ltd
144 Southwark Street, London SE1 0UP

First Titan edition: November 2021
10 9 8 7 6 5 4 3 2 1

A CIP catalogue record for this title is available from the British Library.

Printed and bound by CPI Group (UK) Ltd, Croydon, CR0 4YY.

What did you think of this book? We love to hear from our readers.
Please email us at: readerfeedback@titanemail.com,
or write to Reader Feedback at the above address.

To receive advance information, news, competitions, and exclusive offers
online, please sign up for the Titan newsletter on our website:
www.titanbooks.com

In memoriam, THG.

Prologue

Archivist's Note

The following manuscript has been held among the JHW papers since at least 24 June 1921. A handwritten addendum of that date thought to have been made by Watson himself advises that it is "NEVER for publication".

However, one hundred years having elapsed, the executive board take the unanimous view that there is no longer any public interest in this testimony remaining secret. For more on its author, see files JHW 4112-17 and also her service record held at Kew.

Chapter One

By the first week of December 1917, I thought myself quite inured to the horrors of war. The men in our care had been variously torn up by bullets, shells and barbed wire, and there were often problems of infection, as well as from exposure to that perishing cold. In short, the demands on us in the hospital a few miles from Rebecq were constant and wide-ranging. I had been well schooled in the myriad ways that men might suffer.

Be assured, Dr Watson; I had not grown indifferent to the soldiers on our ward. As I am sure you must know from your own battlefield experience, one learns to roll up one's sleeves and pitch in. As a lowly VAD – a volunteer – I undertook tasks as dictated by the qualified staff of the Medical Corps. We worked long and challenging shifts in a fug of carbolic. I mopped, I scrubbed, I fetched and carried. Patients and equipment often had to be transported, and I pride myself that I mastered those recalcitrant wheeled beds. There was always something to be done – and I found it was always best to keep busy. No use to dwell, as others might, on what we could not alter.

That December was particularly harsh, with the conflict sure to drag on into yet another year. The weather was no less relentless, veering from gale to thunderstorm, which kept us largely trapped indoors. We did our best to keep chipper for the sake of the men.

Looking back, I realise how jittery we were, on the hop with nerves and edging towards crisis. There was never any respite. The persistent boom of artillery just two miles east would rattle the beds and equipment, and jog us as we handed out tea. One didn't hear the guns so much as feel them in one's bones and teeth. That and the work and just holding oneself together... Well, it was all rather exhausting. Days and nights bled together, and I almost sleepwalked through my duties – until that particular night.

I'd endured a twelve-hour shift and then, in the evening, stayed on to help Jill Sullivan, a kind-hearted RAMC nurse who had got behind with the medicines. She knew I could handle injections – and, unlike most of the qualified nurses, didn't resent me for it. I was glad to be useful, but by the end of all that it was well past nine and I was ready for some dinner and my crib. However, as I headed off the ward, Dulcie O'Brien caught up with me.

"Matron wants to see you, Gus," she said with cruel relish. "What can you have done?"

I couldn't think of anything, which didn't make me feel much better as I headed to the office.

Until hostilities started, our hospital had been a grand old country estate, all typically French faded grandeur. The army had taken it over, converting the kitchen and stables for use as operating theatres and knocking through the ground-floor galleries to form our enormous ward. It would never have done to lug injured servicemen up the grand staircase so the spacious rooms on the first floor became offices and accommodation. (The nurses got billeted two floors above that, in what had once been servants' quarters, and us orderlies had beds along the furthest wall, where there was the draught.)

I left the bustle of the ward, crossed the echoing marble of the magnificent entrance hall, and made my way up the stairs. The pretty cornflower wallpaper had begun to peel, discoloured with oblongs where huge paintings had once hung. I ascended into a whole other world: the lowing of wounded men giving way to the staccato clack of typewriters, even at such a late hour. Bulky metal filing cabinets filled the landing at the top of the stairs, enclosing the desks of the secretaries. One of these formidable maiden-aunt types knew I was expected and ushered me through into what had once been the library, the books now all cleared from the shelves and the space partitioned into narrow stalls that each contained a telephone. Beyond this was what had once been a boudoir. Now, an engraved metal plate declared it the domain of "Sister Gloria" – who we referred to as Matron.

I dusted down my apron, straightened my cap, knocked, and went straight in, as was the form in those days when we couldn't afford to waste time. The small, square room was wreathed in cigarette smoke, curling against the huge chart that filled the nearest wall. This chart was divided into narrow columns and rows, delineating the hours of all staff from consultants to cleaners. I always found it utterly captivating, having long had a passion for maps and timetables, but knew from experience that people found this alarming – an embarrassment to my class and my family. Thus, I made a determined effort to ignore the chart and focus on the diminutive figure enthroned behind her desk.

Matron was a tiny, wiry woman whose age I could never have guessed. A terrifying, compact mass of authority, we used to say

11

she was higher than God. Her deeply lined, expressive face was framed by a spotless coif headpiece. She never looked less than immaculate in the pale grey tunic of the Order of St Citha. Even the cigarette was poised elegantly in her hand.

"Augusta," she tutted. "You should be off-duty."

I wasn't sure how to respond. Did I really face reprimand for putting in a few extra hours? "Yes, Matron," I said.

"Well, I have need of you now."

I realised I had just lost even my paltry allocation of sleep. "Of course, Matron," I said.

She peered up at me, and I thought my tone might have betrayed my real feelings. It would not have been the first time I landed myself in trouble that way. I endeavoured to look suitably penitent.

"You will look after our guest," commanded Matron.

Until that moment, I had not been aware of anyone else in the room. The tall, gaunt man had been standing by the window the whole time, so perfectly still that I'd completely overlooked him. He was old, perhaps in his late sixties, silver hair slicked back from an expansive forehead. There was something familiar about this willowy, old figure, as if a character from Dickens had been rendered in flesh.

"G-good evening, sir," I said, annoyed to be so shaken. He said nothing but his dark, intelligent eyes picked over me. It was chillingly unnerving, like being watched by a spider. I turned back to Matron, who regarded the man sourly.

"You will show him the ward, answer his questions, and render all service," she instructed me. "Let him see how we meet the challenges of the work here. We have nothing to hide. And we welcome any suggestions on how we might improve."

This last part she said quite acidly but the man did not respond.

"It's late," she told me crossly, as if this were somehow all my fault. "You had best get on."

"Yes, Matron. If you'd care to come this way, sir." The man bowed almost mockingly at Matron and followed me out.

We frequently had visitors, of course – men from the Home Office and its various satellites, bigwigs from the army, sometimes even relatives of the wounded men. The official lot would trail round the ward with their clipboards, trying to spot our lapses of protocol. The important thing, Matron drilled into all of us, was that we demonstrated our ability, and left the dignitaries with the sense that a great deal more might be possible with only a little more resource.

Even so, it was highly unusual to have a visitor call so late at night and without any warning. Also, I could not think of a single occasion when a visitor had been put in the charge of a lowly VAD such as myself, rather than a senior nurse or even one of the doctors. It was all very irregular and would only give the nurses another reason to accuse me of not knowing my place. I rather relished the prospect of annoying them as I led the old man down the grand staircase.

At that hour, things on the ward were relatively quiet and subdued, which was the worst luck, I thought. We spent our working hours battling to achieve such orderly calm, but it hardly conveyed an impression of hard graft.

"You'll have to remove your jacket," I told the man as we stopped at the main desk. There were sanitary reasons, but this was also an old trick I had seen the nurses use to establish authority. Some visitors objected, but the old man gamely slipped off his suit jacket and was already rolling up his shirtsleeves before I had the chance to say so. I took the jacket from him to hang up on one of the hooks, and noted something odd. Though I am hardly an expert on gentleman's tailoring, I could tell immediately that it was an item of quality and tastefully cut. Yet one sleeve was rough against my bare hand, the fabric discoloured by an old stain. As a VAD, I knew the damage that can be done to clothing – and the people inside – by certain volatile chemicals. I had, however, never met anyone who would suffer such a thing and then continue to wear the same suit, no matter how well made.

Had he bought a damaged garment cheaply? No – I couldn't believe that. Like my brothers and their friends, he exuded that easy self-confidence only money can provide.

Recovering myself, I headed to the sink. The man joined me and watched the manner in which I thoroughly scrubbed my hands. As I reached for the towel, he repeated the procedure himself, without needing to be prompted. His fingers were long and rather graceful, but with that unnerving, spider-like quality. I glanced round and saw some nurses watching from the desk. They, too, had never known a visitor – a man – wash his hands so diligently without being directed to do so. He had still not said a word.

"Can we help you?" asked Dulcie O'Brien, stalking over and entirely blanking me.

"Matron asked me to show this visitor the ward," I told her. Dulcie sighed at our guest, as if this were completely unthinkable.

"Someone properly qualified should show you round," she said.

"Is there such a man on duty?" asked the visitor, mildly.

Dulcie's smiled faltered. "Not just now, sir, but one of the nurses…"

"I'm sure one girl is as good as another," he sighed.

Dulcie now turned to me as if, in his rude way, the visitor had accepted her offer. Had she been a little nicer, I would have gladly surrendered him into her care. As it was, I thought she could go to hell. This man might be hatefully chauvinist, but he was also *mine*.

"Matron instructed me specifically," I said. "You could take it up with her."

Dulcie glared at me. "Oh, I will," she said.

I would surely pay for it later, but it was a thrill to watch Dulcie skulk back to the desk where the other sour-faced nurses waited. Under their withering gaze, I led the visitor on to the ward proper, heading down the aisle between the lines of beds.

"There are thirty-two beds on each side," I told him. "Equally spaced to maximise the number we can accommodate, while allowing us space to get around each patient and administer to their needs. It's also important to maintain some distance to stop the spread of infection."

He didn't seem to be listening. Many visitors had the same reaction, a visceral shock on seeing what we dealt with. There were the missing limbs, the damage to men's faces, the smell you got from trench foot. It was all the more uncanny at that late hour, the men sleeping but hardly at peace. They muttered and twitched in their beds.

I ought to have led the visitor through to the side corridor where he might compose himself. There were private rooms there, reserved for the officers or the most horrifically wounded, but it was also quiet and out of the way. Most visitors needed only a short pause to rally themselves; it was simply that our work took some getting used to.

But the old man didn't seem in the least bit appalled. His features were taut, his lips thin, his eyes glittering with interest as he took in every detail. He looked with *fascination* on one patient, Sergeant Oberman, who'd lost a leg and most of one arm. Oberman glared back at him, rightly indignant at being treated as an exhibit.

"We do our best for them," I said as I led the visitor away.

Behind us, Laurence Oberman blew a raspberry. "That en't even true."

The visitor turned back with interest but I caught his arm. "Pay it no heed," I told him. "The wounded are often irascible."

"It is one thing to feel aggrieved at one's own ill fortune," said the man, "but that is not what he claimed." Lightly, he extracted his arm from me and went over to Oberman. "What," he said, "is not true?"

If he'd had any sense, Oberman would have apologised, but cornered like this he decided to stick to his guns. "She said they do their best for us, din't she? But really all they do is what's best for the machine. They patch us up so they can send us back to the trenches. 'Alf of me's gone and yet they're on about finding me something so's I can still be useful!" He tried to sit up, over-balanced and almost fell out of bed.

"Now, Sergeant Oberman," I chided, hurrying over before he could do himself a mischief. "It's after lights-out and you need to recuperate." A man missing a leg and most of his arm is still surprisingly heavy, and Oberman resisted my efforts to help. I got an arm under his shoulder and braced my body against his to stop him falling out of bed, but with the sheets rucked up behind him, I couldn't move him back. We were left prone, in an awkward stalemate.

Then the visitor was on the other side of the bed and curtly tugged the under-sheet out from beneath Oberman, the action tipping the balance so that he fell away from where I held him and rolled back across the bed. The old man neatly stopped him with just the tips of his fingers on the young man's shoulder and hip. I tucked in the blanket and we had Oberman securely back in bed – as quick and smooth as a conjuring trick.

"Obliged, thank ye," said Oberman, quiet now from embarrassment, and settled back as if asleep. The old man looked keen to ask more questions, but I ushered him away,

"The thing is, Oberman would go back to the trenches in an instant if he could," I said, keeping my voice low to rein in my anger. "We keep him here and we care for him, and we get all his resentment as thanks. We really don't just patch them up and churn them out again like some blessed factory!"

The man brooded for a moment. "What makes you think he is so keen to return to the front?"

"I know, it's insanity, but I think he feels so wretched as he is."

"And he is thinking of his friends out there," said the visitor. "They signed up together, didn't they? Right at the start of the war."

"I gather there are only three of them left," I said. And then it hit me. "However did you know?"

The visitor glanced back at Oberman, now lying quietly in his bed. "I observed," said the man.

I looked from him to Oberman but could discern nothing of note. The visitor saw me struggling – and failing – to see, and he sighed.

"To reach the rank of sergeant," he said, "Oberman must have been in the army for some time. Yet he retains the dialect and accent of his native Wiltshire. That would have been drummed out of him in officer training, where they like things to be uniform. Therefore he did not attend officer training of the old sort, but was promoted on merit while here. Indeed, his accent has withstood time spent among men from all the regions of the kingdom, and all the classes, too. That is suggestive of his having a core around him, of men of his own sort and from the same area. One has read of the pals who signed up together. And then your remark that he would gladly return to the front, despite what he has clearly already been through."

He rattled through this explanation speedily enough, though it was not of the least consequence. But when he finished, he seemed most put out that I did not applaud.

"This brave man's story should not be used as the basis for some amusing parlour trick, Mr Sherlock Holmes," I told him plainly.

Chapter Two

Oh yes, I knew Sherlock Holmes all right. He had seemed familiar that first moment I saw him, and then there had been that show of contemptible chauvinism. Yet it was only now, in showing off his powers, that I placed exactly who he was. The great detective. The famous misogynist. A man to whom violent crime was as amusing as a crossword.

Naturally, this was not the response that Holmes expected, or indeed was used to. I delighted in seeing him lose that insufferable smile. He was older than the familiar portrait used in *The Strand*, of course. In the flesh, Holmes is less heroic in aspect, more gaunt than angular, less arresting to the eye. He was – or he had the capacity to be – rather unremarkable, a man not worthy of a second glance. I suppose that fits: such facility must be of great value in his line of work.

His dark brows furrowed. "I usually have a good memory for faces," he said, irritated that he could not remember me. "I take it we have met before."

"No," I told him. "Never."

"Then you take against my judgement in one or other case. You feel I should have allowed some particular criminal to abscond, or there are those whom I did not detain that you know should have gone to the gallows." He flapped a hand dismissively, for he had no time for the opinions of the hoi polloi.

"Such matters are not a game," I told him. "That is what offends me – not a particular case but your attitude as a whole."

He studied me for a moment, picking over the details I presented. Without make-up – which staff were not permitted to wear – I felt rather exposed, and was ever more self-conscious as he scrutinised the way I tied my hair beneath my cap, and the brooch partially hidden by my apron. Yet whatever he deduced from these clues, he only smiled. Of course, I wanted to know his conclusions but I would rather have died than ask him. This was all a divertissement to him and I refused to play along.

Instead, I swept past him to continue the tour of the ward. Holmes came after me but had little interest in the arrangement of beds by relative ailment.

"You really are offended," he said. "We have never met and yet your antipathy could not be clearer. That is a disappointment, as I thought..." He trailed off.

Now I really was astonished. "You thought we might be friends!" Then I realised why, and could barely hide my fury. "Because my name amused you! Another of your games."

"Nurse Watson–" he began.

"You are wrong there, Mr Holmes," I told him. "I am just a VAD."

He clearly did not like to be corrected. "Miss Watson," he said impatiently. "Since you know my reputation, you must surely know that my friend Dr Watson is the very best of men."

"Must I?" I responded coldly. Holmes seemed hurt by this.

"He is at least a better man than me. My spirits rose upon seeing your name on the board in Sister Gloria's office. I am not by custom one for good omens, but in these dark days one must take what small comfort one can. Therefore, I suggested to Sister Gloria that there was some familial connection between you and my friend."

"You lied," I said. "There isn't one."

"Not by blood, perhaps," persisted Holmes. "But I can see you share something of his temperament. His military and medical background, too."

I whipped round at him, angrily. "You don't know the first thing about me! I am not a soldier, and I am not a nurse, just some silly girl who thought she might escape the tedium of home and instead ended up mopping floors. Orderlies are very much *not* on the medical staff – as you will find the nurses only too glad to tell you."

Yet that insufferable, awful man shook his head. "The brooch is the giveaway, of course," said Holmes. "Women's Volunteer Reserve. A most singular organisation, established by a pair of radical Suffragettes keen to prove that women are the equal of men, and so their recruits were drilled just as ordinary soldiers, trained as mechanics and whatever else. By some margin, the WVR offered the most interesting engagements to any woman seeking to enrol for war work. Yet this radical outfit also did not start with much money, so recruits had to supply their own uniforms and kit. That, of course, limited their intake to the wealthier classes. I expect that must have led to quite an education for all parties – the well-to-do in with the radicals!"

"We already campaigned for the vote," I said. "Besides, the reserve was more practical than that. They taught us to shoot, and drive, and how to mend an engine. Though none of that's done me any good out here – my training might even have been a hindrance for being so unconventional. Matron has rather old-fashioned views about that sort of thing. I thought I'd be nursing or even driving an ambulance, saving men from the thick of the fighting and learning skills I could use after the war. There's barely been any of that."

"You're still doing a valuable and much-needed job," said Holmes.

"Are you offering to help?" I was angry with him, and impatient to be rid of him, but he only smiled.

"If I am able, then yes. I am here to observe the important work you do here and, where I can, make some suggestions for improvement. Any small advance would be of value to the war effort and, more importantly, lessen the suffering of the men." He studied me for a moment. "You don't believe me," he said. "Perhaps you'd care to explain."

Cursing myself for this inability to hide my true feelings, I decided there was little to lose by telling him exactly what I thought. "We have hosted plenty of visitors before," I told him, "and they have all faced the same problem. We are not a typical hospital. The shape of the building means we have had to adapt certain procedures. That has the consequence that any observations you might make here, any suggestions for improvement, cannot be more generally applied. There are model hospitals further down the line that would better suit inspection of that kind. But you, Mr Holmes, have come here."

"I could have been to these other hospitals first," he said.

"With all this rain and mud? Your suit and shoes are much too clean. Then there's the time of your arrival. Why be here so late, unless you travelled with the post van from the dock. That suggests you came directly from your ship."

Now his nostrils flared. "I came in an aeroplane. A most singular experience; I rather recommend it. But on all other points you are correct. Very good, Miss Watson. Very good indeed."

"Then you are here, at our particular hospital, on a case. Has there perhaps been a murder?"

This I said with heavy irony because it seemed quite ridiculous, given the ongoing slaughter. Yet Holmes stroked a finger over his lips, considering what he might divulge. His eyes darted left and right to ensure we were not overheard.

"Not quite, but it is a matter of some singular interest – and of a sensitive nature, given the war. You were on duty on the night of the first of November."

I almost laughed. "That feels like an age ago, Mr Holmes. I would have to check."

He smiled that thin-lipped smile. "The staff rota is perfectly simple. One need merely read the arrangement for the present week and then count in reverse."

It took me a moment to understand the implication. "That's what you did in Matron's office. It is why you asked for me – not just the coincidence of my name."

He nodded. "It felt auspicious. You were on duty on the night of the first of November, when a young officer died here. I should be obliged if you could recall the details."

I stared at him in astonishment. "You think I'm a witness," I said.

"That remains to be seen. But you have already demonstrated some skill in observation, so I should be grateful for your memories of that evening and any insight you might share."

"I've already told you, it might as well have been another age. One shift is very much like another." I stiffened. "A lot of young officers have died."

Holmes snorted, frustrated by this response. "Nothing remarkable stands out in the memory?"

"What was the young man's name?"

To my surprise, Holmes walked smartly away from me and headed out of the ward, not even sparing a glance to the nurses at the desk. They stared in astonishment, wondering what on earth I might have said – since they knew my ability to say exactly the wrong thing. To escape their scorn and questions, I hurried after Holmes, my face hot with annoyance.

He made for the coat stand, but left his jacket hanging and merely pulled from the pocket a bulging pocket book, from which he plucked a photograph. The oval image showed a bright-eyed, handsome young man in uniform.

"Captain Philip Ogle-Thompson," said Holmes. "Average height, a physique from playing rugby, which also left him without his upper left canine. You can't see that in the picture, but I'm told the missing tooth gave him an engaging, raffish look. The sort of fellow who might make an impression on a young lady."

Holding the photograph in my hands, I willed myself to draw some small scrap of memory, anything at all. But I'd meant what I had told him: a lot of young officers died, and they soon blended one with another.

"I could show this to the nurses," I suggested. "They often have more direct contact with the men." Holmes seemed torn, uncertain that he should share the nature of his enquiry any more widely, but also keen for information. Reluctantly, he consented, and I left him by the coat rack while I went to the main desk.

I was not exactly made welcome. Dulcie O'Brien was no longer with them, but they smarted from the way Holmes had spoken to her before. It was, of course, somehow my fault.

Jill Sullivan saved me, reminding them that I should be in bed and had only been caught by Matron because I'd helped Jill after the end of my shift. The other nurses didn't like that, and one said I shouldn't do nursing work anyway. But they contented themselves to look at the photograph, if only to tell me that they couldn't help. Jill, again, was kind. "Tell his dad of course we remember, and that he was very brave."

I did not want to correct her and explain who Holmes really was, so I patted her arm and said this would be of great comfort to our visitor. Returning to Holmes, I said rather loudly, "Of course we remember Captain Ogle-Thompson. A very brave boy, an inspiration to some of the other men who were here at the time." Holmes, to his credit, played along with this, bowing his head in the manner of a grateful but grieving father.

"Thank you," he told me softly. "There is nothing more to be done if you cannot remember. You may deliver me back to Sister Gloria."

That was like ice through me. He would surely convey to Matron that I had failed to provide what he wanted, and thus confirm her prejudice against me. Entirely out of pride, I wanted to prove myself to this insufferable man – and an idea suddenly struck me.

"We'll just see," I said loudly, so Jill and the other nurses would hear, "which doctor attended him, so you know who to thank."

Holmes beamed at me, delighted, and then remembered his role. Meekly, mournfully, he followed me to the bank of filing cabinets at the end of the ward. A number of thick, leather-bound ledgers were arranged on top, and I quickly found the relevant volume. The leather cracked as I opened the front page, and dashed through the pages to the end of October. I ran my finger down the long list of names, pausing at each red X, which indicated death. There was no Ogle-Thompson.

Holmes leaned eagerly forward to scrutinise the list. "He died on the first of November," he said.

"Yes," I replied archly. "And if he was ever on the ward, it would have been before he died. So we check the preceding entries."

Holmes flashed a smile – he enjoyed either being challenged or my lack of patience. We turned again to the book. "No Ogle, no Thompson, and nothing that might be a misheard or misspelled version. Might we skip a little further back, in case he was on the ward for some time?"

We checked all of October, and September – which meant looking in the previous volume. Then Holmes looked through the lists for November, just to be doubly sure.

"Nothing," I concluded. "I'm afraid he can't have been here."

Holmes considered, then took out his pocket book and withdrew a folded piece of paper, which proved to be a handwritten letter – but from whom I could not tell, because he concealed much of it with his hand. All he allowed me to see was a sentence towards the end, in clear and elegant fountain pen:

> *Philip died at peace, on the ward of the hospital on*
> *Rue St Julienne, a credit to his battalion.*

I read it over more than once just to be quite sure.

"It's not an official account of his death," I concluded. "I don't suppose you can tell me who wrote it."

Holmes gave the briefest shake of his head with an apologetic smile. I studied the sentence again.

"Why say this if it isn't what happened?" I said.

Again, Holmes smiled. "Exactly. Perhaps it is perfectly innocent, or at least well meant. But there is a mystery here, and it is not the only curious aspect."

He was thrilled by the problem before us – and, I realised, so was I. More than that, I enjoyed him being dependent. In that moment, I was greater than his equal. This brilliant, exasperating man relied entirely on my assistance – and, in fact, I could help him.

"Mr Holmes," I said, "I think I know where we should look – but it is rather against the rules."

He beamed at me. "Miss Watson, you have my attention."

Chapter Three

❧

The shadow cast by the grand staircase in the entrance hall concealed a door in the wood panelling below. When closed, the door would be imperceptible to anyone who did not already know it existed, but since the house had been converted into a hospital, we kept it propped open with a statue of an ancient nymph caught in a state of undress. She was a favourite of the men, a lucky totem they said, and those in charge saw fit to indulge them.

I made every effort to exude confidence as I led Sherlock Holmes past the nymph and into the service corridor, hoping that my bearing alone would suggest we had reason to be there. After all, I told myself, Matron had instructed me to assist our eminent visitor in his enquiries. I was merely following that instruction – even if it meant going somewhere out of bounds.

Our luck held and no one interceded. We passed swiftly through the hidden door and into the passage beyond. Our footsteps were loud on the bare stone floor and it felt immediately cold. Naked bulbs hung at intervals, the stark light glaring. The walls were dusty with whitewash, a series of horizontal gouges revealing old grey brick beyond. The damage had been done by beds wheeled through in haste, on their way to theatre – that is, the kitchen as it had been in the days before the war. The powerful, chalky odour was tinged with blood and disinfectant.

I had often been down this passageway when my duties required, ferrying patients on their way to and from operations, sometimes even remaining in the theatre with them if so instructed by the doctors. Yet it was no less disquieting for being familiar. Indeed, the smell conjured images of many awful scenes I had witnessed. Every time I entered the passageway, my skin prickled with goose flesh. Now, being here without express permission, my heart skipped with apprehension – and, I admit, some excitement.

We followed the passage, joining up with another corridor and then heading right. I knew the route through this rabbit warren by heart, but Holmes could have easily followed the gouge marks in the wall that led us to the theatre. The double doors stood open and Isaac Robinson, one of my fellow orderlies, shunted a mop across the tiled floor, too caught up in his task to notice us sweep past. We continued down the passage to what looked like a dead end of impassive grey brick. Inset into the corner was an ordinary, unadorned door.

I reached for the bulb of the handle, mindful not to make the slightest sound with Isaac close around the corner. The handle turned easily but the door held fast. I tried again, turning in the other direction, and still the door would not budge. I dared to rattle the handle, as if it would yield to insistence. Then I stepped back, biting my lip in frustration.

"Locked," I said, mouthing the word rather than speaking it.

Holmes stepped neatly forward and crouched in front of the lock. His joints cracked loudly in the echoing space, yet he moved rather nimbly for his age, that spider-like grace I had observed before. He studied the keyhole as if appraising an Old Master's brushwork, then produced a twist of wire from his pocket and prodded it into the gap.

"Whatever are you doing?" I said, appalled, but keeping my voice low.

"A simple enough mortice lock," he concluded. "As if they do not really intend to keep anyone out."

"Mr Holmes," I whispered urgently, "you really can't think to break in."

He looked up at me in surprise. "Miss Watson, this was your suggestion. I merely follow as you direct."

My cheeks burned but I refused to let him turn this round on me. "This is criminal! We will both find ourselves in a great deal of trouble!"

His eyes glimmered with mischief. "Only if we are caught." He turned his attention back to the lock. It took a little jiggling, but I heard the catch turn and the door squeaked inwards. Had he not done it so quickly, I might have made a better case for returning to the ward. As it was, the door stood open before us, and the answer to our mystery surely lay beyond.

Holmes leant on the wall for support as he got unsteadily back to his feet; I knew better than to try and help him. Sweat beaded on his brow from the exertion, but he looked elated, enjoying this nefarious enterprise. He also saw my disquiet.

"You could return to the ward," he said. "Perhaps say you have mislaid me. I am sure I can convince them I am a confused old man who went and got himself lost."

Resenting the implication that I was afraid, I folded my arms in the stern manner I reserved for the men when they showed too much cheek. "You seem willing to commit burglary while I am standing right with you. Who knows what you might stretch to if I allow you out of my sight?"

Holmes beamed. "Who indeed? Very well then, you had best stay at my side. Follow me…"

But I pointedly went ahead of him into the dark. This was my hospital and, as he said, it had been my idea. I would not now surrender territory, especially not to this man.

There was no illumination and I could not locate a light switch, but the lights in the corridor were enough to see the top of the spiral staircase leading down into further murk. A rope banister hung loosely from metal hoops set in the wall. I took this in one hand and with the other held on to the damp-slick wall. Then there was nothing for it but to descend into total black.

I went gingerly, tracing each step with my foot before committing my weight to it. Holmes followed close behind, I'm sure smiling conceitedly. The steps were a little uneven. My heart was in my mouth as we went on.

Then there came a rising stench, a stomach-churning, meaty tang. I felt my gorge rising, my mouth suddenly dry. Had I been able to see anything in that pitch darkness, I'm sure my vision would have swum. All I could do was cling tighter to the rope.

My eyes had grown more accustomed to the cloying dark by the time we reached the foot of the steps and emerged into a wide space under a low, vaulted ceiling. Ominous blocks were arranged at regular intervals before us.

I started at a sudden sound behind and to my left, but it was Holmes, exploring. He found a light switch and suddenly we were blinded. The harsh light from yet more unshaded bulbs did not make the room any less unnerving. The blocks I had seen in the gloom were rows of narrow tables. On most of them lay corpses, not all of them covered by sheets. One boy lay in his muddy uniform but without his boots, his bare feet sickly blue. Instinctively, I wanted to find him a blanket, to offer some little comfort. His sightless eyes stared accusingly up at the bare-brick ceiling.

Yet Holmes spared barely a glance for the morgue's unfortunate residents. At a nod from me, he stalked over to the desk in one corner.

"What should I be looking for?" he asked me.

"They have a register of the same kind as we use upstairs."

I made to help him go through the papers and files arranged at one side of the desk, but Holmes raised a finger in warning. "It might be better if you were not involved."

"It's a little late for that, Mr Holmes."

"If someone comes in, you can be over there and not quite realise what I've been up to."

"The next shift doesn't start until six. You do not need to protect me. I am not some damsel in distress."

"No, indeed. But it is perfectly logical, Miss Watson. There is no reason why we should both be in trouble when one of us will suffice. Your duties aid the war effort, whereas I am more expendable."

Annoyingly, I could think of no argument against this. I do not think he acted from gallantry, however; he wanted me out from under his feet. When he withdrew his twist of wire again, I felt the same sudden chill at the prospect of criminal enterprise. "Wait," I said, before he could prise open the cabinet. "Why not put this matter before Matron? She could permit us to search – and give us the key."

Holmes stood perfectly still, the wire at the lock on the cabinet. "Indeed she could," he conceded. "We could have done that as soon as we found the discrepancy in the register on your ward. Yet your immediate thought was to lead me down here – in a manner verging on the clandestine."

I stared at him in astonishment. "I was trying to help you."

"Precisely. And the singular fact is that you thought it would be of more assistance to my inquiry *not* to consult the authorities. Isn't that so?"

"I do not know what you are talking about!"

He grew impatient. "Miss Watson, I cannot help you if you will not be honest with yourself."

I hated him. How dare he presume to know my thoughts better than I did.

"You are wrong," I told him. "There is nothing at all. Only…" The word slipped out unbidden and I saw Holmes's eyes light up. "It is nothing, really," I added quickly. "You saw it with Laurence Oberman, and perhaps with the nurses as well. Ill-feeling pervades the very air. I don't know how to characterise it more precisely, just a pall of something wrong. But then I suppose that's to be expected. We are weary, in the midst of winter, and it has already been a long war. What else might one expect?"

Holmes regarded me indulgently. Again, I felt that anger at him for treating this all as some amusing pastime. He seemed to read that, too, and meekly bowed his head.

"Miss Watson, you have already demonstrated some skill at observation. I advise you to trust your instincts. There is something afoot here and I suspect it may be very serious. If there is indeed some reason not to trust the authorities, it will have considerable bearing on the conduct of the war." Then he smiled a wolfish smile. "Or, as you say, it may be some trifling error and easily explained. How satisfied you will be when I am shown to be wrong. Yet to uncover the truth either way, we must have more data. Thus, I must continue."

I barely nodded but that was all the licence Holmes required. He inserted the twist of wire and smoothly unlocked the first cabinet. Despite his words to me, I felt suddenly afraid, watching this violation carried out with such cold efficiency. Holmes at least worked quickly. He scoured through files, then closed and relocked the cabinet before moving on to the next one.

A row of cabinets awaited his attentions. Had I tried to help, I would only have got in his way and made the endeavour take longer. Instead, I dared to look again at the room around us – not at the bodies, but at the furniture that served them. On the previous occasions when I had been in this room, we were always busy and had no opportunity to look round. Now I could take in the workings. A hoist operated by great wheels brought the bodies down from the theatre directly above. There were garage doors at the back of the room, which I knew led out to a ramp behind the building. Ice glittered on the window frames. We prided ourselves on the care we provided to the men upstairs but this all felt coldly mechanical. The poor men laid out in this dismal place deserved better. Of course, the officers did: the men here were all ordinary soldiers, an underclass even in death. I felt it then, a powerful resolve – we *would* do better for them.

"Ah, I think this might be it," said Holmes. He had uncovered a leather-bound book very much like the index we kept up on the ward. I joined him as he traced a finger down page after page, checking the long list of names. Methodically, he checked every entry from the end of August to midway through November.

"No Ogle-Thompson," he concluded. "Again, nothing that could possibly be him, either."

"That can only mean he wasn't at this hospital," I concluded. "He was neither brought in alive and taken to the ward, nor brought in dead and delivered down here. Perhaps he was taken somewhere else – central records ought to hold that information."

"They do not hold any such record."

"Then he might have died out on the field. I'm afraid we don't recover all the bodies. It's ghastly, but it's true."

"Supposing that were the case, why then were the poor man's family informed that Ogle-Thompson died on the ward? That surely suggests a slower, more agonising death than to be killed in action. It would be needlessly cruel."

Yes, the very thought appalled. "Who wrote that letter?" I said.

Holmes brushed that aside. "We should go back upstairs before we are missed."

"Up there, we cannot talk freely. Please, the least that you owe me for risking my neck and bringing you down here is to tell me what this is about."

He considered, his eyes fixed upon me with that same unsettling, cold scrutiny as before. Then he reached into his jacket for the pocket book and withdrew the notepaper. This time, he did not attempt to conceal any of what it contained and simply handed it over. That was, I readily understood, a significant show of trust.

The thick paper was of good quality, the copper plate impeccable.

Convent St Citha
Near Rubecq
France

Monday, 5th November

Mrs Raymond Ogle-Thompson
Tomb Acre House

Belgravia Square
London

My dearest Julia,
A few short words cannot convey my depth of feeling in this awful moment but truly I am sorry. I also know all too well from experience the cold effect of that telegram, and that one pines for more information. So:
At a little after 4 o'clock on the morning of Thursday, 1st November, Philip and his unit came under enemy fire. I am assured they fought bravely but that casualties were sustained. You should be proud to know how Philip helped carry one wounded man back to safety and returned for another — whereupon he himself was wounded. His injuries were grave but he remained cogent, issuing commands that helped save the lives of his men. They have sorely felt his loss. Philip died at peace, on the ward of the hospital on Rue St Julienne, a credit to his battalion.
Be proud of him. When I am next in London I would be happy to call upon you and perhaps answer any questions, though as I am sure you intuit, I cannot tell at present when that might be. With much sorrow,
·R —

I did not want to stoop to asking Holmes whose illegible signature closed the letter. Just to spite him, I approached the question as logically as he might. First, there was the matter of who would have been in a position to write it. The letter made no indication that its author had known this Ogle-Thompson in person, yet they had the authority to elicit information from those who had been with him as he died. There was an obvious candidate beginning with R.

"General Rayner Fitzgerald," I said, handing the letter back to Holmes, and was gratified by his look of surprise.

"You know him well, I take it."

"We have never met," I said. "To the best of my knowledge, the general has never been to the hospital."

"I see. You rather think he should."

Once again, my tone had betrayed my true feelings. "I am sure the general has many demands on his time," I said. "Yet not to once visit the men in our care does seem a little brusque."

Holmes responded with interest. "Then that is his character. A man not known for social graces. He is therefore not the sort who would normally, without prompting, write to a grieving mother."

I almost laughed. "Mr Holmes, I really couldn't say. I do not know the general."

So saying, I refolded the letter and handed it back. Holmes tucked it into the pocket book but he wasn't finished yet. He withdrew a second slip, this time on paper of lesser quality, ruled with lines. "This second – anonymous – letter was received the day after the one from the general," he said, showing me the blocky scrawl across it.

Sirs
Whatever you is informed dont believe it.
In truth, your son Cpn Thompson was a good
man and soldier, as his full record will show.
He saved my life and others to my knowing.

A honest friend

"You note," said Holmes, "that it gives no details as to the manner of the death, yet begs the family not to believe what they might be told. It is unsigned, but the style and novel use of grammar are suggestive. The author either has or wishes us to believe him to have only moderate education."

"It doesn't say the general is lying," I said.

"Neither do I," said Holmes. "We should be very careful on that point. But somewhere in all this, we are missing the truth."

"Someone has muddled things," I said, "perhaps mixed up two different men. That can easily happen, I'm sure." Then another thought struck me. "But you must have considered that. And yet here you are, in France."

Holmes smiled again. Yes, he rather liked to be challenged, even by a woman – a thing rare indeed among men of my acquaintance. "Ogle-Thompson's father is himself a distinguished officer. He served in Afghanistan with Watson. I mean, *my* Watson. It was on his behalf that I hoped to help dispel the family's concerns with a few discreet inquiries."

That made a certain sense – so much of men's business was conducted through such personal connections. I could well imagine the matter being arranged over port at one of their odious clubs.

"What will you report to them now?" I said.

Holmes looked surprised. "Oh, I have not completed my investigation. However, I do not think there is anything more to be learned down here, and I would not wish to land you in hot water. We should return upstairs."

He placed the register back in the cabinet, which he locked, and we made our way upstairs. Holmes led, darting up the steps so I had to run to keep up with him. Try as I might, I could not think where he might try next in his inquiries – but I was eager to find out.

At the top of the stairs, we stopped just inside the door and listened keenly for any sound. There did not seem to be anyone in the passageway, so we dared to step out and Holmes used his wire to lock the door behind us. He seemed exhilarated by this chicanery and had to make an effort to calm himself, adopting once more the persona of an old and respectable dignitary. In that guise, we hobbled back to the ward.

We emerged from the passageway under the stairwell without being intercepted. There were nurses on the desk at the entrance to the ward, and as they saw us there was an edge to their smiles that I didn't like one bit. Perhaps because they were watching, Holmes turned to me and bowed.

"It has been very informative, thank you, Miss Watson," he said, with a tremor in his voice that made him sound rather frail. "Now, I had best allow you to return to your important work."

Of course, I should have expected nothing more. Who was I to this famous man and his investigation? Merely a potential witness who was no longer of use. Yet I confess I had allowed myself to get caught up in his mystery, and it came as quite a wrench to be so easily dismissed. I endeavoured to maintain my composure, not wanting to make a scene.

"You are very welcome, Mr Holmes," I said. "Should I show you back to Matron?"

"I don't think that will be necessary," he said, and pointed.

The cluster of nurses had obscured my view. Now they hurried back round the desk and I saw why they had watched me with such interest. Two figures were on the ward, coming forward into the light. Straight away, I recognised the diminutive silhouette of Matron. The towering bulk beside her took me a moment longer. He was a large, solid man, his round, red face framed by impressive whiskers. I had seen them caricatured in the 'papers passed between the men, the great fellow made to look like a walrus. There was nothing in the least bit comical about him in person, on the ward at long last – and bearing down upon me.

"A general," said Holmes to me, reading the insignia on the man's uniform as he approached. Then he turned quickly to me. "Could this man possibly be..."

"Yes," I told him. "This is General Rayner Fitzgerald."

Chapter Four

∽

"We feared we might have lost you, Mr Holmes," said the general, extending a pudgy, thick hand. "Rayner Fitzgerald. This is my patch, so to speak. No offence to you ladies. Well, Holmes, I trust you've peeked into all our cracks and crevices, and found nothing untoward."

For all the jollity of his words, he was a big man and stood a little too close to Holmes, his height and bulk enough to intimidate most people. Indeed, I took a small step back from this imposing figure. Holmes merely smiled agreeably.

"This is a very fine facility, general. A credit to its staff." He bobbed his head respectfully at Matron, who glowered back at him but did not respond. This was not, I realised, out of respect for the detective. Rather, Matron hovered behind the general, demurring to his authority. I had never seen the small, steely woman like this with anyone else, practically cowering behind him.

"We're well served by Sister Gloria and her girls," said the general. Matron preened at him – not that the general was looking.

"Yet she couldn't recall what it was exactly that you wanted to look at."

Holmes looked quizzical. "Is there something of particular interest you feel I should see?"

The general barely missed a beat but I saw that the question riled him. "Old man, we're keen to help your inquiry, whatever it might be. Tell us what you're all about and then watch us pull out the stops."

"That is most accommodating," said Holmes. "But really, there is no need – especially given the many demands on your time, general. I would not want to put you to any trouble."

They stood, smiling coolly at one another. Outwardly, it all seemed so cordial – indeed, the nurses on the ward were no longer trying to eavesdrop and had gone back to their duties. Yet I noted how the general clenched his fists.

"That's good of you, Holmes," he said, at the limit of his patience. "Even so, this building is under army jurisdiction in a time of war. It would be remiss of me not to know the business of every visitor. You'll forgive me, but I must ask plainly: why exactly are you here?"

His tone brooked no argument and I began to realise my predicament. I might have argued with Matron that I had merely followed her instruction to "render all service" to Holmes, and believed that had given him leave to poke into whatever he pleased. But that surely wouldn't wash with the general, who was known to be ruthless. Holmes had only to mention where we'd just been, how I'd helped him through a locked door, and I would be put on a charge.

Yet Holmes continued to smile placidly. "Why, I am here to help you," he told the general. "I do not think it too immodest to state that my skills in observation and logic have, on occasion, been of some service to the Crown. Perhaps those same skills can be turned to the war effort in some minor way. Small amendments to administration, the slightest tweaks to procedure. Anything that might provide material benefit."

"I see," said the general, darkly. "You have listened to your brother."

Holmes flinched at this and didn't quite recover himself. "You are acquainted with him."

"From the club. One hardly likes to repeat it, but he recently expressed some concerns about your sense of duty to the war effort."

"Those concerns have been expressed for some time," replied Holmes acidly. "It is only recently that he has expressed them to other people. All right, that is in part why I am here. As you say, my brother has long believed that I should play a more active role in affairs of state. The war rather hardened that view. I told him I had retired, that my powers are not what they were, and that besides, my forte has always been the metropolis. This modern, industrial war in a foreign clime is quite outside my scope." He tailed off, a pained look on his face. "Yet he would insist."

The general appraised him and then smiled warmly. "You didn't think you'd be up to it, yet here you jolly well are all the same."

I wondered how many scared young men he had encouraged like this. Holmes swelled a little, feigning gratitude.

"My brother impressed on me that even finding some small advantage would be of value, given the scale of proceedings."

The general barked a laugh. "I should prefer a more sizeable advantage, if you might see your way."

Holmes considered seriously. "That might be possible, yes."

"I am relieved to hear it." The general laughed, and exchanged a look with Matron. Holmes saw it, too, but before they could notice him watching, he quickly turned to me.

"I certainly have much to think about," he told them. "It has been an education. Miss Watson is a patient and knowledgeable guide."

The general seemed to see me for the first time. "I hope Mr Holmes was fully satisfied," he glowered.

"Yes, sir," I said, refusing to let him intimidate me. His eyes bore fixedly into mine for a moment, then he relented and turned back to Holmes.

"They're good girls," he said. "There are times it takes its own kind of courage to work in a place like this."

"Indeed," said Holmes. "Again, I apologise, general. You're a busy man, and yet you have had to come out of your way just to see me!"

As he said this he caught my eye, but I did not need any prompting: I knew this was significant.

The general broke into a grin. "Not in the slightest," he said. "I was coming here anyway, not for you especially."

"I've really not taken you out of your normal routine?"

"This *is* my routine: I call in here at least once a week."

"That is a relief," conceded Holmes.

But, of course, I knew what he had seized on. I had told him, honestly, that the general had never been to our hospital in all my time there – so the general had just lied to us all. I glanced at Matron, who shook her head once at me, meaning I should not contradict what had just been said. She was clearly bothered by this deception, too.

I could not fathom why the general would want to deceive us, and I longed to ask Holmes as he had surely deduced further details. The chance to do so was then snatched away.

"Given the late hour," said the general, "perhaps I can offer the use of my car to take you to your lodgings, wherever they might be."

"I must confess," said Holmes, "that I had not yet arranged anything."

The general clapped his hands together. "Good lord, man. We can't have you sleeping in doorways! I've a very good secretary who keeps track of all the billets. I'll get you up to the Chateau and Monty will soon see what's what. There might even be some dinner left if you've not partaken."

Before Holmes could resist, the general had an arm round his shoulder as though they were old friends. Holmes barely had time to say a brisk word of thanks to Matron – not to me – before he was bustled out into the night.

It was all over so suddenly. I had played a small role in the great detective's latest case but now he had gone ahead without me. Of course, I was hardly in a position to expect any more, and yet I felt it dreadfully. It took me right back to when my brothers enlisted and I could only wave from the front step of our house. Even the servants had more of a role to play, busy preparing tea afterwards while I sat in meek silence with Mother. Now here I was, surplus to requirements once more, this time on the shelf with Matron. I stood watching the open main door of the hospital, willing Holmes to return.

Yet it was the general who came back inside. He marched towards us, dusting his hands, a fearsome look in his eyes. "I should like a quiet word, if you'd be so kind."

There was none of the warmth from before. I had never seen anyone speak to Matron in such a threatening tone. She positively quailed – though it might have been anger at his effrontery, speaking to her in this manner in front of a subordinate. Now Matron turned her anger on me.

"Get to bed," she told me.

I had barely a chance to nod before the general interceded. "Both of you, I think. Perhaps somewhere not quite so exposed." Matron set her jaw and asked us both to follow her.

Even though he was fuming, the general remembered his manners and made a point of letting me go before him up the stairs. On the landing, I followed Matron between the now silent desks and filing cabinets, the secretaries all gone for the night. We made our way through the oppressive dark to Matron's office.

"You will have a drink," she said. It was not a question. From the cabinet in the corner she extracted a bottle in wire mesh. Neatly, she poured whisky and soda into three heavy, crystal glasses, the like of which I'd not seen since leaving home. The general had already plumped down into the armchair opposite the desk. At Matron's bidding, I settled into a straight-backed chair to one side. We raised our glasses to the men in our care.

Matron offered the general a cigarette from a pristine new packet but he preferred his own cigar. She did not think to pass the pack to me, but then I already knew her views on us smoking in uniform.

We sat in uncomfortable silence, them smoking and me cradling my whisky. I at least had the nous to take only a modest sip, sure they meant to interrogate me. Soon enough, the general began, for all his mild, avuncular style.

"What's your name, girl?"

"Augusta Watson, sir."

"And you've been with us some time?"

"Yes, sir. Came over in 'sixteen."

He turned to Matron. "Any black marks in the copybook?"

Matron smiled thinly. "She's a bright and able girl."

I don't think I'd ever received such a compliment from her. The general looked me over, as if appraising a horse. "You're proud to serve your country?"

"Yes, sir," I said, resenting that he even had to ask.

"The work here is vital to the war effort," he told me. It was a statement of fact but he seemed to expect an answer.

"Yes, sir."

"Our visitor. Bit of a queer fish, all told. What did you talk about?"

He said it mildly enough, but his eyes were in deadly earnest. Matron, too, watched me hawkishly. This, then, was the test.

"He didn't say anything to begin with," I said, and told them about how awkward it had been as I'd taken the silent Holmes round the ward. "Then he warmed a little and did this thing, like one of the accounts in *The Strand*, deducing all sorts of bits of my life just from the brooch that I'm wearing." The general glanced at the brooch, but it seemed to mean nothing to him. "That was rather fun," I continued. "Then there was some unpleasant business." Dutifully, I reported the altercation between Holmes and Sergeant Oberman, and then about Holmes asking after a particular patient, and how even the nurses had been unable to help.

Let us be plain: I rather played up my dislike of Holmes. A sip or two of whisky loosened my tongue, and it hurt that I had been discarded. But I had not forgotten myself completely, and I did not mean to betray him. My mind was racing, trying to make sense of what I had been part of and what it could all mean. I was conscious that Holmes and I had met Matron and the general as they emerged from the ward, where they had been looking for Holmes to establish his reason for visiting. It stood to reason that they had spoken to the nurses, asking what they had seen of us and might have overheard. They might also have spoken to Oberman – or they could still do so. It was only provident that I be candid about matters that could be easily verified.

The general seemed pleased by my honesty. "What was the name of this patient he wanted to know about?"

"I'm afraid I can't remember," I said, truthfully enough. "Mr Holmes had a photograph of the young man which I showed to the nurses, one of them might know. But, as I told Holmes, we've seen so many men."

The general masked his irritation that I could not offer more. "You weren't on the ward when we got there," he continued. "You took him into the passage under the stairs."

"Yes, sir."

"What did he want to see?"

This was a more difficult question to answer without landing myself in the stink. I reasoned that we had probably been observed heading into the service corridor. After that, I felt reasonably sure our movements had gone unnoticed. Only Holmes could contradict whatever account I now gave, and I could not believe he would incriminate himself in the matter of that locked door.

I only hesitated a moment, but the general seized on my reluctance to continue. He turned to Matron, who peered at me with impatience. "The general asked you a question."

I had either to lie right to their faces, or drop Holmes and myself right in it. Really, I knew that my first duty was to the general, but there was something very wrong here. I decided I had to test him.

"Sorry sir," I told him, shaking my head as if to clear my senses. "Gosh, this Scotch is rather strong." That, I hoped, would excuse me saying something impertinent. "I'm not sure how familiar you are with the setup here."

I said it casually enough, but the general again glanced at Matron.

"Honestly, girl," she chided me. "The general is well acquainted with everything we do."

The general nodded. "I visit every week."

There it was again: the lie. I knew it and so did Matron, but she could hardly contradict him. Instead, she stubbed out the end of cigarette for longer than was quite necessary, which gave her a reason not to meet my eye. "Surely you've seen him here," she told me, still not looking up.

I felt suddenly very sober as I turned to the general. "I'm not sure that I have, sir."

The general glowered at me. This huge man was evidently not used to being argued with, especially not by some upstart of a girl.

"No, I don't suppose you have," said Matron mildly. "There is no reason you would, what with your duties on the ward." She turned to the general, one hand on the crucifix hanging from her neck. "We do keep them busy, you know."

"Of course," said the general, his eyes still set on me. "You may take it, girl, that I look in on things frequently and know the arrangements here. I would also remind you that I am in authority and we are at war. It is your duty to answer me truthfully. What else did Holmes want to see?"

In that moment, I felt more furious than scared. It may well have been the whisky, but I thought, *How dare he?* Questioning my loyalty when he was the one who had lied! Well, it rather decided things.

"I took him into theatre," I said.

That surprised the general. "He asked to see it?"

"He didn't ask anything. It was all rather awkward because we hadn't been able to help him with the patient he asked about. He wasn't very good about that, and the implication was that we weren't very professional. So I thought I would cow him a little by taking him down to theatre. That's what I meant, sir – if you know what it's like in there. The sight of the instruments, the saws and everything, can have a chilling effect on even the bravest of souls."

The general studied me closely. "And what effect did it have on Holmes?"

I bowed my head in embarrassment. "None in the slightest. He thought it serviceable enough. But I don't think he would have even flinched had we walked in on an operation. The man must be ice inside."

That was, of course, true enough – Holmes had been indifferent to the bodies in the morgue. The most effective falsehoods contain some grain of truth.

For a long while, the general didn't say anything. I felt sure he'd seen through me from the start. Then he began to laugh.

"Capital, capital. All right, very good. Sister Gloria, this girl is a credit to you."

Matron did not smile. She sat there, stroking her crucifix, then looked over at the huge noticeboard with the rota for all the staff. "You should get to bed, Augusta," she told me. "It's late and you're on duty in… well, it ought to be in little more than two hours. Given tonight's additional activities, start on the ward at eight."

This was quite unprecedented: the rota had always been sacrosanct. "Thank you, Matron. Good night, sir." I drained my glass and got to my feet. Matron's beady eyes watched my every movement as I made my way to the door. The general didn't spare me a glance.

"One last thing," he said before I left, still without looking round. "We're at a vital stage in the war and the last thing the men need are distractions. I would be grateful if you kept these matters to yourself. No one else here needs to know who our visitor was. I will thank you not to even mention the name Sherlock Holmes."

"No, sir."

"Sister Gloria and I rely on your discretion."

Chapter Five

You might well imagine the frenzy I was in as I picked my way upstairs to the dormitory. Oil lamps gave a little dreary, puttering light so that I could find my way through the snoring nurses to my own small crib and its single blanket. The company of so many others helped only a little to keep out the perishing cold, and we often slept in our uniforms just to hold on to some warmth. That night, I was simply too weary to change out of my clothes.

I lay there, utterly exhausted and yet my mind all of a whirl. At some point I slipped into fitful, anxious dreams. It felt as if I'd barely nodded off when Lobelia Darlington shook me awake.

"Come on, darling," she beamed. "We're due on at eight."

I felt groggy and sore, the first hangover I'd had in an age, just from a few sips of whisky. My insides clenched with apprehension and I didn't dare let Lobelia get even a hint of my breath. She showed little sympathy and chivvied me into the shared washroom.

Ice had formed in the basins, which we smashed with a piece of brick set aside for that purpose. It's funny, the privations that soon become part of life. Tooth powder was also running scarce so we used a portion between us. Once I'd washed, I took a new uniform from the stack and felt a lot better to be in clean things; then I did the best I could with my hair.

My apprehension grew as we headed down to the makeshift canteen. We wended through the other diners to queue for our breakfast, and I was aware of eyes on my back. When I turned, people looked hurriedly away – but I saw Dulcie O'Brien mutter something and the nurses round her laughed.

As always, Lobelia was a brick – or she didn't notice, being too keen to see what slops were on offer that morning. We were granted a single stringy sausage and gloop of egg, and I didn't think I had any appetite until I started, then wolfed it all greedily down. There was coffee, too, gritty and lukewarm, but welcome just the same.

As we ate, Lobelia gassed about the letter she had had from a cousin, whose forthcoming wedding kept on being disrupted by the inconvenience of war. She delighted in sharing with me every last detail of the flowers, seating arrangements and some extended family feud. You would never have guessed from listening to her go on that we had met in the WVR, and that Lobelia could strip down and rebuild an engine better than anyone I knew. I had once told her grandly about my plans to go into medicine, so it had been a bit galling to then end up skivvying with her on the ward, but she was my one true friend.

I let her chatter on, making appropriate noises and enjoying the distraction, these fond thoughts of home. It helped me ignore everyone else in the canteen and avoid being noticed.

As a result, we arrived on the ward in good spirits and

immediately set to work. We had barely got into the normal list of things to be mopped and wiped when an ambulance arrived with six wounded from the front, one in a very sorry way. That all kept us busy until well into the afternoon, with no time to think except on the job in hand. It was a blessed relief.

In fact, the arrivals gave me a chance to check something I rather took for granted on the ward. While they were still being carried in through the main door, Anj Bakrania went over to the cabinets and collected the register. She had it open and ready as the men were brought onto the ward. Those who could speak gave their names, otherwise the ambulance crew provided details. Anj put them into the book and assigned the beds. One of the doctors looked over her shoulder as she did so, and thought one patient might do better in a bed closer to the main desk. With a sigh, Anj ruled a line through the entry she had written and wrote it out again – the fact she wrote in pen meant no record could be entirely erased.

The new arrivals were then assessed by the doctors. As this went on, Anj copied the details she'd just entered in the register onto printed forms. Lobelia and I distributed these to each of the doctors, who ticked off the boxes pertaining to different treatments, supervision, meals and so forth. The nursing team's response to each patient in our care was predicated on those forms, and the forms all sprang from entries made in the register.

I knew the process but wanted to satisfy myself that no exceptions could be made or records excised from the book. The fact that the young officer Holmes had enquired about did not appear in the register meant he had never been on our ward. Whatever had happened, whatever concerned Sherlock Holmes, it had not happened here. Well, that was rather the end of the matter, I told myself.

Things were less frantic by the evening and, feeling more easy in myself, I helped Jill Sullivan and some of the other friendly nurses to dole out the dinner trays. We joked with the men and lit their cigarettes, and I put out of my mind completely the events of the previous night. That was until the dinner trolley reached the bed of Sergeant Oberman.

"I hope ye gave that ol' bloke what for," he said to me, and of course then Jill wanted to know everything that had been said. Oberman needed no encouragement to recount the story himself, building up his role.

"You really threatened to punch him?" said Jill, enthralled.

Oberman flashed a quick, guilty look at me. "Might 'ave, just so them in charge had a piece of my mind. But then the bleeder was so ancient! Who was he then, anyhow?"

My blood ran cold at that. It felt worse to lie to Jill than to Matron or the general, who I knew had lied themselves. Jill was one of the nurses who didn't treat me as some lady amateur, pushing her way into the hallowed profession of nursing. She encouraged my interest in medicine rather than trying to stamp it right out. "You don't really think they'd tell the likes of me," I said. "Civil service, I think."

Oberman ventured that the man must have come from the ministry and that such people were all alike, and just as bad as the enemy. That sparked something in Jill, who had once had to look after a visitor herself. "He must have been ninety at least, but he had a thing for the nurses..."

I let them go on with salacious stories, relieved to have dodged the bullet with only the tiniest fib. Work continued, and I lost myself in the chores.

Content and weary, I wended my way to dinner and then bed.

Yet, reaching the top of the stairs, I found the dormitory abuzz. Nurses clustered in a corner, Dulcie O'Brien presiding. To my horror, Lobelia Darlington was with her, somehow part of that gang.

"Did you know, Gus?" she asked me, eyes shining bright. "Did you even guess? That old man you were put in charge of last night was none other than Sherlock Holmes!"

I gaped at her in astonishment, which only made her and the others laugh. Dulcie wanted me to confirm that I'd not had the least idea. It was all they should expect from an orderly, after all.

Floundering, I suggested they might have it wrong about the man's identity. If I could introduce some doubt, perhaps this wouldn't reach Matron – who would no doubt assume that any gossip about Holmes had originated with me. However, Lobelia had had it from one of the secretaries, who had overheard Matron, and now word had gone right round the building. I felt giddy, sure I would be for the high jump, and had to perch on the edge of the nearest bed while Lobelia let us in on yet more. Her father was something grand in the Foreign Office, she explained, and she had an inside track.

"There have been questions of late about old Sherlock," she said – with casual familiarity, given she had never met the detective. "Pa says the man has always been too clever by half, and not exactly a straight bat. He used to oblige with jobs for Queen and country, and then for the late King, but that all sort of dried up and he retired and left the country. Pa didn't exactly say so, but there might have been some kind of scandal, I gather it was all rather hush-hush. But then, summer of 'fourteen, just as things are hotting up in Europe, Holmes is back in England."

"He broke up that spy ring," said one of the nurses. "It was in the 'paper."

"Oh was it?" said Lobelia archly. "Maybe he did. But then how do you explain his reluctance to take any further part in the war?"

This caused a little consternation. Some heads turned to me, as if I might offer an answer.

"He must be involved in some form," I said. "I mean, if that's who it was here last night."

Lobelia folded her arms, as if I'd just confirmed what she knew. "Shamed into it," she said. "I shouldn't say, but old Sherlock has a relative high up somewhere in the offices of state. Pa says this fellow has spent the last three years trying to get Sherlock to play an active part in the war. Our secret weapon – imagine!" She let that hang in the air. We had all been brought up on reports of Sherlock Holmes, so it was an intoxicating idea that he might somehow charge in and help us win the war. "Unfortunately," said Lobelia, dramatic timing impeccable, "the answer has always been 'No'."

"Is he a conchie?" asked one of the nurses.

"Or just a coward," said Dulcie. That caused quite a stir.

"Perhaps he's not as smart or brave as he always liked us to think," said a third.

Again, some looked to me for an opinion. "He's quite old now," I ventured. "He might not be up to that sort of thing any more."

"Maybe," concluded Lobelia. "But there's a cloud over old Sherlock. Questions have been asked. That relative I mentioned, his own brother, called him unpatriotic."

Around me, people gasped. I felt an awful, cold fog inside. Some clamoured for me to say something but I could barely order my thoughts. Dulcie pointed it out to the others, telling them how badly I must have been taken in by the old man. She made out as if she only had my welfare at heart, but she revelled in the drama that had been so perfectly staged.

I didn't respond to the questions, saying I didn't know anything – and that I couldn't even confirm that the old visitor really was Sherlock Holmes. Anyway, I said, he was gone now and I didn't think we would see him again. I lied and lied and lied.

Later, when they'd finally exhausted themselves with talk, I lay awake in my crib, worrying over how much of this would get reported to Matron. No matter what I had said to deny it and distance myself, she would surely conclude that I had broken my word to the general.

Six hours after the end of my shift and having had barely two hours' sleep, I returned to the ward almost itching with dread. It proved much worse than I'd feared. Whispers pervaded the feverish air, and the subject spread like infection. As I made my way round with the mop, patients sat up eagerly to ask what I had made of the infamous man in our midst.

I plunged into my work as best I could, ignoring the chatter, downplaying and denying events again as they were put to me directly.

My efforts did no good and only led to ever more fanciful speculation. They now said Holmes had brandished some ingenious miniature gun of his own manufacture. One could hardly blame them: they seized on this distraction from their own woes, and it no doubt lifted spirits. But I felt an impending sense of doom.

Given this mounting anxiety, it was almost a relief when the catastrophe finally came. I was with Jill as she changed a dressing on a very nasty head wound, struggling to concentrate on exactly what she did while feeling rather queasy, when a chill seemed to run through the ward. The chatter died away and I realised people were looking in my direction. Dulcie advanced on me, a triumphant look on her face.

"I'm sorry," she said, for the benefit of those earwigging, "but Matron wants to see you. I get the feeling she isn't best pleased."

With legs like lead, I stalked out of the ward, everyone's eyes on me, and made my way upstairs. Typewriters clacked as I cut through the haze of cigarette smoke. Matron stood waiting for me, an inscrutable, sour look on her face.

I followed her into the office and she closed the door. The blinds were half-drawn and the room was dark and foreboding. She took her seat behind the desk but did not motion me to sit. I stood, hands behind my back, aware of how much I was shaking.

"Mr Holmes," said Matron, with a sigh.

I wanted to deny the accusation, to defend my behaviour since she'd last seen me, but I knew it was better to hold my tongue. "Yes, Matron," I said, meekly.

"He says he still hopes to be useful and that perhaps his skills could be applied to conditions at the front. The general has granted permission for him to be accorded a tour later this morning of a section of trench. Of course, there are concerns for Mr Holmes's safety. It wouldn't do, says the general, for so eminent a figure to go and get himself shot."

It was all so astonishing. I really didn't understand why Matron thought it worth telling me any of this. Yet she seemed to expect a response. "No, Matron," I said.

Her face twitched with distaste. "The general asked me to organise transport. The enemy, he says – no doubt correctly – are less likely to target an ambulance showing the Red Cross. He thought perhaps you might drive it."

I stared, dumbstruck. Surely she couldn't be serious. Matron noted my befuddlement, with no sign of surprise.

"It's my fault," she said. "I'm afraid I told him about your–" her mouth twitched with distaste "–unusual background in the reserve, and he quite got it into his head. But never mind, it won't stand against you. I told the general that he could not order one of my girls to undertake such an assignment, not with things as they are out there. The war is at a precarious stage. That's the delicate phrase they're using. Very well, then."

I couldn't believe it. It had come out of the blue. Yet, flummoxed as I was, I would not let this chance escape me.

"M-Matron," I stammered. "If the general wants me, I'd be happy to drive Mr Holmes."

A sly smile played across her features. "I say again: the Red Cross may not make any difference. The Germans have shot nurses before."

"Yes, Matron."

She took a long draw on her cigarette while looking me over. Then, decided, she reached for a paper on her desk and held it out to me. I went over to take it, hand trembling. A standard-issue typewriter had been used to write three simple sentences, with a postscript in pen and the angular signature R–. They were orders direct from the general.

"It's not all in that letter," Matron warned me. "You won't just be the driver. Tell me, honestly now: what did you make of Mr Holmes?"

"Sorry Matron, I don't know what you mean."

"Did you like him?"

I couldn't imagine where this was going, but wondered how much she suspected of what had really gone on. "I wouldn't say that, exactly," I said.

Matron did not smile. "No, of course not. A man like that, deplorable views about women…" She considered for a moment. "You will report to me everything Holmes does and says, everything in which he shows an interest, anything odd he might leave out. We're relying on the discretion you demonstrated on the ward this morning. Yes, I know it's all round the building. I also know that you tried to minimise the spread. Miss Watson, we rely on your character and courage. This is a highly sensitive assignment. We are asking you to be our spy."

This time she proffered the cigarettes, and I dared to take one. "Yes, Matron," I told her.

Chapter Six

With my orders tucked into my pocket, I went directly from Matron to the Field Ambulance crew, out in what had been the old stables. The rain came down bitterly, but it was only a short run from the house. Two fellow VADs huddled round a fire, though it offered little heat. Gwen Moss and her laconic companion Patch wore the long, double-breasted blue coats and peaked gaberdine caps that were meant to make them easy to spot from a distance, in the hope they then *wouldn't* be shot at. The truth was, it only took a bit of rain and mud and they looked little different from the coats worn by soldiers.

Even though I knew Gwen and Patch well, they needed to see my letter from the general before accepting what I said I had to do, but after that they were eager to help me. Of course, they had heard all the gossip about our illustrious visitor, but I think what clinched it was that aiding me meant they had a day indoors out of the rain.

Their ambulance was a cumbersome block, a Rover-made Sunbeam of a type I'd not driven in at least a year. Gwen gave me a quick refresher course on the essentials – the tricks to start the ignition, the awkward double declutch, and the importance of staying in low gear when slewing through the mud. It all made sense until she spoke of the "poor weather" in Rebecq, which I was a bit slow to realise was her way of warning me that things had got pretty bad down that way. We checked over the engine together, Gwen offering counsel on the most likely things to go wrong.

"*Is* it likely to go wrong?" I asked.

She grinned. "If it can do. It's always weather like this whenever we have to get out and push."

My resolve was further dampened when it took Gwen a few tries to get the ambulance started, and the great machine coughed and rattled however much she adjusted the choke. Gwen assured me that this was quite usual and said part of the problem was the quality of the fuel.

"If you're in with the general," she teased, "you could have a quiet word. He won't hear it from the likes of us."

"I'm not really in with the general," I said.

"Oh yeah," said Gwen with a smile. "Just running this little errand. Nothing out of the ordinary. Whatever you say, m'lady."

With the rain still thrumming down, Gwen offered me her long coat. I gratefully accepted, the distinctive blue at least a kind of talisman against harm. Patch found me a pair of leather gloves as my hands would freeze otherwise.

"Still might," she said, drily.

Then, fully briefed, I clambered up into the open cab, propped myself on the narrow, padded bench, and battled my way into first gear. The ambulance lurched heavily forward, out of the cover of the stable. With no windscreen or protection, I was exposed to the lashing rain. Gwen reached up to present me with her own goggles.

I tied them fast round my head, my hair already bedraggled from the downpour.

That done, I chugged unsteadily off. The Sunbeam was a pig of a thing to steer, and having cleared the stable I nearly took out what remained of the gatepost. In my mirror, I saw Gwen out in the rain, sarcastically applauding.

The lane had become a river but the sheer heft of the ambulance seemed to keep us steady. I puttered on, getting up to third gear. It felt good to be out, even in the mud and rain, after so long cooped up in the hospital.

Once on the main road, I encountered more traffic: supply trucks, staff cars and groups of soldiers on foot. It all moved frustratingly slowly. For much of the route, I got caught behind a truck, its panelling riven with bullet holes. I spied another ambulance coming the other way, and saluted my fellow driver – then immediately regretted taking a hand off the wheel.

Eventually I reached my turn-off, a lane snaking between untended farms. A young corporal on duty at the top of the drive to the Chateau clearly expected me. I was directed down a mud track under a canopy of tall trees until, in a sudden moment that quite took my breath away, I emerged to a view of the great building. It had seen better days and the place buzzed with the military, yet its conical towers lent a fairy-tale air. It was utterly surreal, like driving into a whole other world. Senses reeling, I pulled up in front of the main portico as if some honoured guest.

For a moment, I thought I might have a chance to look inside, but Holmes stepped neatly from the building and climbed up beside me, in a nimble manner that belied his age. He seemed to take no notice of the rain, in part because he wore a storm-grey greatcoat, in immaculate condition, which I felt sure came from the general, and a rather fine tweed cap. His expression was dark and serious until, having folded his long legs into the narrow confines of the cab, he turned to look at me.

"Miss Watson!" he said. "This is a pleasant surprise."

He seemed genuinely pleased and I felt a pang of guilt, given that I'd been sent to spy on him. "Thank you, sir. My orders are to drive you down to Rebecq so you can view the trenches."

"That's right. I have an appointment with a Captain Boyce, whose unit are on the front line."

"Very good, sir. Is this captain connected to the dead chap you wanted to know about?"

Holmes smiled. "You have a sharp mind, Miss Watson. Boyce replaced Ogle-Thompson. It's his unit we're going to see. But, of course, I would rather they didn't know that that is the source of our interest. Better they think, as your general does, that I am making a broader inquiry."

"You can rely on me, sir," I told him – quite fluent in my dishonesty.

We set off, navigating the elegant curve of the driveway without any hint of disaster. The corporal who had seen me in saluted, and this time I gave a curt nod.

Holmes sat back as much as the small space would allow, given his long legs. He had to speak up over the grind of the engine. "You drive more proficiently than the general's man," he said.

"Thank you, sir," I responded.

At the junction, I had to lean right out of the cab, to see what was coming from our left, and then move quickly to take advantage of a gap in the traffic. We joined the slow queue heading to the front.

"The WVR taught you well," he said, and seemed sincere.

"Thank you, sir. It's good to have a chance to put my training to some use."

"I don't suppose there's much call in the medical corps for radical anarchist politics."

I laughed. "I'm an orderly, not a nurse. And the volunteer reserve was hardly ever that."

"You sound disappointed. Was it really all practical skills, no politics at all?"

He seemed to know more about it than most, and I didn't see any point in denying it. "They had quite a thing on the importance of political context."

"In what way?"

I didn't want to open up to him but couldn't resist. It felt so liberating to talk like this. The men of the ward often discussed politics, and some of the nurses could get quite energised in debates with them or after, but I'd learned not to venture opinions. It had the same deadening effect as showing an interest in medicine. Yet Holmes wanted to know what I'd been through in the reserve, and I relished the chance to explain.

"Well," I said. "Look at this lot." We were passing a battalion of sorry-looking men, stooped under their packs and equipment, forlorn as they trudged through the mud. "Most ordinary soldiers don't yet have the vote. Conscription without representation!" I realised I'd said this a little too zealously, echoing my tutors. "Well, that's what they taught us," I continued. "The wider context. It does sort of makes you think."

"There are moves in London to extend the franchise," said Holmes. "It could well happen in the new year."

"Yes, sir," I said. "I've heard something like that. And how the war will be over by Christmas."

To my great surprise, Holmes laughed. "You may well be right. But I think recent events in Russia have focused certain minds.

Even the government are coming round to the idea of concessions to the ordinary man – and perhaps woman, as well. But you're out here with ordinary men, Miss Watson, and you have your political training. As a socialist, do you think such concessions will be too little too late?"

This was all most unexpected. It is not often that a man asks one's political opinion. When they do, it is usually so they can proceed to lecture one on the correct point of view. Yet Holmes seemed to have genuine interest in what I thought, and what my experience might have yielded. I was sorry to disappoint him.

"I'm really not a socialist at all," I told him. "I'm from a wealthy family in Richmond."

"That would not preclude you."

It was my turn to laugh. "I'm not much of a revolutionary."

"What a shame," he said with, I think, a smile.

"Whatever my mother might say, I just wanted to get out of the house and find something I could *do*. Yes, I know – quite scandalous!"

He laughed again. "I take it your mother did not approve of you joining the WVR."

"She was proud when I did, and largely relieved, since it stopped all my talk of going to university. It was only once I was well into my training and she learned what it actually involved that she did not approve. I tried to explain it, but she didn't want to hear about engine oil or how to strip a rifle. She somehow didn't think such things appropriate for my sex or class. Then there was my temerity in having political views."

"Is that why you avoid politics out here, as well? I imagine you need to exercise some care discussing certain topics."

"Not at first. The brass have been more on it in the past few months. They banned a 'paper being printed by the men because one short article looked forward to us all living in peace after the war, which they thought dangerously socialist. But talk of that kind of thing is rife among the men. We hear it a lot on the ward. They all want to get home and back to things as normal. Ending restrictions on pub opening hours, that's the source of most of it. You can't really hold that against them. But lately there's been this feeling..."

But I tailed off, leaning forward as if concerned about some aspect of the road. The truth was, Holmes had been absolutely right: some topics it did well to avoid.

Holmes was, of course, in no way deceived. "You can be candid with me, Miss Watson," he said agreeably. "I understand that it would be merely hypothesis, not your firmly held conviction."

I swallowed. "Well, sir. Lately, there has been this feeling that the brass are in the way, prolonging the war for who knows what reason. I mean, I don't believe it – it doesn't make any sense – but it's what has been doing the rounds."

"Then you've no thought where this idea might have come from."

"Not exactly, sir. But put yourself in the place of a soldier, facing all this mud and potential death every day. One might ask oneself what one were fighting for." Holmes did not respond. I hurriedly filled the silence. "As you say, sir, that's a hypothesis, not my view personally. Quite the opposite. I mean, look at me now."

Holmes still didn't say anything. I dared to glance at him and he was brooding, his long fingers steepled in front of his face. He saw me looking and I turned quickly back to the road.

"You enjoy this," he said. "Driving an ambulance headlong into the war."

"Well, sir," I said, "I suppose it does feel good to be a bit more directly involved."

"Our feelings accord," he said at length. "This case made a good excuse to venture out and see things for myself. It seems my brother was right."

I caught my breath. "Sir?" He did not respond and I knew I could not press him further. Then I had to concentrate on the perilous state of the road. Rain lashed at us and I would have been blind without my goggles. Holmes seemed not to mind the onslaught, peering defiantly out into the murk. His tall frame barely fitted in the cab, and I was conscious that any jolt or sharp turn would send him flying out. Yet he showed not the least concern.

After a while, the rain petered out, and the open, flat farmland was bridged by a glorious rainbow. Holmes showed no interest in the landscape and instead withdrew a folded page from his coat, studying it closely. I had to keep my eyes on the road, but managed to glance at the paper – a list of names that Holmes now recited under his breath.

I concentrated on the rain-slick road, the potholes and other hazards. The rumble of war became steadily more distinct, but it hardly seemed possible that we were heading into danger as we made our way through picturesque countryside. Yet how quickly things changed. The sight of pretty French houses soon gave way to structures with broken windows or fully boarded up, and then pitiful ruins. We bucked a little on the worsening road. The world around us turned more hellish. A few sorry, ruined trees stood bleakly in ravaged ground. There were awful details, too: a dead horse half submerged in a pool of green water, and what might have been the body of a man.

It had been a long while since I'd last ventured out this far and I'd forgotten the sudden stench, at once rotten eggs, rancid meat and the sharp, sweet tang of cordite. I instinctively covered my mouth and nose with my hand, then had to grab the wheel for fear of losing the road. Holmes kindly passed me his handkerchief and covered his own mouth and nose with his hands. Eyes streaming and with a hacking cough, I took us on. A light fog descended, or perhaps it was smoke. We remained in first gear, grinding slowly through the mud, squinting to pick out the path of the road ahead. The rumble grew steadily louder.

Then we came upon the strangest sight. It looked at first like a hill, except that the angular slopes gleamed. There were more beyond it, hill upon hill of spent artillery shells, piled up to the heavens, a vast rubbish tip of war. Tiny, ant-like soldiers worked the lower slopes, dumping more spent shells from a toy-sized truck.

Soon after that, we came upon a tangle of makeshift structures caked in mud. Again, it took effort to comprehend the vast scale, until I spied the ruin of a church tower in among this ramshackle slum. As we approached, we could see the place was alive with activity. The road took us round to one side. Sentries in tin helmets and heavy, leather waterproofs directed traffic. More soldiers gathered round the back of a truck that had got stuck in the mire, trying to impel it onto surer ground. They made little progress.

A sentry flagged me down and I came to a stop, looking down at him from my vantage point in the open cab. He was slight, punctilious, with a neat moustache. I showed him my letter from the general and he examined it closely.

"Righto," he told me, handing it back. "You can park up by the main dressing station and then go on by foot. Watling Street will take you right through. Then there'll be someone to meet you. Grab a helmet as you go, and for God's sake keep your heads down. There'll be no end of grief for everyone if a pretty girl like you ends up shot!"

He winked at me, then moved off to deal with the next car coming in.

I got us through the organised chaos of reversing trucks and, as bidden, found a space behind the tent marked "MDS". Holmes sprang lightly down from the cab; I clambered out with more decorum. Away from the warmth of the ambulance, the cold instantly cut through me. The ground was treacherous, deep and slick with mud. I gathered up my skirts and batted Holmes away when he tried to take my forearm. Pointedly, I made my own unsteady way to the trail of duckboards, though they were no less hazardous for being so wet. Holmes missed his step and I caught his arm, supporting him as we skittered uneasily into the noisy, bustling slum.

There were tents and shed-like structures, but I realised we were following the route of a broken stone wall, a surviving fragment of the decimated town. I had been here before but recognised little – so much had been obliterated. The noise and activity around us were overwhelming. I stopped a soldier to ask for directions to Watling Street. He grunted with disdain that we were already on it.

We followed the duckboards through the squalid, makeshift dwellings. Soldiers rushed past, or ferried equipment. The pervasive gunpowder stink made my sinuses itch, and there was the queasy flavour of humanity, too – sweat and blood and ordure. I felt giddy and Holmes also seemed shaken by it, a pained look on his face. Nevertheless, we went on.

A sentry manning a tumbledown hut had been told to expect us, and nipped inside to fetch a couple of tin helmets. I glimpsed the cosy den he had made for himself, a blanket pinned up against the far wall giving the effect of a souk. Now I'd seen it, I began to notice how other spaces had received a personal touch – the word "Belleview" painted ironically on a toilet block, the pub sign fixed to the mess hut. Anything to make this bleak domain in some small way less grim.

Holmes looked decidedly odd in a Tommy helmet and his greatcoat, and I'm sure I looked no less peculiar. The helmets were heavy and hard and uncomfortable, but we could hardly complain. We continued down the lane of duckboards, weaving in and out of soldiers, and were soon in a brick passageway, modern fortifications perhaps eight feet tall but open to the elements.

The walls of brick soon gave way to earthworks, lined with neat and well-tended layers of sandbags, zigzagging so that one could never see more than a short distance ahead. It was horribly claustrophobic, an animal panic inside me as we proceeded into this deadly trap. We had to dodge round a team of men repairing a section, bracing the wall with a wooden scaffold. It seemed that the weather did just as much damage as the enemy's guns.

Suddenly, there was a deafening *rat-a-tat* of gunfire. Holmes and I both froze, but the men in the trench barely flinched and got on with their duties. They were not merely hardened to the war, I thought, but numbed to its effects. I folded my arms, tucking my hands into my armpits to hide that they were shaking. To my mortification, Holmes saw – but mercifully did not say anything.

Then we came to a stark warning sign: a skull and crossbones, its top section crudely shorn off. There was no mistaking its meaning. A boy in uniform and a tin hat emerged from a dugout and scampered over.

"Mr Holmes? I'm Joe. I'm to take you on to the unit. And I'm to warn you it gets pretty hairy from here."

"Thank you, Joe," said Holmes warmly. "I'm sure we're in no danger so long as we have you as our expert guide." The boy glowed at this, even standing a little taller. Holmes then addressed me. "I suppose if I told you that I am now in safe hands and you could wait for me at the ambulance…"

The wretched thing is that I wanted to go back. I would have gladly sat it out in my little cab, and it's silly to say I was more scared of Matron than of the trenches. But it was the thought of her waiting for my report that made me decline the gallant offer.

"I would remind you, sir," I told him sternly, "of my orders not to let you out of my sight." To his credit, he made no attempt to argue. My bravado failed to impress Joe.

"They all say stuff like that, miss," he grinned at me, good-naturedly. "Until they see what's down there. But suit yourself. Follow me, and keep low."

Stooped and awkward, we followed Joe into trenches that became ever more dismal and unsanitary. There were few enough rooms cut into the earthworks. Instead, men largely sat around in the open air, often huddled at stoves or crude campfires.

"Does the smoke not make them a target?" Holmes asked Joe. "I would have thought it could betray their positions to the enemy."

"Oh, they know where we are, sir. They sometimes try a mortar. But it's generally all right so long as we keep our heads down. Their snipers are pretty good."

We ducked lower and went on. Enormous rats passed languidly by, entirely unafraid. The human stink grew worse. I tried not to think what the practicalities might be, without proper WCs or plumbing. The men we passed all had the same haunted look, with sharp, hungry features and sunken eyes. It was hard enough for us just to pass through this pitiful corridor, but the men had lived here for months.

Joe knew where it was safe for him to babble at us about life in the trenches, and where we needed to proceed in silence.

In places, Holmes shook hands with some of the men that we passed. I don't expect they knew who he was – just some suit come to view conditions – but his bluff good wishes clearly cheered them. What a difference it made, just to show a bit of interest. It didn't matter their rank or class, Holmes had an easy affinity with them all.

A man's man, I thought coldly. With infamous views about women.

I could also see that expending this effort took its toll on him. Joe's youthfulness only made more plain Holmes's great age. I'd guessed he was in his sixties when I first met him, now I thought he might be older. The going was unsteady, even on the duckboards, and there was so much to take in. The sections where we had to go in silence were especially grim, my stomach knotted with apprehension and my every sense alert, yet nothing but the mud to fix on. That constant, intangible threat quickly drains all reserves of energy. I saw it draining Holmes.

Then, suddenly, there was more gunfire, deafening and surely on top of us. Joe and the men around us dived to the ground, so we really were in danger, and we instinctively dropped with them. We lay, pressed against the bitterly cold and sodden earth, as bullets tore overhead.

Eventually the assault died off, though we took our cue from Joe and the other men and did not dare move. It seemed eerily silent after all the shooting, but the men listened keenly and kept still. Being close to Holmes, I could observe his own response, and almost saw the cogs of that great intelligence turning over as he assessed every detail of sound.

Then one man, a cigarette at his lip, crawled slowly over to a tall, rectangular box built into the wall of the trench, peering into the lower part. The periscope gave him a view over the side of the trench without him risking his head. He angled the periscope to take a wide perspective, but could make little out.

We continued to wait in the damp and freezing mud. I yearned to be able to stretch again, to move at all. Beside me, Holmes's breath sounded ragged. He looked pained, his eyes darting back and forth, his cheeks flushed. On the ward, such restlessness often preceded more explosive bouts of shell shock.

"We're all right," I assured him and tried to take his arm, but he pulled gruffly away from me.

"That's hardly what the evidence suggests."

Up the line, a soldier gestured for us to shut up. We did as we were bidden. The man at the periscope had also raised his hand in warning. He had apparently seen something.

We waited. The men readied their rifles, fixing long bayonets. I dearly hoped that we had not had the poor luck to arrive just as the Germans advanced. Holmes seemed quite thrilled by the prospect.

Then someone shouted, "Hallooooo!"

The word echoed around us. I looked back and forth up the trench but couldn't tell which of the men had shouted. Then again, it came: "Halloooo!"

Holmes held up a finger, pointing up, out of the trench and across to the enemy lines. The Germans were calling to us!

"Hallooooo Tommy! How are you this fine day? I hope we find you dead!"

The clarity of the voice was unnerving, the enemy almost on top of us. It clearly disturbed the soldiers, too. They shifted uncomfortably, readying for attack.

Then one of the men near us bellowed, gruffly: "We're just dandy, thank you, Fritz, you sack of s–!"

In an instant, the tension was gone from the air. I admit I

laughed. Even Holmes cracked a smile.

"That is very excellent, old bean," called the German voice cheerily. "I shall share this good news tonight – with your mother!"

I am hardly a bluestocking but I gasped at that. The men ahead of us seemed to acknowledge its skill as an insult, as one might recognise the prowess of an opposing side in cricket. They whispered among themselves, agreeing the perfect response, which the gruff man then called out. It would not do to repeat his words here, but suffice to say that I had been in the company of soldiers for some years and was still rather shocked.

Joe evidently decided that this foul-mouthed sport meant we were safe to move on. Holmes and I followed him into ever more dismal trenches.

"How often do they call to you like that?" Holmes asked.

"Yeah, it 'appens most mornings, sir," said Joe. "Nothing else for them to do though, is there?"

Where part of Watling Street had collapsed, we took a detour through some newly dug trenches barely wider than myself, let alone a soldier carrying kit. The new trenches had not been dug as deep, either, and for one section we were obliged to go on our knees. I was already cold and drenched from sheltering in the mud, so it made little difference to trawl through it again. I kept my attention on Holmes. His coat had not protected his suit or expensive brogues, yet he seemed quite in his element, alert but with none of the mania I had sensed before – when, surely, he'd been in *less* danger.

Not sure what to make of this, I crawled on. It was a blessed relief to join the trench proper once more. Weary and now extremely cold, we trudged rather slowly, Holmes still glad-handing and charming soldiers as we went, offering encouragement and general good cheer. I found it all exhausting and could only stumble behind him. Then, at last, Joe led us into the low, dark hole of a dugout.

A bulb flared harsh dirty orange. We found ourselves in a squat, dank space, the first of a number of rooms hollowed from the earth. There were odd bits of old furniture and even a fireplace inset in the wall, a hovel they'd tried to make homely. Yet to me it felt awfully precarious. Wooden props creaked and water dripped from the muddy ceiling. There was also a dense, earthy smell, like being buried alive. When the walls began to move I staggered back in fear, sure the whole place was collapsing – until I realised there were mud-caked men emerging from their quarters.

Holmes took off his tin helmet and looked helplessly round for somewhere to hang it. Politely brought-up lads would have rushed to assist him, but the etiquette was different in that dark, forbidding hole. The soldiers resented our presence in their den, until Holmes pulled out a fresh pack of cigarettes. Then, at last, we were welcome.

They stirred the embers of the fire and added more scraps of wood, which was damp and struggled to catch. Even so, just the sight of it was a comfort after so long out in the open. My clothes were wet through, I felt cold to the bone, but slowly I started to thaw.

Holmes was ahead of me, his eyes darting over the details all round us. Pinned to the wooden struts supporting this den were photographs, prints and cigarette cards – a motley collection of images. I recognised a view of St Paul's Cathedral, and the woman in fine eveningwear might have been Marie Lloyd.

I must have been the first real woman to ever step foot in that drab room. The men were wary around me, but I sensed not from coyness. They were suspicious of us as invaders. Despite the cigarettes Holmes had offered, they did not trust us at all.

"Captain Boyce," said a scrawny young man, stepping forward. "They said you'd be coming, Mr Holmes, and of course we know your reputation, but they gave no indication what this is all about. I'm afraid we can't offer you tea. Or rather, we could, but the beastly stuff takes a bit of getting used to. But please, perhaps you'd care to sit."

They found a stool for Holmes and dragged out a cane chair for me that looked like it might break at any moment. I perched as demurely as I was able, at least grateful for a place by the fire. The men clustered round us, Joe among them and smoking one of Holmes's cigarettes.

"Well, gentleman," said Holmes. "This is all very pleasant. Thank you for making time to see us." This at least earned a few smiles, though I suspect they were used to tolerating this kind of thing from the brass. "So then, why am I here? You plainly do not require some elderly visitor to come and tell you your business. I know that to be a fact. I have studied the records of the whole division, and this unit has played its part with particular success. You seem surprised but I assure you it is so, working only from statistics."

He spun the lie all too easily, fluent in deception. Yet he had surely chosen the wrong story, as the men looked openly sceptical.

"You mean in the numbers," said one of the men. "Not in actual fighting."

"Indeed," Holmes demurred. "But perhaps those numbers can be made to fight on your behalf. The use of statistics could ensure better planning by Command, resulting in great victories and at less cost in men. That, at least, is the idea."

The men looked no more convinced by this. They exchanged doubtful glances – though, I noticed, not with their captain.

"Sorry, sir," Boyce said to Holmes, clearly discomforted by the way his men behaved. "Precisely what do you want us to do for you?"

Holmes laughed. "Nothing whatever! You have already rendered great service. I have written my report for Command. They now wish me to present my findings in person, to all the generals great and good. In short, they require a small show. I suspect they, too, are not persuaded that mere numbers can match actual fighting, so they will want to know more about the men involved. Thus, here I am, hoping to know you all a little better, so that I might sing your praises."

Oh, his confounded gall! There were still some doubters, but several of the men relished the idea of getting their names in front of the brass. They began to talk eagerly among themselves, but Boyce called for hush.

"That would be a singular honour, Mr Holmes," he said. "How would you like to proceed? Perhaps you have questions to put to my men."

Again, the men exchanged glances. There was something more going on here, I realised. They did not like to think of themselves as Boyce's men.

Holmes seemed not to have noticed, and rubbed his hands together eagerly. "My dear captain, I thought you said you knew my reputation. I have no need to ask questions; I can read your lives quite plainly where I am. Congratulations, Jack Walker, by the way. You recently became a father – to a boy. He has your eyes, I think. Oh, but perhaps that is unfair to say when you have not yet had the chance to meet him."

The man who had been sceptical of numbers, Jack Walker, gaped in wonder at these details that Holmes rattled off with such ease.

"Did I have that correct?" Holmes continued. "Any detail wrong? No? Then good. Now, George Ludders – it is George, isn't it? I'm afraid I do not know the name of the sweetheart – forgive me, fiancée – to whom you proposed in Brighton. I can tell you that she has curly red hair and her father is a groom, or at least tends several horses. You should not allow him to intimidate you: he will approve of the match, given time. And then who here is the artist? Yes, you Mr Kovacs, of course. This is not your first time in France. You visited Paris before you attended the Slade."

The effect was electric. They stared open-mouthed, and then spontaneously applauded. Holmes waved off their praise. "It is simplicity itself, I assure you."

It was extraordinary to witness but I knew how at least some of the trick had been done. First he had prepared; the paper he had studied in the ambulance listed the men in the unit, which he had committed to memory. That register of names could then be matched to the cards and photographs round us. These were pinned up in separate clusters and it seemed logical to assume that each man had a space of his own. The nearest such collection boasted a small photograph of a startled-looking baby, and below it "11.10.17" had been carved into the wood. Near this, a cigarette card showed a man in cricket whites, his name written over by hand to say "Walker", because he resembled the man Holmes had congratulated.

I endeavoured to make sense of the other deductions, while Holmes continued in the same vein. The artist Kovacs could be identified from three dog-eared postcards showing Impressionist paintings, no doubt all displayed in Parisian galleries – which an ordinary soldier would hardly get leave to visit in a time of war. On the next strut, a postcard was pinned up the wrong way round, to show the words not the picture. From my chair, I could read the printed caption "Brighton"; Holmes was closer and must have been able to read some of the handwriting, too.

Yet while I could just about follow his technical prowess, the men were entranced by what seemed to them like magic. What was more, the pictures and souvenirs that Holmes drew from were displayed for a purpose, bridging the impossible distance between the trenches and home. In teasing out and stating those connections, Holmes made them that much stronger. I, who had never met any of these men before, had a vivid sense of their lives, a world away from the war.

Holmes looked again round the dugout, his eyes picking over a desk in the corner, a standard-issue typewriter in its box, paper and pens on the shelf to one side. A field telephone had been set up beside the desk, its thick cable trailing to the door. Holmes seemed to recognise something of particular interest in this.

"Now," he said with relish. "Which one you is Dutton? Is Bill Dutton here? If he might step forward…"

In an instant, the spell had been broken. As one, they looked embarrassed and awkward. Holmes had unwittingly committed some awful faux pas.

"I'm afraid not, Mr Holmes," said Boyce. "You've got it wrong."

Holmes looked quickly back round the room, and I thought I saw panic in his eyes at the thought that his powers had failed him. In that moment, he was no longer the great detective of legend, just an old man out of his depth. "Surely not," he said hollowly. "Unless…"

"Private Dutton is dead," said Captain Boyce. "Poor man bought it just three days ago."

Holmes looked genuinely stunned by this. He floundered, trying to find the words. I could see it distressed him to have made such a mistake.

"Of course, Mr Holmes meant no disrespect," I said quickly.

They seemed to accept this, begrudgingly, but we had lost their good will. Holmes, still floundering, looked round at them, taking in the mood.

"I take it he was a good man," he said.

There were a few mumbles of assent. Then Walker laughed. "Not exactly what you'd call 'good', sir. Bit of a character, all told."

"A good soldier, though," said Boyce. The men grunted agreement.

"Stubborn," added another. "Man could out-sulk a mule."

"No fan of the brass," said Ludders.

"And yet fiercely loyal," said Walker, again to general consent. "Even to the old boss."

He instantly regretted saying this. The other men, too, looked aghast. I saw Holmes watch their faces curiously, then turn to Captain Boyce.

"I've been with this unit for a matter of weeks," said Boyce, thinly. "The man before me…" I noticed, as did Holmes, Boyce glance round at his men, and how they would not meet his eye. "… well, he bought it too," Boyce concluded.

No one objected to this, and no one volunteered anything further, yet it was evident there was much more to be said.

Holmes withdrew the list from his pocket and ran his finger down the names. "A Captain Ogle-Thompson," he said, as if the name were completely new to him. The men positively recoiled.

"Good riddance," muttered Walker.

"Walker!" snapped Boyce. The two men glared at one another, and things might have turned nasty. However, Walker opted not to challenge his commanding officer and shuffled a step backwards. Boyce seemed uncertain how to proceed, given the animosity of the men towards him. He turned back to Holmes. "It would be fair to say that the late captain was not universally popular."

Holmes looked round the men again. "Your expressions, gentleman, suggest that is an understatement."

Boyce forced a tight-lipped smile but said nothing more. The silence hung in the air.

"A lot of men get shot," growled Walker.

"Walker, I have already told you," snapped Boyce.

But Walker wouldn't be quashed. "It's just," he sneered, "that some of 'em deserve it."

Chapter Seven

⟲

Holmes had shown me a photograph of Philip Ogle-Thompson, the handsome young officer. He had told me as well that the captain had lost a tooth playing rugby, which gave him a slightly rascally smile. I'd a rather vivid sense of him. And yet the men in his command had detested him, and were glad of his death.

It seemed utterly horrific, such hatred directed towards a dead man. What could possibly warrant it? Surely things were bad enough in the trenches without the soldiers turning on one another. Their captain clearly thought so, too.

"It is not done to speak ill of the dead," said Boyce firmly. To my astonishment, some of the men turned their backs on him. "It's meant to be unlucky," Boyce told them.

Those words, at least, affected the men. The trenches were well known to be rife with superstition. Yet they apparently resented it coming from Boyce. They hated Ogle-Thompson and disliked his replacement. It was the most extraordinary thing to witness, and I could see Holmes watching with interest.

Walker seemed to notice this and glowered back at Holmes, as if daring him to ask for details. Holmes beamed benignly back.

"It is also quite beside the point," he said, amicably. "I don't have any interest in this, um…" He held up the list of names again. "…whatever his name even was. As I said, the whole reason for being here is to glean details that I can share with Command, so they have a sense of this exemplary unit as something more than a column of numbers. Mr Walker, what are you calling your new baby boy?"

I didn't think this tactic would work. Yet, wary to begin with, Jack soon warmed to telling us about the son he was yet to meet. Letters from his wife related how the boy slept and laughed and was fascinated by a local cat. Again, that vivid connection with home acted like a tonic. Holmes asked more questions, of all the men, and they told us of their families and loved ones, their lives back in England and the simple pleasures they would return to when the war was finally over. Holmes for his part made no more deductions, just showed an interest in the things that were precious to the men. They were glad to share. Then, emboldened, the men wanted to know what he had done to read their lives before. He turned instead to me.

"Miss Watson knows my methods," he said. "I believe she can tell you."

I felt my cheeks colour under their scrutiny, but made a good fist of explaining how Holmes had identified Jack as the new father and Kovacs as the artist. Holmes seemed pleased that I noted the importance of prior research as well as observation. Yet the men were underwhelmed.

"It's not like a trick at all!" laughed Boyce.

"Oh you think so," said Holmes, indulging him. "You will note, captain, that I have not applied my talents to you. And you are of some special interest, since you have no personal items pinned

86

up in here." It was a simple statement of fact but some of the men were impressed by it. I thought it again demonstrated the divide between Boyce and his men. "We require new data," Holmes continued, "from which I can build a hypothesis and demonstrate my art. Or, in your parlance, turn my trick. Captain, perhaps you would oblige by turning out your pockets."

To the men, this seemed good sport at the expense of their captain. Boyce obliged magnanimously, producing items from his jacket pocket, one by one.

"A handkerchief," said Holmes. "Good quality – too good to have been issued by the army." That earned a knowing laugh. "No monogram or emblem. And it's also spotless. What else? A cigarette lighter. This was a present from your mother and stepfather on the occasion of your twenty-first birthday – the engraving says so. Please, we can do better than that, I think!"

Boyce tried another pocket and extracted a folded slip of card. It seemed to puzzle him and then, when he opened it out, all colour drained from his face.

Holmes immediately darted forward and plucked the card from the captain's hand. I leant over to study it. Numbers had been neatly printed in a single column:

66/1
76/1
66/1
89/1
54/1
83/1
90/1

"Fractions," I said. "Whatever does it mean?"

"Do any of the rest of you know?" Holmes asked the men and showed them the card, but it meant little to them. Boyce remained ashen, though he tried not to show it.

"It is a betting slip," said Holmes, mildly. "Oh, not a conventional betting slip. It lists the stakes but does not name the competitors. Also, note the ratios: I do not fancy odds of sixty-six to one. These are bets of high risk and therefore high stakes. An anonymous, high-stakes race, one that I am afraid is not wholly legal."

The men stared in astonishment at Boyce, who only shook his head, mystified. Holmes seemed delighted by this and pounced.

"You are going to tell us that you have never seen this card before," he said. "It is nothing to do with you. You cannot even venture a guess as to how it got into your pocket."

"I am not a betting man," Boyce told his men.

"Ah," smiled Holmes. "But I am."

First there was a stunned silence. Then the men erupted in laughter and applause. Boyce, evidently relieved, slapped Holmes good-naturedly on the arm. "Absolutely first class," he said. "You could have been a master criminal. Never felt a thing when you put it there."

"You did say you wanted a trick," admitted Holmes.

Then his eyes caught mine and for the briefest instant I saw that cool glint of intelligence. He slipped the card neatly into his pocket, and I knew better than to say anything. But I also understood that he had not planted the card.

We stayed a little longer, Holmes demonstrating a few more simple acts of deduction and making encouraging small talk. Yet he had acquired whatever knowledge we had come for and, eager to discuss whatever it might be, I was grateful when he finally made our excuses to Boyce and the men. Holmes knew better than to wish them luck – that was also thought unlucky – and instead told them that he would visit again if his duties would allow. "It has been a delight to spend time with you, gentlemen," he said, and they clearly felt the same.

We donned our tin helmets and Joe led us back along the precarious route towards Watling Street. Having sat for so long by the fire, the cold hit me terribly and I was glad that Joe hurried us along. The men we had passed on the way nodded greeting as we went by again, though there was now silence from the German trenches, the insults traded for another day. Men ate from open tins – I do not think they cooked the contents – and huddled together in the hope of warmth. I worried how the old detective was faring, yet he seemed energised by all he had seen.

In fact, once again I saw how his eyes darted back and forth over every detail around us, and his ears had flushed quite scarlet. In part, whatever he had learned in the dugout had lit a fire inside him. But there was more to it than that. His quick, nervous movements were as much about him being in the trench, manically vigilant to all attendant dangers. We saw it with some of our patients, an inability to settle because, after all they had been through, they were constantly alert.

Then Joe began chatting, a sign we had left the most hazardous sections of trench behind us. He wanted to know more about Holmes's methods, but I could see the old man was not quite in the right state of mind to indulge him.

"Captain Boyce seems a good sort," I said to Joe, expecting him not to agree. In fact, the boy thought better than to do down his captain to a perfect stranger.

"He's all right, miss. We've had worse."

"You mean that man he replaced."

Joe looked squeamish. "We're not meant to say nothing about him."

"Of course," I said quickly. "It doesn't matter. As long as Boyce is all right."

Joe considered. "Like you saw, he can take a joke. He's not such a stickler for everything being done by the book. You can't be too much like that out here, miss. It'll get you in the end. Um, just up here and then I can leave you to find the rest of your way."

We thanked Joe and watched him hare back the way we had come, weaving nimbly between soldiers and detritus as if the boy had been brought up in this filth. Only when he was no longer in sight, and having checked there was nobody close, did I dare speak to Holmes.

"They really didn't like Ogle-Thompson," I said.

"No," said Holmes, but would not say more.

Once we reached the main dressing station and our ambulance, I was eager to push off. However, one of the medical corps asked us if we'd missed lunch, and then saw I was shaking with cold. Against my protests we were led into the tent, where they ladled out two bowls of grey soup. I ate hungrily and Holmes brooded over everything we had learned. For all I wanted to quiz him, I had to content myself with morsels of gossip from the medical team. There were no wounded men that afternoon. They had had an idle day, they said, and I could see that as a result they were jumpy – I knew from my own work that it was better to be kept occupied. The waiting, the boredom, could be utterly corrosive.

By the time we had finished our meal it was dark and bitterly cold. Soldiers helped me start the ambulance – or watched, bemused, as I did it myself – and warned of ice on the road. I brushed them aside and got up into the cab. Holmes was still brooding, oblivious to all dangers.

The roads weren't as bad as the men had feared, but the headlamps gave only limited light and I took things steadily. Holmes remained silent. We passed the hills of spent shell casings and escaped the stink and noise of war. In the silence, my ears rang. My thoughts were whirling, too, as I tried to make sense of what we had learned.

"Well, sir," I said at length. "You were saying about Ogle-Thompson and how he wasn't exactly loved by his men."

Holmes didn't respond at once, then let out a slow sigh. "I wasn't saying anything of the sort. But since you seem so keen, I suspect Ogle-Thompson was cut from the same cloth as his father. Not the easiest man with whom to hunker down in conditions like that. I tell you, Miss Watson, I have known better living in the worst of slums. Is this really the best we can do for our men?"

He did not seem to expect an answer. I drove on. Eventually, I could stand the brooding silence no longer.

"Did you learn as much as you'd hoped?"

"In part," said Holmes. "This is proving to be a most singular case. I'm sure you see that yourself."

"The second letter," I said. "The one not from the general. You think it came from that dugout."

I had to watch the road in the gathering darkness, but I felt sure Holmes was smiling.

"On what do you base that suggestion?" he said.

"It was Ogle-Thompson's unit. They knew him and how he

died. And they had papers, a typewriter. They are equipped to send such messages."

Holmes laughed. "It would not stand up in a court of law. Yet we might add that the second letter is of the same paper stock as they had on the shelf in the dugout. More tellingly, there was the note above the desk."

I had not spotted the note. "Could you read that from where we were sitting?"

"I had already read it by the time we sat down. You might remember my fluster over where to hang my hat."

"Very sly. And what did the note say?"

"Oh, some instructions for unsticking the keys of the typewriter. The notable thing was the hand."

"You mean it was the same as your letter."

"I was hardly in a position to compare the two documents directly, but both have a loopless cursive script – the 'g' and 'p' do not join up to the letters that follow them. That is at least suggestive of a single author."

"Whom we must have just met," I said.

"That is possible," he said, though his tone suggested he thought otherwise.

"Then someone else," I said. He did not respond. I considered all I had witnessed. "Oh. The other man who died. They said he was loyal to their former officer. Loyal enough to have written to his parents."

"Good," said Holmes. "Yes, that would fit very well, though it is hardly convenient as we cannot now interview him. You recall the dead man's name?"

"Bother, no."

"Bill Dutton. Private William Murray Dutton on my list of names.

Killed in action three days ago, according to Captain Boyce."

"You don't believe him."

"I see no reason not to. For one thing, the men showed no indication that Dutton's death was out of the ordinary."

"Not like Ogle-Thompson."

"You noticed that. Good. These things are often relative. One can judge the extraordinary by comparison to the run-of-the-mill. Dutton's death was tragic, no doubt, but nothing unusual in the mire of the trenches. We therefore use it as the yardstick by which we can judge their reactions to this other death. The men he served with, the captain who replaced him and the general who wrote to Ogle-Thompson's mother have all reacted unusually. Then there is the added complication of that list."

"The list of names?"

"The list of figures, the ratios." He withdrew the card from his pocket and turned it over, though I could do no more than glance at it while driving through the dark. "Odds of sixty-six to one are really not very promising. And many more of these odds are even worse."

"That's the betting slip," I said, "which you claimed to have put into Captain Boyce's pocket."

"I did not actually say so," said Holmes.

"But you *didn't* plant it on him, did you?"

He was clearly pleased that I had made this deduction without needing to be prompted. "No, I didn't put it in his pocket – but neither did Captain Boyce. Someone else put it there for him to find."

"And you saw his response when he found it. He was horrified."

"Very good, Miss Watson. So he recognised what it signified, even if he didn't know how it came to be in his possession."

"But to be so upset by a betting slip… I suppose he might be religious and see gambling as a great sin."

"That might do well," said Holmes. "Except that this card is not a betting slip. I suggested that to put the man at his ease. You saw how readily he wanted to believe it? He was almost grateful that I took this card away."

"Then what is it really?"

Holmes considered the card. "If I am right," he said darkly, "it is something truly diabolical. Miss Watson, I sincerely hope that I am wrong."

I did not take Holmes back to the Chateau. Instead, he directed me to take a turning that I did not know. We followed a perilous, winding lane but Holmes assured me we were going the right way. It annoyed me that I had no idea where we were, while Holmes had arrived just two nights previously and knew the whole terrain. Of course, there was no use in complaining, and anyway, I had to keep my eyes on the road, so poorly lit by the headlamps. We coursed through the rain-spattered dark, then suddenly came upon cottages and a farmhouse.

As directed by Holmes, I pulled up outside a particular house. Through the window, we could see officers smoking and drinking at a wide kitchen table. It all looked incongruously cosy: I was hit by a primal longing for hearth and home, and sorely envious of Holmes for being billeted in such a place.

"Thank you, Miss Watson," he said. "Once again, you have been most accommodating. I hope it will not be long before we meet again."

"I hope so, too, sir," I said, and honestly I meant it. Despite everything, I had relished this second dose of adventure. But I had to be realistic. "I'm afraid it will depend on the general."

"You had best report to him directly."

He said the words blandly enough but they struck me hard. "Sorry, sir?"

"Please, Miss Watson, do not spare it the least thought. He assigned you as my driver for a specific purpose. I mean to say, he has drivers by the dozen here, men of experience who know the trenches first hand. Yet he assigned me an orderly."

I felt hot with shame. "You knew," I said.

"It seemed logical. You resented my visit the other night. You said as much to the general, or failed to hide your feelings. Perhaps you played up your dislike of me so that he would not suspect you had helped me visit the morgue. In doing so, you showed him you could be trusted in this matter – that you would be loyal to him by default, and not be swayed by my fame. I am sure he quite delighted in pairing Holmes the notorious misogynist with a Suffragette!"

With this, he jumped lightly down from the cab and made an effort to brush some of the muck from his coat. It would do no good; he was utterly caked in it, as was I. I also felt utterly wretched.

"I was never a Suffragette," I told him. "And I did not betray any confidence. The general does not know that we went down to the morgue."

"There was no need to lie on my behalf. I will take responsibility for my actions – and protect you from censure."

Confound him, that hurt. "I did not do it out of self-interest!"

His smile did not falter. "I did not claim you did."

"I was trying to help your investigation. This case, I think it's important."

Holmes bowed politely. "It is."

I glanced around nervously. There was no one on the road. "I still want to help," I told him. "Tell me what I should say."

Now Holmes looked disappointed. "You must tell the general everything," he said. "Present, with my full blessing, all you have observed, every last salient detail. The morgue, the dugout, the whole business." Then he turned neatly on his heel and sauntered to the front door, where he stopped to smile back at me, wolfishly. "The challenge, of course," he said, "is whether you can tell him what any of it means."

Then he was gone, lost to the warm comfort inside. I sat alone in the cab, fuming. No man has ever been more hated! Blast his infuriating smugness!

In fact, that was exactly what I now resolved to do. He had challenged me to make sense of this mystery. All right Mr Holmes, I told myself, crunching the ambulance into first gear, I would do exactly that.

Chapter Eight

A different sentry stood on duty at the top of the drive to the Chateau. This time I wasn't expected and he looked with disdain at my muddy, sodden clothes. Of course, it is considered a sign of hard graft when a man gets dirty from work, but we are held to a different account. I still had my letter from the general, in which this tedious sentry now tried to find fault. Then he behaved as if allowing me to pass were some great concession on his part, and began to say something about his views on permitting women to drive. I put my foot down and he had to jump back to save being spattered with mud.

The route he prescribed led down and round to what had once been a manicured lawn, now churned up by various staff cars. A canvas canopy had been erected to protect the fancier models from the elements; I spotted a rather nice Bentley as I passed.

There was no one on duty to indicate where I should fit, so I took a space overlooking the ornamental garden. The ambulance headlamps swept over the officers sat by the pond smoking fat cigars. The very cleanliness of their uniforms offended, especially coming straight from the trenches. But I was angry anyway and they were just in my line of sight.

Switching off the engine and plunged once more into darkness, I thought I could hear roosting – the first birds I'd heard in I couldn't say when. That cold, crisp evening, that bracing air, felt gloriously clean, even pure. I cringed with guilt, one of the few lucky ones able to escape from the trenches. Sat in the cab of the ambulance, I could still feel myself back there, haunted by the sounds and smells, the tension in my muscles, the underlying fear. How, I wondered, could anyone withstand that nightmare place without going utterly mad?

Then, conscious of the men by the pond watching me, I filled in the log book for the ambulance and climbed down from the cab. Walls of sandbags created an obstacle course up to the house and I followed the zigzagging route to a sentry at a low door.

"Know where you're going, love?" he said, barely looking up from the cigarette he was rolling.

"General Fitzgerald," I said.

The man stiffened, uncomfortably. "Aren't you the lucky one?" he said, and gave me directions. I proceeded inside.

The "Chateau" was really nothing of the sort, an ironic nickname applied by the soldiers out of wounded masculinity. Prior to the war the building had been a convent, and though it had long been past its prime and neglected, it suited the army down to the ground. I passed through plain, functional corridors to a dazzling space lit by bare electric bulbs. At row upon row of desks, men in uniform typed reports and checked paperwork. In the painted frescoes behind them, the nuns were similarly stooped over earnest, charitable work.

The men were too busy to pay me much heed, though a few looked over as I passed through. In the glare of the light, I was even more conscious of my shabby, soiled attire. Here, they fought an immaculate war.

I followed the directions I'd been given to a low, wide corridor positively alive with activity. Two rows of desks almost filled the space, each desk equipped with a telephone and typewriter. Men worked busily, calling to one another, barking instructions into their 'phones and making hasty notes. This, I came to learn, was the nerve centre for our division, the latest information relayed direct from the trenches.

A weaselly man with a greased moustache intercepted me before I could proceed. "Yes, love?"

"I am *Miss* Watson," I countered. "I am expected by General Fitzgerald."

He seemed to find the very idea entertaining. "I see. Did the old man give you a time or were you just to show up?"

"My orders," I said, to put this silly fool back in his place, "are to report to him straight away."

He clearly thought I must have got it wrong, so – again – I brandished my letter. He read if over carefully. "Nothing here about 'straight away'. There's other people as need the general's time. You can wait over there and he'll get to you when he can."

I knew he was fobbing me off. "What I have to tell him–"

"Yes, it's vital to the whole war. That's what everyone says. You take a seat and he'll see you when he can. If he deems it worth his time."

Smarting, I withdrew to the bench in an alcove at one side, under an enormous crucifix. Our Saviour gazed pitifully down on me in his agony.

The minutes crept by. With no clock in sight from my niche, I could not tell how long I sat there, but it must have been at least an hour. In my damp, dirty clothes I am surprised I did not catch a chill. I was in two minds about giving up, going back to the hospital to change, and then returning – but I worried I would miss my chance with the general. Besides, that time helped me gather my thoughts and think through all I had witnessed. Bits of the evidence fitted together quite neatly, while other elements remained mystifying. I puzzled over them, as if sheer effort of will might thread them together.

Eventually, the oleaginous man I'd spoken to came hurriedly over. "All right, you can have a few minutes."

I followed him to a door down the corridor. He knocked but didn't go in, ushering me forward. I went through into a small, square chamber – a cell for the devout. The hulking, walrus-like form of the general sat ensconced behind an incongruously ornate desk that was covered in papers. His teeth ground at the pipe in his mouth, the pungent smoke curling round his bushy whiskers. He acknowledged my arrival with a grunt and continued to read. I stood to attention in front of the desk, trying to hide my impatience.

It was a spartan chamber with few comforts or luxuries. A portrait of the king hung upon the wall, and on the desk there was a framed photo of the general and his corpulent family, all looking rather awkward.

At last, the general sat back in his seat, muttered, "At ease" – as though I were one of the men – and gestured at the only other chair, in a corner. I dragged it over and sat nearly in front of him. Only now did he seem to notice me and the state I was in.

"Oh dear me," he said, amused. "Have we been in the wars?"

"I thought it better to see you directly, sir," I said.

"Yes, very good. It's Augusta, isn't it? Do you mind if I call you Augusta? Did they offer you tea?"

The obsequious man – Montagu – was duly summoned and told to rustle up some refreshments. Montagu gave me a scathing look but rushed off to oblige. "Door!" barked the general, and the man scampered back to close it.

Now the general leaned forward towards me. "Abominable fellow. Manners of an ox. He has quite the head for logistics and all that, which is dashed useful to us just now. But there's something lacking where his heart should be. I dare say like your own Mr Holmes."

"He is not *my* Mr Holmes," I protested, then remembered to add, "sir."

The general glowed with satisfaction. "Knew I was right to put you together. Well, you'd best tell me everything."

I'd been so fired up with the prospect of reporting to him, yet now it actually came to it I find myself struggling for words. For one thing, there was the tricky matter of my confession.

"General," I said, "when we met before, I'm afraid I left out some details of the tour I gave Holmes." I thought it best to get through this sticky business as soon as possible, and sketched out Holmes's initial inquiry about the man Ogle-Thompson. At the mention of that name, the general's nostrils flared.

"The old cove," he said. "Statistics be damned. That was why he took you out to the unit today – his interest in that lad!"

At his bidding, I went on, detailing what we had not found in the register, and then my thought about where else we might check, the locked door, and what we failed to find in the morgue. The general listened in silence, his shrewd, dark eyes fixed on me, his teeth grinding at his pipe.

"Then we returned to the ward, where we found you with Matron," I said. "And you know the rest, sir. I don't think there's anything else, until you asked me to drive for Holmes today."

He regarded me coolly, his expression stern. Without moving a muscle, he seemed utterly different: no longer avuncular but all ruthless power.

"Why did you not tell me this before?" he said.

Before I could answer, a sharp knock at the door gave me a start, and Montagu bustled in with a tray, the cups and saucers tinkling. The tea set was one of those overly lavish, Victorian styles with gold-plated rims. It didn't match the modest convent cell in the slightest. Montagu poured, not asking me how I might take it but dropping two sugar lumps into each cup. Then he retired, with another hateful smile at me.

The general picked up his cup and saucer and sat back to regard me. "Why did you lie to me?" he asked.

I dared to take my own cup and saucer, though my hand was unsteady. "I think I was in shock, sir," I said. "I felt incriminated. And I'm afraid I'm not used to Scotch. It all went to my head, I suppose. I can only apologise, sir – and make a clean breast of it now."

I was throwing myself on his mercy, and he pressed his advantage.

"This anonymous letter," he said with pleasant menace. "The one that seemed to contradict mine. Did Holmes have any clue who might have written that?"

"We think we know who it was," I said. "As a result of our investigation today."

"I see. Does the identity of this person exonerate me?"

That took me by surprise. "Well, sir. Not exactly."

His eyes twinkled. "Then you still think I might be a wrong 'un."

"No, sir. I mean, sir, I regret not being entirely honest with you when we spoke the other evening."

"You're an accomplished liar," the general told me. "If I'd caught any hint of this, I wouldn't have paired you with him today. And there I was, thinking myself a sound judge of men. Well. You had best tell me what took place today, and then we can decide what to do with you."

Perturbed by this, I gave him a concise account of my journey to the trenches and back. He listened attentively, refilling his pipe and lighting it as I unfolded my story. I sipped my tea and even helped myself to one of the delicate biscuits, trying to convey a fearless air.

The truth is, I felt nothing of the sort, and as I spoke my mind tumbled over with all the dreadful possibilities he might have in store. I could be put on a charge, even face court martial. As I sat sharing tea and biscuits with this walrus-like man, was he coldly deliberating on whether I should be shot? He decided the fates of thousands of men out in the trenches every day, and I was nothing, no one.

"Well, young lady," he said when I had completed my narrative. "It all sounds pretty mystifying – and of very little consequence given what else is going on." He eyed me shrewdly. "Or perhaps you think differently."

I should have denied it. How much more sensible to play dumb and then meekly withdraw. That is what Mother would have counselled – but she was not in that room.

"I think, sir," I told the general, "that you wanted to be kind."

He didn't speak, but a smile played across his face.

"That's at the heart of all this, sir," I went on. "You wrote to Captain Ogle-Thompson's mother on familiar terms, so you know her socially or have some other connection."

"Let us say, for the sake of argument, that you are correct in that aspect. Go on."

"You sought to comfort her for the loss of her son. It was kinder to say that he died on my ward though he was never even brought to the hospital."

He didn't flinch. "That is quite an accusation. Why would I lie to poor Julia?"

"I think rather that you spared her," I said. "Her son died out in the mud, in the cold and wet and horror. You painted a more comforting image: him in bed in a well-ordered hospital, surrounded by caring staff. What mother would not prefer that?"

The general nodded slowly. "You make me sound almost noble. But it's a jolly serious accusation all the same."

"That wasn't my intention, sir."

"And there are other ways to explain what might have happened. I could have muddled up the details of the specific case. You know, I write a lot of letters to a lot of mothers."

His tone made plain I was not to challenge him further on this point. "Yes, sir," I said.

That seemed to satisfy him. He chewed on the end of his pipe and I sipped demurely at my tea. "This second letter you mention," he said idly, as if only continuing this conversation out of politeness. "I take it that was some silly blighter stirring trouble."

"We don't think so, sir."

He couldn't hide his interest. "You spoke to the person responsible?"

"I'm afraid not. We think the second letter was written by Private William Dutton, but he died a few days ago." That gave the general a start, so I pressed on. "There was nothing suspicious about it, just the ordinary course of the war. By all accounts, Dutton was a good soldier and not the sort to make a nuisance of himself."

"Hmm," said the general. "Then why write?"

"He didn't know of your connection to Ogle-Thompson's mother, and couldn't be sure what you'd write to her."

"Dashed impertinent to think it was any of his business!"

"He might have worried, too, that someone else in the unit would say something, and that word might get around. The men in his unit told us today that Ogle-Thompson was strict and not exactly everyone's favourite. No one wants to hear that their son is unpopular."

The general's brow furrowed. "Hmm. I suppose it more or less fits. Anything else?"

"There's this business of the betting slip, but I can't see how it fits with Ogle-Thompson. Unless one reason his men didn't like him was that he came down hard when he caught them gambling. They might have lost money as a result. Dutton might then have worried that they would ask the family to make up the debt. But really I'm guessing there, sir."

The general brooded over this for a moment. "I dare say it explains things. Well, all good. Capital. I shall write again to the family and apologise for the mix-up. And yet one hardly wants to stir this all up for them. They have just lost their son."

We sat for a moment as he puzzled over the options, and then he looked quizzically at me.

"Perhaps you have a suggestion."

"No, sir!" I protested. "Well, hardly…"

He smiled. "Go on."

"It's only that it strikes me that you could use Mr Holmes. He undertook the case for the family. Let him go back and explain that the second letter was sent with good intentions but based on a misunderstanding. The family can feel confident – and relieved – that the great Sherlock Holmes has got to the truth."

The general seemed quite taken by the idea. "You think I should ask him to lie."

"Oh no," I said. "But he might be selective in what he tells them, to spare a grieving family any further pain. Even he would understand that."

The general smiled. "You really don't like him."

"I wouldn't say that, sir. He's brilliant in many ways. He's also well aware of that fact."

He laughed. "Of course. Well, Miss Watson, this has all been rather illuminating." He slurped at his tea and, since I hadn't finished mine, filled time with good-mannered questions about my family and background, and my people seemed to pass muster. We made easy, idle talk, though inside I felt aflutter at having survived the ordeal. Immodestly, I thought I had rather impressed him.

We were not quite finished when Montagu knocked and came in.

"General, Mr Holmes is here to see you."

The general bestowed a benign smile upon me. "The condemned man. Miss Watson, I suggest that Montagu demonstrates how you might leave without Holmes seeing you."

I got up from my seat and was ready to go, but Montagu hovered in the doorway, grimacing.

"Begging your pardon, general, but Mr Holmes specifically requested that Miss Watson remain so he might address you both."

The general grinned. "The absolute cheek of him! Miss Watson, you are not required to be part of his charade. By all means go if you so wish."

I admit I considered it, just to irritate Holmes. But I also wanted to see his response to the general instructing him what to tell Ogle-Thompson's family, so I retook my seat.

A moment later, Holmes strode boldly in, brandishing in one hand a cane chair which he dropped down neatly beside me and seated himself, without being invited. He was immaculate, his suit and shoes pristine, his grey hair windswept like some romantic poet, but no longer flecked with mud. What a contrast I made, in my soiled and sodden uniform.

"Miss Watson, a pleasure as always," he said breezily. "General, I hope she has been entirely candid. You have been told about the registers on the ward and in the morgue, what we were told of Private Dutton, and our discovery of what I told the men was a betting slip? Good, then you have all the evidence before you."

As he spoke, he withdrew from his suit the pocket book he had shown me before. He riffled through the loose papers tucked into the back and selected a folded sheet. It was not any of the documents I had seen before. Instead, he unfolded a crisp banknote.

"Now, general. Are you a sporting man, by any chance?"

I suspect few people ever spoke to the general in such a cavalier manner, or at least had not done so for some time. The general, cheeks flushed and eyes wide, stared back at this extraordinary man. Holmes continued, holding up the banknote.

"Five pounds," he said.

"I can see what it is," snapped the general. "And you seem to labour under a misapprehension, Mr Holmes. We have no need of your conjuring tricks. Miss Watson has told me everything – including your decidedly questionable behaviour regarding the morgue. She has also solved your case for you."

Holmes, eyes wide, turned to me. "You made sense of it?"

"Yes," I told him.

"Every bit of it? Even the betting slip?"

"Yes," I said, exasperated now.

"Excellent," he said. "No, don't tell me – as long as the general remembers what was said."

"Of course I do," snapped the general. "What on earth is this?"

Holmes waved the banknote. "A wager. You have Miss Watson's explanation of the case. Five pounds says she has it entirely wrong!"

Chapter Nine

"**M**onty!" barked the general – and I thought he meant to have Holmes thrown out. I would not have blamed him. Yet Holmes showed no sign of concern, sprawling back in his chair, long legs splayed in front of him in a manner hardly fitting the office of a general.

Montagu appeared at the door. "Sir?"

"More tea," barked the general. The secretary scurried off. "All right, Mr Holmes," said the general. "Impress us with your version of events. Though it is only fair to warn you that Miss Watson has made the most compelling case."

Holmes bowed his head, in mock respect to me. "I should expect nothing less," he said. "Yet the fact she is still seated is evidence of its own sort. She has not exposed your lie."

This he said with relish, but it did not achieve the intended effect. The general and I both laughed at once, and for a moment I delighted in seeing Holmes wrong-footed – but only for a moment. He looked utterly distraught. Perhaps I was sensitive to that because I had spent so many months tending young men who had been robbed of their strength and ability, and had to come to terms with the loss of so much they had taken for granted. As I had observed in the dugout earlier that day, Holmes seemed to be genuinely terrified by the prospect of losing his faculties. It struck me then that his smug demeanour was only a kind of mask, projecting a confidence he did not honestly feel. Despite everything, I felt sorry for the man.

"I am honoured indeed if I have matched part of your deduction," I said. He did not seem to hear. I changed tack, knowing the kind of bluff humour that got a response from my patients. "Do I win all of the five pounds, or should I split it with the general?"

Holmes smiled. "I rather think that is up to him."

The general did not seem amused by any of this. "I should remind you, Miss Watson, that I did not accept your accusation."

Holmes sat forward with renewed interest. "Then you claim you did not lie."

The general shifted uncomfortably. "I said there might have been a mistake."

Holmes turned to me. "And how did that stand with you, Miss Watson?"

I knew better than to be drawn. "How does it stand with you, Mr Holmes?"

He beamed. "Touché. The telling detail, I think, is in the second letter received by the family of the late Ogle-Thompson." He withdrew from his pocket book the page I had seen before.

Sirs

Whatever you is informed dont believe it. In truth, your son Cpn Thompson was a good man

and good soldier, as his full record will show.
He saved my life and others to my knowing.
A honest friend

"Our working hypothesis is that this came from the dugout and is the work of Private William Dutton," said Holmes. "The intriguing detail is the word 'informed'. Not 'said' or 'told' or what have you. 'Informed' suggests official notification. Then this appeal to the dead man's 'full record'. He means, surely, that some event or incident should not tar an otherwise exemplary career in the service. How much do I follow you in all this, Miss Watson?"

I stared at the words in the letter, furious. Yes, of course that was their meaning.

"I did not have the letter to refer to," I told him, hotly.

"No, of course," said Holmes. "But now add to this what you saw today, the response of those men in the dugout."

"They hated Ogle-Thompson," I said. "They thought him too strict, but that is hardly a reason for hatred. There must have been something else. Something shameful."

"Good," said Holmes. "And to counter this, Dutton says that his life was saved by Ogle-Thompson. That is a similar story to the one in your letter, general."

He produced the first letter, and passed it to the general – who dismissed it with a wave of his hand.

"Just come out with it, Mr Holmes."

Holmes sighed. "Both letters want to insist Ogle-Thompson was brave. We can therefore suppose that this had been called into question. That is the source of the shame: some act of gross cowardice."

I gasped. But the astonishing thing was the general's silence. He did not deny it. He simply stared back at Holmes, levelly.

"Such a thing would, of course, lead to court martial," said Holmes. "But that would appear in the service record. And, if he had been found guilty and delivered to a firing squad, something of this would have been included in the official notification telegraphed to the family. What we have here is an *accusation* of serious cowardice, but then Ogle-Thompson died before the matter could be properly dealt with. The result has been uncertainty, and that void is what these letters each sought to fill."

Still the general didn't say anything. "Was he a coward?" I asked.

The general slowly nodded. "And worse. Oh, that other letter is quite correct. Philip had an exemplary record, mentions in Dispatches, that stuff it says about saving lives. But lately the boy had been spreading wild stories about the conduct of the war. Pure hogwash, exaggerating how bad things are out of all proportion. Well, a respected young officer... you can imagine the effect on the men. Oh, they vehemently deny that they listened to him. But I'm career army, worked my way up through the ranks. I know what that kind of poison can do, just being spoken out loud. So. Charge of sedition. And you're right, Mr Holmes. He would have faced the firing squad. But he got wind of what was coming, or used up the last vestige of his wits. Word is that he simple charged over the top. No gun, no helmet, nothing, shouting to the enemy as he ran towards their trenches, calling them his friends. Not that that did him much good."

"Then he was shot by the Germans," I said.

"There were a lot of witnesses to say so. He made quite a show, out in No Man's Land as if taking a stroll through Hyde Park. But I wouldn't have blamed any of our lot for shooting him first. Might well have done it m'self."

I felt hollow inside at the thought, all too easy to visualise having stood in those trenches only hours before.

"You recovered his body," said Holmes.

"No one went to get him, if that's what you mean," said the general. "He crawled back to the trench himself, and died shortly thereafter. They say they did what they could for him."

Holmes held up the second letter, the one from Private Dutton. "In what you told the mother, you used the same story as in this – that Ogle-Thompson saved Dutton's life."

"I could have taken that from his service record," said the general.

"I've checked his records and it's not mentioned," said Holmes. "No one else seems to have been keen to defend the dead man's honour, therefore you must have been acquainted with the details by Dutton himself. I can't imagine an ordinary private had the chance to appeal to a general in person. I suppose he wrote you a letter."

The general stared back at Holmes, his jaw set grimly.

"I burnt it," he said.

"Very wise," nodded Holmes. "What a curious letter it must have been. We can see from the example here that Dutton was no master essayist. He clearly did not expect to persuade you of anything, or he would not also have written to the family. And yet, as your own letter shows, you were indeed persuaded to lie." The general wanted to protest, but Holmes held up a hand. "It is hardly credible that you would be swayed by a single document, whatever the source. I put it to you that Dutton's entreaty served only to confirm what you already understood. There is something more to all of this, a greater injustice."

I had sat in rapt silence and now waited on the general to respond. Yes, Holmes had blown my simple theories entirely out of the water, but in doing so he had laid out a much stronger version of events, and one with very grave implications.

But before the general could address any of these, the door burst open and in marched Montagu with the tray of tea.

"Out!" bellowed the general. Tea things rattling, Montagu turned neatly on his heel. "Put the tea down first," snapped the general.

There followed a light farce as Montagu scurried over, cleared space on the desk, and dutifully – but at double speed – poured out our tea.

"Thank you so much," purred Holmes. "Pray, what kind of cake is that?"

"Madeira," said Montagu. "Only we're running a tad low on lemon peel so Chef has to improvise…" He would have said more but caught the general's steely eye and promptly made himself scarce.

"Door!" shouted the general, but Montagu already knew to close it firmly behind him.

Holmes, with great pleasure, cut thick slices of cake for the three of us. We had cake in the hospital but nothing like this, with a glorious, soft aroma. The privations of war make one especially appreciative of food, and this was heaven itself. It had also been a long while since I'd had anything to eat. What would the men at the main dressing station have made of me feasting like this, I thought. It was another world.

"Where were we?" said Holmes agreeably, sitting back in his seat. "Ah yes. General, you already knew there was something rum about the business with Ogle-Thompson and the circumstances of his death."

The general sipped his tea quite politely. "Not entirely," he said. "But I'm an old soldier and have been through a few scrapes before this one. And I have some doubts about these accusations of cowardice. Oh, it can happen. I've dealt with some shoddy behaviour in my time. But here, this madness that comes so out of character…" He shuddered. "Philip hasn't been the only one."

"And you can't explain it," said Holmes.

"No one can," said the general. "It seems a unique response to the scale of this sorry war. The remarkable pressures it places on the men, unlike any previous conflict. There's cases of it among all the Allied forces, I'm afraid. The quacks think it must be psychological. In all truth, Mr Holmes, I am not sure what use that is to anyone. I mean, if it's all in the mind, what in heaven can we do?"

Holmes turned to me. "You have training as a nurse. What would you do for these men?"

"We would help them," I said, not sure what else could be said.

"But prevention is better than cure," said Holmes. "The problem is that until now we have seen only symptoms, not any cause for such erratic behaviour."

"The cause is the war," muttered the general. "How exactly does that help us?"

"Wait a moment," I said, heart beginning to race. "Mr Holmes, you said, 'until now'…"

He withdrew further documents from the pocket book. "Perhaps I should tell you that I suspected something of all this from the moment I saw the two letters. Of course, I could not be sure, but the repeated detail of the heroism, that use of the word 'informed', were at least suggestive and so my initial thought was simply not to proceed with investigation. My friend Dr Watson had asked me to look into the business as a favour to Ogle-Thompson's father and I saw no useful purpose in exposing the family to this hidden shame. However, when I met with Ogle-Thompson's parents, they presented me with the few personal possessions sent home to them from the trenches. I obliged with some deductions from the wristwatch, his wallet and a miniature, framed photograph of the young man's fiancée. Now, this last item struck me as curious. The misshapen clasps and a pattern of scratches showed that it had been tampered with. 'He was devoted to this Ann,' I said, and they confirmed that the two had been childhood sweethearts, that there had never been anyone else, and that this framed photograph had been her gift to him when he left for the war. If his affections had not altered, why then would the young man open and close the frame?"

He asked this of the general and me. The general harrumphed, eager to get on with the story. Holmes turned to me. "He put something else in the frame," I said. "Behind the photograph, for safekeeping."

Holmes's nostrils flared and his eyes glittered. "Excellent, Miss Watson. Yes, that was my conclusion. I made an excuse to the family, saying I wished to ponder the various items before taking on the case. They allowed me to take the watch, the wallet and frame back to examine more closely. In the back of the frame I found this."

He placed a card on the desk in front of us. Immediately I thought he had made a mistake, for it looked like the card of figures, the "betting slip", that he had taken from Captain Boyce earlier that day. But now Holmes produced another card, and placed it down next to the first. "This," he said, "was in the pocket of the captain who replaced Ogle-Thompson, though he had no idea how it got there."

The general and I leaned forward to examine the two sets of numbers.

71/1	66/1
44/1	76/1
64/1	66/1
58/1	89/1

63/1	54/1
101/1	83/1
65/1	90/1

"Another betting slip," I said. "Except you told me it is not a betting slip."

"I wish it were," said Holmes. "Note that he hid this card in the photograph frame, not his wallet, suggesting that he knew it was important to keep secret. That frame was too delicate to be constantly used for hiding documents, so this was not a regular hiding place either, but a one-off. Therefore, I supposed, if the slip were some kind of record of bets, it had to be a uniquely significant wager – or something else entirely. This, with the mystery relating to the manner of the young man's death, was enough to convince me to take this case."

I studied the cards. They were both the same size, in the same form, and used the same typeface. The first card, from Ogle-Thompson's picture frame, was a little more creased and worn, presumably where the young captain had himself studied it. As for the numbers, I could make no sense of them other than that they presented ratios or odds. As Holmes had said previously, odds of sixty-six to one were hardly favourable – and many of the stakes were much worse. Then I counted the rows.

"Seven rows," I said. "I suppose that could signify a week."

I turned to Holmes for confirmation, but his eyes were fixed on the general. The general stared down at the cards in abject horror.

"You recognise what they are," said Holmes.

The general nodded, dumbstruck. Then he got up from his chair.

"For G—'s sake, put those away before anyone else has to see them!" he said. "You had best come with me, Mr Holmes. But I must impress on you that this is a matter of the greatest secrecy, in the national interest." He glanced again at the cards and quickly looked away, as if they caused him physical pain.

Chapter Ten

Holmes neatly folded the cards and papers back into his pocket book, but passed the five-pound note to me.

"But–" I began to say.

"My wager was that you had it *entirely* wrong," he told me. "But your logic was sound and some deductions correct. I underestimated you, Miss Watson, and it is right it should be to my cost."

It was, I realised, his way of apologising for his earlier rudeness. I plucked the note from his fingers with a nod of thanks. Something more than money passed between us in that exchange: an acknowledgement of a kind of kinship.

The general, looming over us, did not share this regard for my skills. "Miss Watson might care to remain here," he said – to Holmes, for all that he phrased it as if it were my own choice.

Holmes clearly saw my reaction to this. "General," he said, "I think she should come, too."

"Out of the question."

"Miss Watson is an intelligent and resourceful woman, an asset to my investigation. You yourself credited her insight. I am sure she can be trusted." In fact, I felt my loyalties had been, at best, divided in the case so far. Nevertheless, I was glad he felt I had earned my place through merit – even if it also rankled that this access would come as his gift. The general regarded me sceptically, and my soiled and muddy uniform did little to bolster my appeal. Yet he evidently concluded that it was not worth an argument with Holmes.

"I hardly need to remind you both," he told us, "that unauthorised disclosure of anything you are about to see could land you both in hot water."

He might have meant to put me off but it only hardened my resolve. "Yes, sir," I said firmly. That seemed to settle things.

The general led us out into the low, wide corridor of desks. Montagu hurried over to intercept us but the general brushed the little man aside. "Hold the fort," the general told him, indicating the small, square desk to one side. "We have a small matter to attend." Montagu regarded me acidly as he took his seat.

We followed the general through a series of passageways. Holmes caught my eye and smiled encouragement. I tried to look serious and determined, not some shrinking violet. That seemed to amuse him.

We turned into a nondescript corridor. Halfway up it, a soldier idled on a chair. Only as we approached did the man leap to his feet and salute the general. The general nodded at an innocuous door to one side and the soldier hurriedly fished keys from his pocket and found the right one for the lock. He had not at all looked like a guard, but I suspect that was rather the point.

The door opened onto what looked like a cupboard, but the general marched inside and shoved his hand against the back wall.

With a click, a panel of false bricks opened inwards and revealed a flight of stairs. Holmes beamed with delight at this ingenuity. We followed the general down the secret stairs. The soldier made sure to close the door behind us.

The narrow stairwell was quite unlike the one that had led Holmes and I down to the hospital morgue. Here, the steps were neat and even, perhaps newly repaired. Electric lights meant we could see our way easily. For all this route was secret, I thought it must be well used.

Another soldier waited at the foot of the stairs. He saluted the general and allowed us to proceed into the claustrophobic network of cellars. Holmes had to stoop, but looked thrilled by this secret world. There were cabinets and files in some of the small rooms we passed, yet most rooms were bare, and eerie. Our footsteps echoed around us and I had the uncanny sense of being watched.

In fact, we were closely observed. Sentries emerged from the darkness to verify who we were. They knew the general, of course, but still stopped him to be sure. Each sentry that we came to scrutinised Holmes and me closely. They were especially suspicious of me, in my muddy clothes. Each time, the general gave our names, which the sentries recorded in their log books before we could proceed any further.

Around a corner and we could hear a thrum of machinery. Soon, this resolved into voices and activity – a human machine of men working. We emerged into a room rather like the one I had observed upstairs: rows of desks and typewriters, and the clamour of industry. The general swept through and we followed in his wake. Our destination was another locked door at the back of this great room.

The soldier on guard asked our names and logged them in his own book, which the general made a point of examining. But the soldier did not himself have the key for this door. Instead, the general produced one from his keychain. He had to pull with some force before the heavy, thick door swung outwards. We went through into a long, narrow space, the walls, floor and ceiling bare concrete. Two filing cabinets awaited us, and a chair and desk.

We followed the general inside – had there been anyone else, it would have been quite a squeeze. Now I saw, inset into one wall, a bulky metal device. The general operated a switch on this and the machine started up with a terrible rattle and roar. A vent in the side began to puff with a hot, metallic odour. The general studied the air-conditioning unit for a moment and then, satisfied, pushed between Holmes and me to go back to the door and close it, shutting us in with an ominous clang.

I felt a sudden animal panic at being trapped in such a small, unnatural space. Holmes seemed unaffected, though his eyes picked quickly over the surrounding details. I followed his example, trying to take it all in. The general eased himself between us once more.

"It's soundproof, more or less," he said. Then he gestured at the rattling, puffing machine in the wall. "And that thing makes enough racket to drown out anything else. No one can hear us or see what goes on in here. So…"

He produced another key and with it opened a drawer in one of the filing cabinets. Then, using both hands, he hauled out an enormous, leather-bound book. It was many times bigger than the registers we had seen in the hospital. The general hefted the huge book over to a desk in the corner, dropping it down with an almighty crash. He reached for the cover to open it, then stopped and placed both hands on top of the book.

"I remind you," he said to us, "that this is extremely confidential. Pain of death and torture."

"You are not obliged to show us anything," Holmes told him. "But there is something very serious afoot and we will do all in our power to help you."

Perhaps against his better judgement, the general opened the book and flicked through a handful of pages. Each page was printed with a grid of compact squares. Onto these were written two long columns of handwritten figures. I do not recall the figures exactly but a general impression will suffice:

11.10	12/1
12.10	9/1
13.10	63/1
14.10	24/1
15.10	8/1
16.10	11/1

Holmes had brought the two cards with him and placed them in the book, next to the column of numbers. I'd already deduced that the seven ratios given on each of the betting slips corresponded to days in a week. On that basis, it was easy to read the first column in this ledger as days, the repeated "10" signifying October. In the second column, the ratios were clearly in the same form as on the cards.

"It's impossible," said the general under his breath.

But Holmes did not share his horror; indeed, he studied the cards and the figures in the book with renewed fascination. "How many people have access to this book?"

The general fished out the key on its chain. "There are four keys: this and three others, held by men whose honour I would not dare to question. They are all kept on chains. And anyway, you have seen the way things are arranged here. You could not get through that door without being seen and your presence recorded. I checked the names in the book outside. No one else has been in here. So how could they possibly have copied this intelligence?"

Holmes considered for a moment. Then, fishing a magnifying glass from his pocket, he began a methodical examination of the room around us. The walls, the floor and ceiling were all of bare, coarse concrete, and he tapped and prodded but could find no exception. He studied the air-conditioning machine and the furniture, checking they did not conceal any break in the concrete. Then he examined the door, asking the general's permission before opening it so that he could inspect the lock, the hinges and that it fully sealed the doorway. I watched with interest, enjoying this sight of him, glass in hand, just as in the stories. He took a slip of paper from his pocket and attempted to pass it under the door. It would not fit, whatever he tried. He closed the door and tried feeding the paper above the door or along its side. It could not be done.

He turned back to us, eyes glittering with interest. "A locked-room mystery," he told us. "How very intriguing. With the door open, there is no way that a person in here could hide themselves from those working outside. There is no way to enter without being observed. I take it there are people working in the room out there at all times?"

"Exactly," said the general. "It should be impossible for anyone to get at this book."

Holmes brooded for a moment, then ducked nimbly between us to get to the desk. He bent over the book and ran a long index finger down the column of ratios. He quickly moved on to the next column, then turned the page to continue the trail.

"You're onto something?" asked the general.

"Possibly," said Holmes, working his way down the page. "If I can find the sequences as written on the cards, we will have a better idea when the information was copied. We can then cross-check against your register of those who accessed the room." He turned another page, but that huge volume would take him some time to work through. The general shifted impatiently.

"Only three other fellows have the key," he said. "So they must be the suspects."

"You are also a suspect, general," said Holmes with a smile. He continued to work.

"Is there anything I can do to help?" I asked Holmes.

"I doubt it," he said, his attention focused on the book. Then he stopped. "Miss Watson, do you understand what the numbers show?"

Without waiting for my answer, he continued to trace through the column of figures. The general watched me quizzically. Holmes had once again put me on the spot, but I had, of course, been working on this question. The seriousness with which the general treated the numbers made it plain that they were related to the conduct of the war. Both captains had recognised their significance, and been horrified. Then there was the fact that each card listed seven figures, surely corresponding to a week.

"They're daily tallies of some kind," I said. The general snorted – annoyed that I had decoded this highly secret material. "You record the success or otherwise of each day on the front. But I am not sure what it is being counted."

Holmes seemed pleased by my deduction – and that I admitted where I had got stuck. "We might reverse the problem," he told me in an encouraging tone, still working his way through the figures in the book. "What statistic could be collected on a daily basis?"

I imagined myself back in the trenches, alongside Captain Boyce. What would I be able to measure? "It's not territory captured," I said, "because that does not change every day. It would also be difficult to measure. As would the number of enemy killed or wounded." It was in saying these last words that the awful realisation hit me. "But the officers out there would know how many of their own men had died."

The general snorted again – because I had it exactly. "Each unit calls in their daily numbers," he said. "We total them up here, but the totals can make grim reading. On one day of the Somme, we lost sixty thousand men in a single day! Well, I can tell you, we were all in a funk here about that – and of course it got out and caused merry hell among the men. Morale is four-fifths of how we'll win this war."

Holmes wagged a finger at the columns in the book. "Hence this cipher. You total the numbers lost, but as a ratio against some given number of men to begin with. The ratio means something to you and your administrators, but not to the men out in trenches, so the information cannot spread."

"But Ogle-Thompson," I said, "and Captain Boyce both realised what the cards meant."

"They both supplied the daily figures for their unit," said Holmes. "My guess is that they supplied those figures once a week." He looked to the general, who nodded to confirm this. "That is why a week's figures are given on each card, so that they would make the connection. Of course, without knowing the given figure of men from which these ratios are calculated, they would not have a true picture of losses. But then, I do not think that was the intention of whoever produced these cards. In effect, each ratio is a man's chances of surviving to the end of a given day."

No wonder the officers had been appalled. Sixty-six to one against was no chance at all!

Yet Holmes did not seem to share this sense of horror. Indeed, he traced his finger down a final column of figures with mounting satisfaction.

"You've found it?" asked the general.

"On the contrary," said Holmes with delight. "Yes, individually, some ratios correspond to those in the book, but at no point does the seven-ratio sequence on either card appear."

The general did not understand and looked to me to explain. "Then," I said to Holmes, "the cards have been faked."

"Worse than that," Holmes told me. "The cards match the format of the centralised records, so an officer in receipt of one of these cards would think it was an official tally. Yet the odds are very much worse on the cards that the mean average of those in the book. Now, imagine the effect on an officer finding such a card."

Of course, I didn't need to imagine: I had seen Boyce's reaction first-hand. "They would think the war is going very badly," I said.

The general now leaned over to study the cards again. Beneath his whiskers, his features coloured with anger. "They would think it was all hopeless!"

We turned to Holmes, who looked energised, elated by this awful revelation. "That, I propose, is what happened to young Ogle-Thompson. Someone secreted this card upon his person. He found it, understood its significance, and it broke his spirit. This man, this strict stickler for rules even in the mire of the trenches, and he saw it all as futile."

"They meant to do the same to Captain Boyce," I said. "And general, you said this was happening throughout the Allied forces."

Holmes raised a finger in warning. "That is speculation. Boyce and Ogle-Thompson are the only men we know to have received one of these cards, both of them in the same unit. We have no evidence that this goes any further. We must have more data."

The general growled. "Who? Who would do this?"

"That we shall have to establish," said Holmes.

"But I don't understand," I added. "There are surely much easier ways to disrupt the war." The general shot me a look I will not quickly forget. "I mean to say," I said, "one reads about spies they have caught, the efforts at direct sabotage."

"Efforts that have failed, given that they were caught," said Holmes.

"Those are the ones we know of," I continued. "But there must a thousand ways to disrupt the war effort. You might blow up the docks or supply lines, or sabotage equipment..."

The general still had his eyes on me. "Quite the little Suffragette..." he said darkly.

Holmes flapped his hand to wave away the general's concern. "Miss Watson is entirely correct to put herself in the position of whoever is doing this," he said. "That is how we will outwit them. We must think as they do, and ask ourselves what our actions are intended to gain."

"Anarchy," said the general. "That's what anarchists want."

"It is very well-organised way of bringing about chaos," said Holmes. He turned to me. "Think of what we saw in the trenches, how the men were with Boyce. What did you observe?"

"They were awkward around him," I said. "But really, one should expect that, given that he had not been with them very long, and after what happened with their previous officer..."

"You must put yourself into their heads," he told me. "Take

yourself back to the dugout. How it felt. The sound and smell and everything. No detail is too small."

I felt self-conscious with the general watching, but did as I was bidden, closing my eyes and willing myself back to that cold, damp room under the earth.

"It is not done to speak ill of the dead," said Boyce firmly. To my astonishment, some of the men turned their backs on him. "It's meant to be unlucky," Boyce told them.

Those words, at least, affected the men. The trenches were well known to be rife with superstition. Yet they apparently resented it coming from Boyce. They hated Ogle-Thompson and disliked his replacement. It was the most extraordinary thing to witness, and I could see Holmes watching with interest.

With a start, I opened my eyes to find Holmes triumphant. "Tell the general what we both observed."

"Sir," I said. "The men… they can't trust their new captain because they're still smarting from the way the last one behaved. They worry the new one could turn out just the same. They're waiting for him to flip. What was done to Ogle-Thompson, it gets at the bond between officers and men, so it affects everyone in the trenches."

"More than that," said Holmes. "Officers are often of the middle and upper classes, so the effect is to undermine the very heart of our society." He held up one of the cards. "These are tools of revolution."

I thought the general would be appalled by this, but he seized on the idea. "Mr Holmes, it's well recognised now that more officers than men suffer from shell shock. The doctors cannot account for it: they would expect those of good families, good backgrounds, good blood, to be hardier in weathering these things. Are you saying you can explain it – that the officers have been targeted, and anyone suffering this kind of breakdown has received one of these cards?"

I could see why he wanted to believe that to be so. As he'd told me before, he wrote to a great number of families. Perhaps, as with Ogle-Thompson, he had connections to some of the relatives. But what words would ever do to tell grieving loved ones about the wild-eyed horror of shell shock or accusations of cowardice?

Yet Holmes's smile faltered. "We have only found two of these cards. Surely more would have surfaced if what you say is true, given that shell shock has been observed and even studied for some years. No, I think the people behind this are exploiting a phenomenon that already existed; they have developed a means to induce the same effects. But then perhaps, in what we have deduced about their dreadful scheme, there is the key to understanding shell shock. Officers gather the daily figures and are briefed on operations. As a result, they have a wider sense of context, a greater perspective on the war than the common soldiery. And the cold truth is that the scale of everything out on the front – the volume of munitions, of men, of loss, of unrelenting pressure – can be overwhelming. Thus officers succumb more often than the ordinary men."

I remembered the symptoms Holmes himself had presented in the trenches: that extreme vigilance of darting eyes and breathlessness as he tried to take it all in. His intelligence, his skills at observation, made him *more* susceptible.

"Then," said the general as he made the same connection, "you're saying shell shock is explicable – even logical."

Holmes looked uncomfortable. "I sincerely hope it can be explained and then remedied, but I merely posit a hypothesis that seems to fit the facts we have observed. Yet, having seen conditions in the trenches for myself..." For a moment, he seemed lost, imagining himself back there. He soon shook himself out of it but something haunted still remained.

"In the madness of such conflict," he told us, "I should say that a breakdown was a rational response."

We left the concrete room, Holmes pocketing the two cards and the general locking the door behind us. My mind was racing and I wanted to ask who could possibly be behind the cards, and what Holmes suspected of how far their conspiracy went, and how we might catch them. Of course, outside the locked room and in hearing of all the staff, I could not say a thing.

Without a word, we made our way back to the general's office. I was jittery with excitement, eager to pick over all we had uncovered and its significance. Yet when I turned to Holmes, he held up a finger to indicate that I should stay silent and nodded to the general.

The general had seemed so domineering when I first met him. Now he dejectedly poured out three glasses of the very best Scotch. Holmes and I took our seats, from where we watched the general drain his glass in one go and pour himself another. He looked awfully tired and old, his whiskers drooping glumly. I exchanged a glance with Holmes, who clearly shared my concern.

Then the general unlocked a safe on the far side of the desk, withdrew a bundle of papers, flicked through them, and found a document that he passed to Holmes. It looked little different from countless other missives I had seen, spelling out formal orders. What was more striking in that moment was the general's demeanour. His head was bowed, his eyes averted to the floor. He looked thoroughly ashamed.

"The wretched thing is," he said, "I thought Ogle-Thompson had saved us all a lot of bother. Much better to die on the front, like a proper soldier, than… than…"

He could not finish the sentence. Holmes showed me the document.

From: Gen. Rayner Fitzgerald
To: Corps of Military Police

Sir,

I do not understand your inquiry. If Captain Ogle-Thompson is guilty of the charges, he should jolly well face the firing squad. No reference to his former record and no familial connection should have bearing on that first duty.

R–

When I had read those stark words, Holmes placed the document face down on the desk. Then he sat back in his chair and sipped his whisky.

"You could not have known any better," I told the general.

He rounded on me angrily. "Couldn't I, indeed? The military police had their doubts! They even put them in writing. What would you possibly know?"

Chastened, I mumbled, "Sorry, sir."

"The military police could offer no evidence," said Holmes blithely. "They presented you with only a *feeling* that something did not add up. Anything more, and you surely would have been swayed."

The general seemed grateful for that consideration. "I would like to think so. Miss Watson, I apologise: I am angry at myself rather than you. Several people have expressed doubts about what's been going on. But I was vehement that any officer who betrayed his duty should be taken out and shot."

"For the encouragement of others," nodded Holmes.

The general nodded slowly. "Morale is crucial out here. We have to be strict and maintain discipline in all ranks if we are to win. At least, that was what I thought. That was what made this case so galling. Philip and I had discussed this very issue. Don't mistake me, I barely knew the lad. But I well remembered, when we'd had some officers together for an encouraging chinwag, how much he took that imperative to heart."

"It did not make him very popular with his men," I said.

"I bet it didn't!" said the general.

"Yet he did his duty," added Holmes, "as he understood it. I imagine Private Dutton said something of the sort in the letter that he wrote you. And, of course, he mentioned this heroic service, how Ogle-Thompson had saved lives."

The general sighed. "Dutton was an ordinary soldier, describing exemplary soldiering. I burnt his letter but I remember a particular phrase. 'What drives a man like Ogle-Thompson to act so out of character?'"

"A very good question," said Holmes. "That straightforward appeal got through to you. I suspect you looked up Ogle-Thompson's record." The general nodded. "And on the basis of what you read there," Holmes continued, "you gave him the benefit of the doubt. But that meant you had been gravely wrong in your judgement on him. So, as a matter of honour, you undertook to write to the man's family and assure them of his good character."

"He *was* a good man," said the general. "Wasn't he?"

Holmes nodded, then raised his glass. I understood the gesture and raised mine, and the general joined us in toasting the late Ogle-Thompson.

"It is a good thing," said Holmes, "that you did not reply to Private Dutton, or tell him you would write to the family."

"I do not answer to the ordinary soldier," scoffed the general.

"Indeed," smiled Holmes. "That delineation between officers and men! And if you had, Dutton would not have felt compelled to write to the family himself, and we should never have had cause to look into this criminal case." He drained his glass. "General, the register of numbers you showed us is designed to conceal the true cost of the war. How much damage can these people do?"

"Until you laid it out for me, I did not even know there was any plot," said the general.

"Now you do," said Holmes testily. "Is it having an effect?"

The general considered. "As I say, we've had too many cases of shell shock, of acts of cowardice by officers otherwise of good character. But I can't think it is having that much of an effect on the progress of the war. At least, the enemy are no more successful as a result."

Holmes didn't answer this. His eyes narrowed, his fingers steepled in front of him, and I could tell he saw something of interest in this answer.

"Perhaps they have only just started," I suggested.

"Well, I want them caught," snapped the general. "Whoever is behind this, I want *them* up in front of a firing squad. You will find them, won't you, Mr Holmes? Your country is counting on you and all that."

"What talents I have are at your service," replied Holmes.

"Then get on with it," said the general gruffly, and drained his glass. He didn't say anything more, and Holmes and I came to realise we had been dismissed. I thought better than to finish my whisky and instead got to my feet.

"Where do we begin?" I asked Holmes.

"I thought first of all–" he started to say, but the general cut him off.

"I really cannot sanction that," he said. "We're dealing with dangerous saboteurs of the worst kind. Anarchist maniacs! I can't send a girl into that. Thank you, Miss Watson, you can return to your ward."

"But sir!" I protested.

"Reading secret files is one thing," he told me. "But I cannot knowingly send a young woman into danger. Were the worst to happen, whatever should I write to your family?"

I didn't have an answer to that. When he'd asked me before about my people and background, I thought I had passed a kind of test, proving myself worthy because of my connections. Now I saw those connections were, as always, holding me back. A young lady had her place.

Damn him, Holmes said not a word in my defence. I stared at him in outrage, then turned to the general, determined to plead with him if I could only find the words. His expression brooked no argument. He firmly held my gaze.

"What you have been privy to here is in the strictest confidence," he told me.

"Yes, sir," I protested. "But really, I want to help if I can."

"Then do your duty in your designated role. Go back to the hospital." I didn't say anything but it must have been plain what I thought. "I've your best interests at heart," he told me. "You'll thank me in the long run, if you've any sense."

I didn't. I wouldn't. But there was nothing to be done.

Chapter Eleven

I fought my way along that accursed, dark road, the ambulance crunching through the layer of ice already formed in the potholes. More than once that great, cumbersome vehicle tried to get away from me and, swearing, I had to heave against the wheel to keep from plunging off into countryside I couldn't even see. It did me good to have something to fight, for I welled with righteous anger at having been dismissed. There was also frustration, that same deep-rooted indignance on behalf of all my sex. Then there was the crippling shame.

Damn it, these men had used me and then thrown me aside. Worst of all, I had allowed myself the unforgivable indulgence of thinking I had been accepted, even granted equal status by Holmes. Oh, I hated him more than ever for scorning me. Now, somehow, I had to return to my ordinary work.

Hot with anger, I pulled into the stable and hopped down from the cab. The other VADs must have seen the state of my clothes and the look on my face because they did not dare to get in my way. I stalked past them and across the yard. A chill wind swept through, and did something to extinguish my fury. By the time I reached the door of the hospital, more than anything I felt apprehensive. Women of my own rank were one thing, but I had now to face the nurses. Just the thought of their scorn, their condescension, crushed me.

A sympathetic orderly was on duty in the low, comforting light of the entrance hall, but saw the tentative way I crept in and – bless her! – did not speak a word. As I passed, the ward seemed busy, or busy enough that no one paid me any heed. The great clock showed half past nine as I hurried on and up the stairs.

Matron welcomed me kindly. I declined a drink and gave her a brief outline of my day: I had taken Holmes to the trenches, we had spoken to some of the men, then I had reported to the general all I had observed. I glossed over details and made no mention of the betting slips, or our visit to the secret underground room. The general had been quite clear about these being confidential. If he thought Matron should know about them, he could tell her himself.

The result was that I had little of interest to share with Matron, yet she didn't seem the least disappointed. My impression was of her relief that I had returned in one piece and not embarrassed myself – or her.

"You'll be on the usual rota tomorrow," she told me. "I expect you'll welcome the familiar routine. Now, get yourself off to bed."

Alone in the silent dormitory, I could at long last tug off my sodden clothes, dumping them in the basket at the end of our row of beds. In my long under-things, I scampered through to the washroom and did my best to get thoroughly clean with only a basin of tepid water and a sponge. The windows were already frosted and my breath steamed, so by the time I reached the supply cupboard to find myself a clean nightgown, my teeth were chattering. Even then, scrubbed and in clean linen, I could not rid myself of the cloying, awful stink of mud and human squalor from the trenches. Writing these words now, I still have a sense of it – a stench I can never escape.

Conscious that any moment my colleagues would emerge from the end of the shift, I scrambled into bed, tucking the sheet and blanket tightly round my body in a cocoon. I still shook with cold and feared I might have caught a chill. Yet gradually the close confines of the blanket kindled blissful warmth. Bone weary after all the day's exertion, I succumbed to it, and must have been dead asleep by the time the nurses bustled in. That, at least, was a mercy.

Though I escaped their clatter and questions, my dreams took me back to the trenches. Once again, Holmes and I were nose down in the foul-smelling mud as shots cracked overhead. Then there were explosions and the very ground was shifting, walls of sandbags tumbling down on top of us. I clawed and fought but could not get free – then woke, drenched in sweat and still tightly encased in my blankets. A voice from the next bed muttered crossly at me to pipe down. Shaken, a little feverish, I adjusted the blankets and did my best to settle into less troubled sleep. In moments, I was back in that mud.

When morning came, I felt worse than I had when going to bed, my joints stiff and an awful knot in the pit of my stomach. The nurses watched with malicious interest as I struggled out of bed and through the washroom. To begin with, no one dared confront me. They kept their distance, exchanging knowing looks and whispers.

Jill Sullivan, whom I had thought my friend, was finally put up to it by one of the others. She sidled over, trying to seem casual. "Darling," she said to me. "What was it all about, then?"

"I don't know what you mean," I replied sullenly. From across the room, Dulcie O'Brien turned to the others in delight.

"Hear that? Spends a day and a night with Sherlock bleeding Holmes and she doesn't know anything about it! Come on, Gus. What's the old man here for? Is he really on a case?"

Of course, saying nothing at all would have only fanned the flames of their interest. Guardedly, I admitted that I had driven Holmes to Rebecq, where he had spoken to some of the men – though I couldn't be sure what he might have said. I did not tell them that these interviews took place on the front line, but to my dismay they had already deduced that for themselves from the state of my discarded uniform.

"Was it harrowing?" asked Hyacinth Winter, her eyes wide with excitement. She was not alone in hoping that it had been. That is not to say that they wished me to have suffered. With long, repetitive hours on the ward, we all had a tendency to seize on anything different, any prospect of excitement. But being the target of this interest left me feeling sick. I mumbled a response, careful not to divulge anything specific, let alone of particular interest. They wanted to know if I had seen rats, or bodies in the mud, or if I had been shot at. On this last question I shivered involuntarily, and that seemed a more gratifying answer to them than any words I might have said. Yet I did my best to play everything down. I told them I had taken Holmes back to the Chateau, where he had met with the general, but when I didn't say more they assumed that I had not been with them. After all, why would a woman be admitted into the men's confidence? That really wouldn't be credible.

I think they were satisfied. They had, I realised, been sorely envious that I, of all people – a lowly VAD – had been entrusted with the care of such a famous visitor. My answers now only demonstrated that they had been right to think me ill-qualified for such an assignment. Some even said – not to my face but in my hearing – that I must have goofed, that I'd been sent back in disgrace because I hadn't been up to the job. That cut through me, because it was exactly how I felt.

I kept rehearsing it in my mind, what I might have said and done so that Holmes rebuked the general, insisting on my continued involvement.

Nevertheless, I felt better once I'd changed into a fresh uniform and eaten a little greasy breakfast. Then it was back on the ward, where I was quickly lost in cleaning, swabbing, fetching and tidying – whatever I could do to be useful. The men in the beds, though surely interested, thought better of asking about Sherlock Holmes. They were no less prone to the allure of gossip but better versed in the protocols of discretion.

Then, as I made my way round the ward, I came upon a scene. Two days before, I would never have noticed the least thing out of the ordinary; yet now, my attention was arrested by a curious, small detail: three nurses all with the same fixed smiles. It seemed so incongruous, so *wrong* – though I couldn't quite say why. I needed more information.

I also knew better than to let them catch me watching, so I skirted around the beds as if on my way to the next chore, and then observed them from one side. They smiled at one another, kept their voices low and apparently calm – yet now I paid close attention, they were clearly in the midst of an argument.

We had been well drilled, even as orderlies, not to contradict one another in sight of the men, and to take any disagreement off the ward. It was singular, then, that these three experienced nurses did not withdraw to settle whatever might be in dispute. Having been drawn to this fact, I now saw that the senior nurse had her arm tucked behind her back, to conceal the syringe in her hand. She did not conceal it from her colleagues; the angle did not work. No, she hid the syringe from the man in the bed just behind them.

The two junior nurses were, I realised, discreetly but effectively blocking their colleague's path to this patient. Behind them, the poor man twisted fitfully in his bed, whimpering and clawing in distress. That was not unusual on the ward, given all that our patients had been through. The senior nurse evidently meant to administer some sedative to calm him, but for some reason the others objected. I ventured round, getting closer to the nurses but as if I had not heeded them at all, caught up in checking the state of the floor.

"...it's not yet been four hours since his last dose," said one of the junior nurses, insistent for all she spoke under her breath and with a determined smile. "He's already sleeping."

"He disrupts the ward," replied the senior nurse in the same hard-edged whisper. "That affects the other patients – and he is clearly suffering."

They could not deny this, and I could see that the senior nurse had won. By now I had reached the far side of the bed of the patient in question. He was a pale, thin figure, his scalp and one side of his head horribly scarred. His hands clawed at the air above his face, a manic, burrowing action.

And in a flash I understood why, for I had surely had the same nightmare. Without further thought, I moved quickly round him.

"It's all right, my darling," I told him softly. "You just caught yourself up in your bedsheets. You're safe, you're in bed, I'm here to look after you. Let's try to make you more comfortable."

I untangled the sheets and then drew them up over him again. By then, the two junior nurses had come to help, but already the man had stopped twisting. Indeed, he now lay contentedly as the nurses fussed round him. I stepped back, letting them take over. One flashed me a smile, which only dropped me further in it with her superior.

It happened so quickly: I noticed something odd, moved in closer to investigate, and then saw the solution. Anyone might have done the same – I am sure those trained in medicine would think little of what I had done. But I had not been formally trained, not according to the regime in the hospital, and it was not my place.

The senior nurse took me firmly by the wrist and almost dragged me off the ward. We went into the side room where we kept the linen and she pointedly closed the door. Then she whirled on me, very close, her face almost touching mine.

"What the hell was that?"

"Sorry, sister," I told her, acting dumb. "I only did what Matron told us. The men with nightmares about being buried in the trenches. We have to settle them quickly, before they do themselves a mischief."

The woman quaked with fury. "We do," she seethed. "But 'we' as in the nursing staff. Not the likes of you."

I let my mouth fall open in stupid realisation. "Oh! Yes, sister. Sorry, sister."

"Mr Holmes has given you airs," she said. "Don't let me catch you acting above your station again. There are soiled pyjamas in the bin at the end of the aisle. You can deal with those."

She meant to punish me but I relished the chance to escape the ward. The basket in question sat in a wheeled frame, which I walked through to the steam and noise of the laundry.

The army had installed enormous machines to deal with all our washing, but the things still required plenty of labour just to load and unload. A line of baskets had been left for someone else to deal with, so I rolled up my sleeves and got busy. It was slow, sweaty work, and I had to keep stopping to wipe my brow on the back of my forearm. But physical exertion was exactly what I needed. I could take out my frustrations on the innocent clothes, and it gave me space to think.

The nurse had been angry because I correctly diagnosed her patient. She had not liked it when contradicted by two fellow nurses, so how much worse to then have it from me? But I had been right, and I had saved that man from – at the very least – further discomfort. I deduced the cause rather than just dealing with his symptoms because of my direct experience, and because I had *observed.*

I remained in good spirits when I returned to the ward, and blithely ignored the looks and comments of the nursing staff, whether about being above my station or failing Sherlock Holmes, or my red-faced "glow" from the hot laundry room. They could not hurt me. This new perspective, this clarity with which I now took in the world around me, made me powerful.

They imposed more duties that they hoped would take me down a peg or two. I approached it all with the same brisk good humour just to spite them. That attitude also won me favour with the men, who could see I was being ill-treated for all they could not fathom the politics of women.

"I'm glad your mother is over her 'flu," I told Lieutenant Dale as I mopped the floor round his bed. He stared at me in wonder, and for a moment even I couldn't think how I'd known. But on his bedside table was a new copy of Housman's *A Shropshire Lad*, and a week ago I had overheard Dale say that his mother was laid up with influenza so he had only the same volume of stuffy, traditional poems to pore over. When I explained this, Dale thought nothing of my deduction – it was so obvious! – but I had connected the two details by instinct, without any deliberate thought.

The book was a handsome, slim edition, ideal for a uniform pocket. I had not read it, but it seemed to strike some emotional chord with the soldiers, its sentimental vision of English life echoing their own longing for home. But I knew that because I worked among the soldiers: it wasn't something Dale's mother would necessarily know.

"Your mother sought advice on what to buy you," I said.

This time, Dale did not notice that I had puzzled this out for myself. "Yes, she said so in her letter. The old girl doesn't know the first thing about poetry."

"Then she went to some trouble to find you the right thing," I said. He broke into a grin. It was exactly the effect I had intended with my new-found powers. As with Holmes in the dugout, by recognising a connection between Dale and life back home, I had strengthened that bond. I moved on, mopping the floor around the next patient and at the same time assessing his life from the discernible clues.

It was showing off and it annoyed the nurses, but they couldn't deny the positive effect I had on the men. I knew it couldn't last, that there would come a confrontation. But I was spoiling for a fight.

At tea break, Dulcie O'Brien sidled over and took my hand, then began chatting at me with breathless candour about one of the patients for whom she'd developed a "pash". Of course I was suspicious, as Dulcie had never exactly been friendly. But the other nurses took their cue from her and were stiffly cordial, and it went on that afternoon. By evening, I started to think that they really might have deigned to admit me into their club.

"You're one of us," Dulcie told me as she helped me make a bed, though really she addressed her words to the other nurses. "That Sherlock Holmes has brought something out in you."

I shuddered at that, because I did not want to face questions about Holmes. But Dulcie interpreted this reticence as something else.

"I didn't mean it comes from him. Don't let any men take the credit. It's probably you reacting against such an insufferable specimen. But kicking back at Mr Holmes has brought about this wondrous transformation. You're more confident, more in charge! And here, I'll tell you what we can do. We'll put a word in with Matron and see if we can't get you promoted to nurse." The nurses applauded this suggestion, as did some of the men listening in. Yet I must have made one of my faces, because Dulcie laughed. "Oh, are we not grand enough for you now? I suppose it's being WVR – you won't be happy until you've equalled the menfolk as well. All right, why not?" And then she beamed maliciously. "You go and be doctor."

The nurses laughed as if she had made some brilliant joke. And, of course, she had. Dulcie beamed back at me, her eyes cold with victory. Her whole act of friendship had been merely a ploy to reach this tedious punchline and bring all I had accomplished crashing down. They had been laughing at me for the whole day, thrilling to the delicious joke of my pretension.

Because how ridiculous, how fanciful, how downright implausible, that I could ever be Dr Watson?

They could not have known how much that name cut me to the

quick. Of all the things to assault me with, they had chanced upon the very worst. But they saw how I reacted and knew they had struck gold. It would be their weapon from now on.

Chastised, I got on with my duties and tried to ignore them. They continued to call me "Dr Watson" as they ordered me to clean the toilet or mop a patch of floor where tea had "accidentally" been spilled. Then they called me to the desk, where Dulcie had prepared a new torture. The nurses had filled out the day's forms and chits for each patient. These now needed sorting, and then had to be put back in the cabinets. It was a menial job but usually the province of the nurses. Today, they had decided that it was beneath them and so should be done by me.

I know it hardly sounds anything at all. Had they been caught, they could have denied any malice. It was barely more than a light-hearted prank – proof, even, that they considered me a full member of their sorority. Perhaps they really thought it was just a bit of fun. They could surely have no idea how it cut me to the core.

"Are you going to object, Dr Watson?" asked Dulcie with acid sweetness as I seethed, daring me to answer her back. I could not trust myself to say anything at all, so I gathered up the loose and muddled paperwork – surely more than a day's worth – and retreated to the filing cabinets where I had last stood with Holmes. Perhaps that was intentional, too.

In fact, organising those papers had a soothing effect, the monotony working to extinguish my anger, and it kept me out of the way of the nurses. I sat quietly on the floor and put the papers together, sure I could eke it out long enough to last the rest of my shift, when at last I could escape back to the dormitory.

When I was some way into the filing, Matron swept onto the ward, her habit flapping behind her, on one of her surprise inspections. She did not register me over by the cabinet, instead fixing hawk-like on the nurses at the desk and their silly mood. I had never been more grateful to her than when she gave them short shrift for their idleness and found them all menial chores.

Then Matron saw me at the files and marched briskly over. She was a small, slight woman and yet imposing, and now she seemed utterly livid. "You are not a nurse," she informed me.

"No, Matron. I was helping out."

She looked back at the nurses she had only just scolded. For a horrible moment I thought they might deny all knowledge and really drop me in it, but Dulcie at least had the honesty to say she had asked if I wouldn't mind.

"Very well," said Matron. "You may continue, Miss Watson. Then, when you have finished, you might see me upstairs."

With that, she stalked off the ward. My heart sank, and the nurses quickly concluded that I was for the high jump. They didn't think it could be the filing; after some discussion, they decided that my presumption in dealing with Lieutenant Dale's nightmare earlier that day must have been reported. I did not say what this obviously implied: that one of them must have told on me. One small blessing, though, was that they stopped referring to me as Dr Watson.

As instructed, I finished the filing and then made my weary way up to my doom. On the first-floor landing, the secretaries regarded me with cold interest as I passed. That made it easier: knowing they were watching, my pride would not allow me to show any hesitation. With every fibre of my being, I tried to convey that this visit was of the least concern. I knocked on the door to Matron's office and went in.

To my wretched disappointment, Sherlock Holmes was not there. The wizened form of Matron presided alone behind her desk, a cigarette in her fingers. At the sight of me, she sat back in her chair and tutted with disdain. I stood there, waiting for an invitation to sit – but it did not come.

"I expected better," she told me.

"Sorry, Matron," I said, automatically.

"You have valuable work as an orderly, Miss Watson. You make a significant contribution to our efforts here. I am sorry you consider it beneath you."

So, she had indeed been informed of my response to Lieutenant Dale. There followed a pretty grim dressing down, with a list of my shortcomings and the threat to write to my family, as if I honestly cared what they thought any more. Just as when the same threats had been brandished at boarding school, I weathered it stoically enough. She went on sermonising about the war not being a game and that I was not to compete with other women, extolling the virtues of sisterhood, all of us equal for all that we had our particular roles. I had heard this sort of thing often enough, even in the WVR. Finally, the ordeal was over. Matron lit another cigarette and motioned me to the chair opposite her desk. This was her concession to Christian charity: a bit of mollifying calm after the storm.

"What did you make of Mr Holmes?" she asked. It sounded innocuous enough, just making idle conversation, but I was all too aware of my obligation not to talk about what I had witnessed – even to her.

"Peculiar," I said.

Matron chuckled at that. "Is he really as clever as the stories have us believe?"

I shifted uncomfortably. "I'm afraid I couldn't say." Then it struck me that this might imply that I had been instructed not to say anything. "I mean, I didn't see much of what he got up to. I was really only his driver."

Matron drew on her cigarette, her eyes fixed upon me. I tried not to squirm under her scrutiny. "You didn't see anything of interest," she said.

I thought of the general's order, and his threat. "No, Matron," I said.

She smiled inscrutably. "You shouldn't tell me if you did. But you enjoyed trailing round after him – didn't you?"

That was a surprising question. "Yes, Matron. As you said, it was something a bit out of the ordinary."

She nodded. "I won't ask for details, Miss Watson, but I hope you did us proud."

"I think I did all right."

She smiled. "I dare say I shall hear from the general if you didn't – but not otherwise. That is the way with these things. I hope you are not too disappointed if we never hear anything from Mr Holmes again."

"No, Matron," I said – but I am sure my voice trembled. In truth, it was awful to have it put so baldly. I felt terrible for being excluded.

Matron sighed. "If you really want to trail after him," she said, "it's the general you need to convince." I wasn't sure I understood – could she really mean to encourage me? "You're an intelligent girl, frustrated by your work here," she told me.

"Honestly, I'm not. I really do want to be useful.".

She drew on a cigarette, regarding me quizzically. "Write me a letter. Say you were happy to be of service to the general, and that you'd be happy to do so again. I can pass that up to him and add a note myself, asking if there might be some way in which you can still be of use to him or to Mr Holmes."

I really couldn't believe it, but she meant to aid me. "Th-thank you," I stammered.

Matron batted that away with a sweep of her hand. "I hold no sway over the general and he might ignore it. Or worse, he might take you up on this foolish offer. You should be careful of what you wish for, Miss Watson, especially when its focus is a man."

I assured her I would be careful and then quickly wrote the letter – there and then, before she might change her mind.

Chapter Twelve

For all I tried to tell myself that nothing would result from my letter, I felt elated at the prospect – and as a result of Matron's support. I am sure she thought little of my chances, and would not have encouraged me had she given the matter any thought, and yet her kindness shone bright. Completing the letter, I thanked her again and then practically skipped up the stairs to the dormitory.

The nurses were waiting, worried about what I might have said in my defence. I assured them that I had not incriminated anyone else and that it had not been too awful. Relieved, they stole away to their beds, Dulcie telling me – for the others to hear – that I "really had been a brick". Again, she held out the promise that we might yet be friends.

Lying in the darkness afterwards, I longed to be free of them. Yet I had had my share of disappointments in life and knew to be pragmatic. Even drudging work as an orderly, I had more than once had to remind myself, was better than being stuck at home with Mother in London. I now resolved to form bonds and accrue debts where I could, and so knit myself among the nurses. They might never embrace me, but I would do what I could. I thought this would at least give me a focus for the next day or two as I went about my work on the ward. It would keep me from going mad as I waited for a response to my letter – which surely would not come. It was the powerlessness that ate into me. I could endure the derision of the nurses and their needling jokes if I told myself I at least had a plan.

And yet, next morning, before I had even dressed, Jill Sullivan came round with the post, and I had a memo from Command.

```
Watson, A - 81215922
You will transport, as driver, your earlier cargo
as dictated from reference A at oh eight hundred
hours today.
Fitzgerald
```

The hand-drawn squiggle showing reference A proved, on closer inspection, to be a map of the winding road and the house where Holmes had been billeted. I had forty minutes to get there.

Having hurried into my uniform and through the washroom, I went straight down to Matron's office. She had apparently been up all night dealing with some problem of logistics up the supply line to the port, and was not in the best of moods to receive me. I showed her the memo and she snatched it from my hand, holding it up close to those deep-set, inquisitive eyes.

"You'll leave us short, of course," she said, sourly. "We'll all have to work that little bit harder."

"Sorry, Matron," I said.

She sighed, thrusting the memo back at me. "I suppose I cannot object – but it is inconvenient. I hope you keep Mr Holmes in check."

Once she had dismissed me, I raced downstairs – to find a group of nurses waiting. Dulcie O'Brien came forward with a small cardboard tray, in which there was a fried egg sandwich. "Breakfast on the run," she said. "Think you might need it."

I suspected a trap but they seemed sincere, even nervous on my behalf. They were, I realised, feeling guilty now that I had another dangerous assignment. Perhaps they thought their actions had driven me to this course – because, of course, I could not have been given this mission based on my own merit.

"Thanks," I told them. "See you all tonight."

More than one of them winced at that – it was the kind of thing thought to be grossly bad luck.

I stepped outside into a crisp, bright winter's morning, the low sun blinding but beautiful. A pair of ambulances waited in the stable and I chose the one I'd driven two days before, only to find it would not start. Patch heard me cursing and came over to help. Together we probed and prodded the engine and finally got it turning over. I hared off up the road, already running late.

There was little traffic on the main road when I got there, so I tore through serene, frosty countryside. The roads remained treacherous enough that I had to concentrate on avoiding potholes and the like, but for all the effort of controlling that great, unsteady juggernaut, it was something quite wonderful to be out on such a morning.

I heaved the ambulance into the turning and followed the winding lane to the docile-looking cottage. As I pulled up, Sherlock Holmes stepped from the front door, immaculate as ever.

"Good morning, Miss Watson," he said as he climbed lithely into the cab beside me. "This is unexpected. I understood from the general that he did not think it safe for you to continue as my escort."

"He must have changed his opinion, sir."

"That he must." He looked me over suspiciously, trying to fathom how I had connived to bring about this change. "Did the general indicate to you that there might be some risk in what we undertake this morning?"

"I hope you're not suggesting that I will not be up to the task."

"I would not dare!" he laughed.

I put the ambulance into reverse and brought off a pretty good five-point turn in that narrow lane. As we trundled back towards the main road, I caught a glimpse of Holmes, nostrils flared with exhilaration at the impending adventure. I felt it, too: the excitement of the chase – and not some little panic at what I had just thrown myself into.

"Where are we off to, sir?" I asked him.

"The front," he said. "But much further along than the last time. I spent yesterday speaking to officers at the Chateau who have served time on the front line. Two of them had, to their evident surprise, a betting slip concealed in their pockets that they could not explain. I expected more, but I suppose our evidence suggests that those in receipt of such betting slips do not then survive very long. Besides, the most disruptive place for these things is on the front line, so that is where I expect to find further evidence. The key factor is that the men do not get wind of what we are looking for."

"It's all right, sir," I said. "You can pull the same conjuring tricks as before."

He sighed. "That is not how I would describe them."

"No, sir."

"Besides, my concern is more that we don't let on to whoever supplied these cards that we are on their trail. So, the story remains that I am here to see what small improvements I might be able to suggest."

"You just being among them, shaking hands and showing an interest, helps morale," I said.

"Really?" said Holmes. "It's of very little consequence beyond being good manners."

"To you, maybe," I said.

"Well," he said, evidently surprised. "That factor can be at our disposal. We will charm them into revealing their secrets."

"Given what you've learned since I last saw you, do you know who might be behind the betting slips?"

Holmes shifted restlessly. "I have suspicions but no good evidence in that regard. There is much about this matter that eludes me." It was not a complaint; he relished it.

We followed the main road and a trail of slow-moving traffic before Holmes told me to take a right turn, referring to a map he had been sent that morning by the general. The road we turned onto was even more pitted and uneven, and the ambulance protested, threatening to expel us both from the cab. I changed down to second gear and soon took better charge, though we could only make slow progress. We followed a winding route between the undulating fields, stark and bare that cold December day. I had never been this way before: it was literally foreign territory and I knew to proceed with caution.

I expected impatience from Holmes as we cantered slowly on. Yet he seemed content, studying the map against the view ahead. Every now and then he would give a blunt instruction, either to take a turning or to carry on, but I got little out of him otherwise, his attention all on the map. It didn't seem very remarkable from the brief glimpses I took.

"Perhaps," said Holmes without looking up, "you might keep your eyes on the road."

Just in time, I saw the jagged gash where heavy rain had swept away the road. Desperately, I hauled on the wheel and, like some stubborn mule, the ambulance lumbered round and spared us from disaster. I set us to rights again and we puttered on, but it had been a near thing. Holmes had not once looked up from his map.

We continued in silence for a while, me hot with self-recrimination and embarrassment, and rage at Holmes for just sitting there.

"These roads aren't easy," I said, when I could bear the silence no longer. "Neither is this brute of a thing." I slapped one hand on the wheel.

"Indeed," said Holmes. "But as I observed before, you are a better driver than the general's man."

"I suppose he has one leg or something," I said.

"My dear Miss Watson, I am quite sincere. Your training and experience are quite evident to me. I could ask for no finer escort."

The road got ever more precarious and I had a hairy moment with a flooded stretch that proved deeper than expected, but I pulled us through.

"There you are," said Holmes, as if I had only proved his point. But now he looked up from his map. "You are perturbed by something, Miss Watson, and I fear the fault lies with me but I do not know on what account. I am aware that I can on occasion seem callous, even cruel – though it is never my intention."

"It's not that," I said.

"But it is *something*. Please, be candid."

I drew a breath. "You abandoned me the other night."

"You felt I should contradict the general when he gave you a direct order." He said this amiably enough, not taking it seriously at all – which, of course, only made me angry.

"I think," I said, "that you have certain views regarding women."

Holmes shook his head wearily. "Ah," he said. "This."

"I've read the stories about you, I know what you think of us."

This seemed to amuse him. "No doubt better than I know my thoughts myself."

"If I remember correctly, you know of just a single woman with intelligence to equal a man's."

"That is not quite what I said."

But I was warming to my cause. "Oh, she must have been quite exceptional. I mean, imagine, being able to hold her own against the whole of mankind, which I take it includes all the lunatics and criminals and drunks!"

"I believe," said Holmes drolly, "that I have heard this reasoning used in relation to the right to vote."

"Well, exactly," I said.

"And, of course, you're right."

That rather took the wind out of my sails. "You're not serious."

"Miss Watson, I quite take your point. Irene Adler surpassed the wit of the ordinary man; her skills almost equal to my own."

The conceit of him! "She bested you, didn't she?" I asked.

He barked a laugh. "Oh, she was indeed remarkable. It was not only intelligence but courage, humour and resolve. She was exceptional, as you say. I had never encountered anyone quite like her. Or rather, I had not observed such ability in other women."

"Perhaps," I said, "that says more about you than it does about them."

Holmes did not respond immediately. I could not take my eyes from the uneven road, but my sense was that he took his time to prepare an answer. "Perhaps it does," he said coolly. "Pray enlighten me, if you will."

"You like to think that you work from evidence alone," I said.

"I pride myself that I do."

"And you had not seen evidence of other women with such qualities. Yet you hardly troubled to look for such evidence, not in the way you do in one of your cases, actively seeking new data with which to test your hypothesis. I am guessing you do not engage in the sorts of social gathering where you might have met women of particular intelligence."

He smiled. "Indeed not. And I can also see that intelligent women may have little to no interest in conversing with me, either, given my reported opinions."

There was no hint of apology or remorse, just acceptance, after due consideration, of a given theory. I gripped the steering wheel hard, annoyed by his coolness when this subject so enflamed my heart.

"You have come to this realisation rather late," I told him.

"Is there not joy among the Suffragettes over one misogynist who repents?"

That, I admit, made me laugh. "You should meet the Pankhursts," I said. "They would provide all the evidence you could ask for."

"That could well be illuminating for us all," agreed Holmes.

"You acknowledge the tactics employed in their campaigns," I said. "Their courage and determination were quite remarkable."

"Not everyone thought so," said Holmes.

"There are those who did not agree with the cause, or with the methods used," I admitted. "Yet they recognised that the Suffragettes were formidable. That can be judged from the reaction of the government and our police. You must know what they did to us. Some might tell you that the organisation had to dig in *because* of that reaction." I had heard first-hand accounts of assault, force feeding and whatever else, but Holmes seemed not to pick up on my tone.

"An intriguing proposition," he mused. There was the tantalising sense that he might say more, yet we could not pursue the conversation. As we talked, I had been aware of the gradual ascent of the road. Now we crested the brow, and came on the most extraordinary view, looking out across a dun-coloured, ravaged valley for what must have been miles. I struggled to take in the scale. Small dips and hillocks were bomb craters, and a thin, meandering line the road, apparently unbroken as it threaded through the quagmire. A darker line traced the horizon – the slender, crooked network of trenches.

A row of field guns looked down on this commanding view. Soldiers lounged around them, chatting, laughing, drinking tea. As in the trenches, they wore multiple layers and huddled to keep out the cold, yet there was an easy confidence about them in such a strong defensive position. Nor were they as plastered in mud as the men we'd seen before. It was altogether a better place to be stationed.

Presently, we came upon a small community of squat, stocky buildings nestled either side of the road. Between them, a wooden beam wrapped loosely in barbed wire blocked our further progress.

As we puttered up, I saw lines of low defensive walls on the far side of these buildings, one wall concealing the long snout of a field gun. Figures emerged from the nearest brick building, rifles in their hands. They were slumped, wary and unshaven, troglodytes in uniform. One, a corporal in an ill-fitting balaclava, stalked over to my side of the cab. His thin, lined face had an insouciant air.

"Good morning," I told him cheerily.

"You say so, miss. Sure you're in the right place?"

Holmes handed over the printed slip with his orders. The corporal scanned it and couldn't hide his surprise. He looked up at me to check we were serious.

"Is there a problem, corporal?"

Of course, he would never question orders direct from the general. "No, ma'am," he said. "Want some coffee while you're here? We can put something in it to keep the cold out."

I turned to Holmes. "That's very kind of you, corporal, but we should get on."

"Fair enough," said the corporal. He gesticulated to the other men and, begrudgingly, they dragged the barrier out of our path, freeing up the road ahead.

"Thank you," I said.

"I expect you know your business," he said. "No point us trying to warn you."

"'Fraid not," I told him. He didn't look happy but motioned us on. As we passed the men with the barrier, one man saluted in rather slovenly, ironic fashion and another made the sign of the cross.

The road snaked down the hillside gently, but I had to go down to first gear for the perilous bends. Holmes did not say a word but studied his map and the view in front of us closely. Before long, the road had considerably worsened, bumping and jostling us in our seats. The sunshine was lost behind cloud.

Then came a disturbing sight: the burnt-out ruins of squat brick buildings and low walls, in the same formation as those we had recently passed through. For all that we were in the shadow of the hill, it felt eerily as if we had completed a circle and come again on the sentry point, only now destroyed and its troglodytes dead. But no, as we got closer I could see some difference in layout: the place we had stopped before had more defensive fortifications. They had lost this border and retreated up the hill, but learned some lessons in doing so.

Beyond the ruined buildings there were battered, pockmarked hoardings. One showed a skeleton choking on yellow gas, another was all capital letters: "DANGER!", "MINES!" and "NO PICNICS!"

We rumbled on. There was a marked change in the landscape now, churned and ruptured with occasional pools of greenish water, and a lot more barbed wire. In places, the ground had been so ravaged there were great ravines and gorges, one big enough to have driven down. The scale of devastation was astonishing, but just as remarkable was it being so silent and still. There were no clues from which to deduce how long this damaged land had last seen fighting or how far we now were from the front. With the noise of the engine and the effort of navigating that uneven road, I could not discern any rumble of artillery – but that did not mean it wasn't there. I peered ahead, trying to make out the trucks and activity that would mark the outermost part of the trenches.

It was as if we journeyed across the pitted surface of the moon, the ground around us twisted and warped into ever more fantastic nightmare shapes. Ejecta lay strewn across the road. I steered warily round a great chunk of earth, rock and tree root big enough to loom over the ambulance. Again, we could proceed only in first gear, slowly, inexorably advancing into hell.

Holmes looked up from his map to scrutinise the ever less discernible road ahead. "We should be at the trenches soon," he told me.

"Yes, sir," I said.

"It looked closer from up on the hill, but then we had little reference from that vantage point by which to judge scale. The map is also based on aerial intelligence that is at least two days old. The note that accompanied it did say it might be different once we got here."

He meant to reassure me, and I tried to match his cheery tone. "It's a good thing, I expect. Means our boys are advancing."

"Let us hope so," said Holmes.

Then came the first explosion, a powerful *crump* we felt and heard close – even over the roar of the engine – but otherwise did not see. Shaken, I told myself we must be approaching the front lines. Then came another, closer *crump*, followed by loose mud raining down on the canvas sides of the ambulance. I could taste dust in the air.

Our training had instilled in us one lesson: to get the hell out of situations like this. I put my foot down and we bumped and bucked across the road. That made it difficult to see, either ahead or in the mirrors. But we were under fire and had to push on. Holmes clung tight to the edge of the cab. I got us up to third just as the road in front of us exploded.

Had the ambulance been fitted with a windscreen, the glass would have been shattered by the blast and we'd have both been cut to pieces. As it was, open to the air, Holmes and I were pelted with heavy, hot clumps of mud. Searing, jagged grains clogged my mouth and nose. Skidding to a stop, I cranked the gears into reverse. I think I must have been cut pretty badly, but all I felt was outrage.

"This is an ambulance!" I spat. "We're clearly marked with a red cross."

The engine protested but then we were lumbering backward. I could see nothing in the mud-smeared mirrors now, so had to lean perilously out of the cab to look back along the road. Holmes was shouting something but I couldn't hear him for the howl in my ears. Then there came another explosion, flinging more muck at us hard. The air was thick with smoke and dust, and I struggled to draw breath, desperately hoping there would not be gas. I floored the pedal and the ambulance groaned backwards – right into another explosion.

The force of it was incredible, smashing me into the steering wheel. Had Holmes not been clinging on, he would have been hurled over the top of the engine. Stunned, head pounding, I twisted round to look at the road – and saw the buckled flank of the ambulance, strands of canvas flapping and on fire. Even so, I put my foot down and with a ghastly rending of metal on metal we rolled unsteadily backwards. Another explosion sounded, somewhere, rocking the ambulance dreadfully, but we held our course.

Then there simply wasn't a road any more. We plunged backwards down a steep ridge. I slammed the brake pedal but it did no good: we slid helplessly back, the slope eroding under our weight so that an avalanche of mud tumbled after us. That slowed our perilous descent and we slid unevenly to a stop, the ambulance half buried and at a precarious angle.

There, the engine finally guttered and died. Dazed, sore, my ears ringing in agony, I was painfully aware of the silence.

Chapter Thirteen

Holmes was, like me, entirely caked in mud, his coat badly torn. The grime on his face glistened where he bled. Yet his bloodshot eyes moved quickly, taking in our predicament and the surrounding devastation, already concocting solutions. Then he held a finger to his lips – though I knew better than to make a sound – and pointed off to his side, indicating that he would get out of the cab.

Carefully, painfully, he extracted himself from the broken seat and slipped down to the ground. There he waited, poised against the side of the ambulance, like a fox sniffing the air.

He could make little out – I am sure his ears were ringing just as mine were – and we couldn't afford to lose time, so he beckoned for me to follow. I heaved myself out from behind the steering wheel and crawled round, then fell more than clambered out. The mud was soft and warm and I sank some way into it. Loose soil tumbled after us from the ridge we had fallen down. We were in the midst of gnarled-up, broken earth, out of sight of the road we had veered from. There were no more explosions – because, I supposed, whoever had shot at us had achieved their aim. Now they had us at their mercy.

Holmes examined the back of the ambulance. The wheels were almost entirely buried in mud, but Holmes showed me how the panel above had been badly twisted and now pressed directly into the tyre. Working together, we tried to bend the panel back but with little result other than to bloody my hands. We both knew the grim consequence: even if we dug out the ambulance, we would not get it moving again.

Then there came a sound, from up towards the road. Holmes caught my elbow and motioned me towards him, as lightly as if we were dancing. We huddled together in the shadow of the ambulance, concealed from prying eyes on the ridge. I did not dare to try and see who might be up there. Holmes, beside me, crouched perfectly still, his every sense alert.

There were voices, at least two men talking – though I couldn't hear what they said, or whether it was English or German. The voices were low and wary, but surely getting closer.

Holmes dropped to his knees and crawled back along the side of the ambulance to the cab. I couldn't think what he was up to, but watched him carefully, silently, unlatch and raise the flap to look upon the engine. His long fingers moved dextrously inside, but I couldn't believe even the great detective would be able to get it started. Besides, if he did, we would still face the men on the ridge.

He drew something from his pocket, perhaps a screwdriver, and worked something on the engine – but not carefully enough. To my horror, a high metallic note rang out, echoing all around. Holmes froze.

The men on the ridge were now silent. Then something cracked sharply and loud. It cracked again, and something spanged off the side of the ambulance – they were shooting at us!

Holmes scrambled back quickly to join me, nimble and low to the ground like a cat. He seemed more energised than afraid, eyes quickly picking over the ground. As he made his assessment, my nose began to itch. I realised there was the pungent, sweet stink of petrol all around us. Holmes must have opened the fuel tank!

I didn't dare speak but touched his arm and, when he looked around, wrinkled my nose. He winked back at me, then pointed away from the ambulance, to a kind of knee-height crevasse running jaggedly through the ruptured earth. He motioned with two fingers, a "legs walking" gesture, moving his arm to indicate that he wanted us to duck ourselves behind that low rise. I couldn't believe it – the marksmen on the ridge would still have a clear sight…

Yet Holmes was already moving off, on his hands and knees, pressed close to the ground. I glanced back around towards the ridge, sure the men must have seen him – but the ambulance obscured my view. That meant, I realised, that they would not see Holmes, at least to begin with.

I followed in his wake, half crawling, half dragging myself, elbow after elbow. My whole body ached from the crash, blood dripped from my chin, and I wanted to gag from the ever more pervasive stink of petrol. That was when I realised what Holmes planned to do to aid our escape.

Holmes reached the crevasse and now I saw that the ground to the right of it sloped a little downwards, so it provided more cover than I'd initially thought. Indeed, it concealed Holmes almost entirely from the road, even without the ambulance. He folded his long legs up behind him, creating room for me to squeeze in. By the time I had managed it, he had a box of matches in his hand.

We were both still perilously close to the ambulance. Yet Holmes shifted himself round so that he was poised and ready to run. I followed his example, trying to keep low so we would not be seen. Holmes regarded me, checking I was ready. Heart hammering, I nodded. He raised his arm over the cover of earth and deftly flicked a match.

We didn't so much run as hurl ourselves forward. Then I was in the air, carried by a terrific, hot, cataclysmic roar. I crashed into Holmes and we both tumbled down into soft, yielding earth. Instantly on his feet, Holmes grabbed my wrist and we hared into the cover of more raised structures of mud, running and sliding and slipping. He seemed blind, zigzagging back and forth with no destination in mind. I had the horrible thought that this might lead us right back to the men who had shot at us.

I glanced back and saw only the vast, furious blaze of the ambulance, filling the sky with acrid, black smoke. Struggling for breath, eyes streaming, I stumbled desperately after Holmes. There were other sounds beside us – shouts, cracks, perhaps the spang of bullets. I did not look back again.

Soon I could no longer feel the heat of the flames. The smoke began to clear and I could almost breathe. Dimly, I realised I had been wrong. Holmes did not run blindly. He looked quickly back and forth, with that extreme vigilance I'd observed in the trenches as he took everything in. His quick mind could made sense of the devastation around us, using the strange, warped shapes of torn-up earth to provide us with cover.

At one point, he stopped and pressed his fist into the ground, producing a distinctive handprint. He made another print a little further along, and then ducked back to lead me in another direction entirely – having laid this false trail for our enemies.

We kept on. There were no further gunshots, I realised. They had not seen us escape and we were not being pursued. It would be some time before the men on the ridge could be sure that we were not in that inferno. Holmes had outfoxed them and we had got away.

And yet there was nowhere to go. As my senses came back to me, I was horribly aware of our predicament, stranded on foot so far from the nearest available aid. We had lost the road – our one route back to safety. We needed to get back to it, but Holmes seemed set on precisely the other direction.

He hunkered down in another chasm in the ground so that we could catch our breath. Holmes still had my wrist, and I yanked my hand from his. He turned in surprise, then saw the look in my eye.

"Forgive the liberty," he said, his voice low. "I thought it rather expedient."

"We are going the wrong way," I told him in a whisper. "We should follow the path of the road, back the way we came. That nice corporal on the hill must have seen what happened. He will surely send help."

Holmes shook his head. "The enemy will be watching the road. We'd be dead long before help could reach us."

"Then don't take to the road, we just keep it in sight and follow its course."

"Even so. That's where they will be looking. Besides, we don't know who fired at us."

There had not been any question in my mind until that point: only Germans would attack a civilian vehicle marked with a red cross. But with cold dread I realised he might be right. We were investigating a conspiracy carried out by people on our own side.

Of course they would want us out of the way. I felt sick at the thought. We had not wandered into fire accidentally; someone intended to murder us.

I gripped my hands together in an effort to stop them shaking. "All right," I snapped at Holmes. "Where else are you heading?"

He withdrew the map from his pocket, now tattered and worn after all we had been through. "This way, we join up with your supply road. It's slightly longer, but not what they'll expect."

It enraged me that he could deal with all of this so calmly. I snatched the map from him and tried to make sense of it. Scrawled lines delineated roads, with a few sparse intersections. There were no labels or map symbols to help make sense of the area shown, and I struggled to match the drawing to my knowledge of the roads. The top-most edge seemed to indicate the main road from Rebecq, with junctions I recognised – one of them to my hospital. Yet a cross-hatched line ran just south of the hospital and across the paper.

"What does this indicate?" I asked of the cross-hatch.

Holmes started, evidently perturbed by this question. "A rough approximation of the position of the Allied lines. But you should know that."

"Does the map show where I collected you from?" I asked. He pointed to the place and my heart sank – it exactly matched where I had thought. "The position of the lines two days ago is completely wrong," I told him. "It's at least a good inch too high."

Holmes considered the effect of that. "Then the position on the hill…" he began.

"*That* was the front line," I finished.

"It seems we have been led astray."

"Who gave you this accursed map?"

"It was delivered to me this morning by courier, along with my orders from the general." Then he looked quizzical. "If either of them really came from him."

He produced the document he had shown to the corporal. It looked official enough, printed on headed paper with the divisional emblem. I pulled out the memo I had myself received that morning. It was easy to see that they had been produced by the same typewriter. Holmes noted that the top edge of the memo was not quite perpendicular to the side. He held it up to the bottom of his letter from the general, and the slightly diagonal edge matched perfectly. They had been a single document, typed as one, then the bottom section had been snipped off.

"You have my apologies, Miss Watson. I thought our enquires might lead to some counter-action but, in my shameful misogynist fashion, I assumed that such an attack would be directed solely at me."

"I did rather go on about wanting equal treatment," I said.

Holmes smiled, and looked again at the map. "We should not feel so badly about being duped. These people have gone to some considerable lengths to make it all seem credible. They faked these documents very well and delivered them to us through the ordinary military post so that we would not suspect. They selected a route by which we could cross the front line without even been aware. And then there is the other intriguing factor–"

But before he could say more, there was a shout from back the way we had come. Holmes and I both instinctively ducked, pressing ourselves into the cold, damp mud. I clamped a hand across my mouth to hide the sound of my own ragged breath.

We lay there for agonising moments, listening keenly. The ambulance still burned with vigour, a steady grind and roar. But there was nothing else.

Just as I thought we might be all right, a voice suddenly rang out, still some distance away. A man yelled something and someone else responded – in curt, plosive German that carried easily to where we were hiding. It was, oddly, a relief to hear it, signalling that we had not been fired on by our own people. But I knew only a smattering of words in the language and had to turn to Holmes.

"Six of them in total," he whispered. "They know we were not in the blaze. Two will remain here, the other four are fanning out to search."

There were more words spoken, and Holmes looked grim as he listened. One man said something and was shouted down with, "*Nein.*"

"No what?" I asked Holmes. He looked torn, unsure whether to tell me whatever awful thing he had heard. "No what?" I asked again.

"Prisoners," he said. "We are both to be shot on sight."

Chapter Fourteen

⤳

As a child I was frightened of thunderstorms. "Inconsolable," Mother will sigh even to this day, as if a direct line can be threaded from such early fuss-making to my ongoing lack of a husband. She forgets, or neglects to mention, that I long ago conquered my fear. One thundery night, my parents taught me the trick of counting slowly in the gap between the lightning and the noise. The shorter the interval, the closer the storm – but the point is to count each time there is lightning, tracking progress until it has passed. In doing so, you take control. Now, I relish the prospect of a storm, knowing that I can simply count it away.

Lying on my side in the mud, just out of view of the German soldiers, I tried to do something similar. Despite bristling with cold and fear, I made myself close my eyes and pictured myself in the centre of a grid, a chess board. The Germans conversed with each other, one making some ribald joke that earned a little laughter. I used that to place them in squares. The joking man made another comment, his voice louder – and therefore closer, so I moved him one square forward, closer to my position. Concentrating on him, I could hear his squelching footsteps, then the creak and heft of leather, perhaps his coat. Another soldier, to his left, moved two squares further from me. I tracked them all as best I could, resisting the desperate temptation to turn my head and look. They were terrifyingly close and the slightest movement would have betrayed our position. Cheek pressed to the earth, I cursed myself for trembling, sure that at any moment there would be a shout or the crack of a gun going off, and my own weakness would have killed us. The joking man took another step closer, into the square directly next to mine, and I held my breath.

But I couldn't resist opening my eyes.

My first sight was the boots and spats. The soldier wore a grey woollen uniform with red piping and bright buttons. He carried a rifle, finger on the trigger and ready to fire. Crouching a little, leaning forward, he looked like a hunter on the prowl for rabbits, almost comically serious. He had wispy red hair, alert, ratty features, and a long beak of a nose.

Then he turned his head... and looked directly at me.

I froze. In all of history, no one had ever been more still. The red-haired man stood there, the gun pointed to his side, yet he stared right at me and didn't even blink. The winter sun glinted unnaturally in one of his eyes.

A glass eye! I wanted to laugh. The man almost stood on top of me had a glass eye, and so had not seen me at all. Sure enough, after an agonising few moments he moved on, stalking away to my left.

When I was sure the storm had passed, I let out a desperate breath. Closing my eyes again, I listened for the soldiers, plotting their course in my head. Holmes had been right: for all they fanned out, they assumed we would follow the path of the road back towards the hillside. That was their focus, and the reason why the man with the glass eye had not looked round far enough to see me.

I fought the instinct to get up and run in the other direction. We had to stay perfectly still, and not give them any reason to look back.

After a long time listening to them move away across the grid, I was startled by a sound close to the right of me. I dared to look, raising my head just a fraction from the damp, sticky ground, but could not see anything but great, uneven clods of churned earth.

Then something moved, in amidst it. The broken earth served to break up the outline of Holmes, who was anyway so caked all over in mud that my eyes had entirely passed over him. Even as he moved, it was like some strange illusion, the partial sense of a head and face forming from the ground to look quickly about.

I held my breath again, bracing for the sound of a shot. There was nothing.

Even so, Holmes held up a finger, cautioning me to remain where I lay as he slowly shifted himself round for a better view of what was happening. We could still hear the voices of the Germans, but now some fair distance off. Whatever Holmes could see, he nodded with satisfaction. Then, at last, he motioned for me to follow him.

My limbs were plagued with pins and needles after so long without moving. Sore and weary, it took an effort to crawl after Holmes. We moved through rather than over the broken ground, as one with the mud so that we might still be invisible. Yet, as before, Holmes made a point of abruptly changing course, pressing distinct handprints into the dirt to suggest we had gone in one direction, then striking out in another. He evidently thought they might yet pick up our trail.

I didn't dare say anything, but at one point I caught his eye and gave him a look of puzzlement. He nodded, gesturing behind me. I looked back the way we had come but could see little except the devastated landscape under a pall of acrid, curling smoke. Following the trail of smoke to a point on the horizon, I could just make out flames from the still burning ambulance. Then I remembered what he had said: two Germans remaining by the ambulance while the other four fanned out. Those two were surely still there, no doubt watching for movement. I turned to Holmes and nodded my understanding. We kept lower and crawled on.

I do not know how long we continued. For a long while, I focused only on my hands and knees, the deadening struggle to make progress through that uneven, squalid ground. I kept Holmes in sight, who moved lithely as if in his element. His brogues, I saw, were quite ruined.

It started to patter with rain, which made the going harder. I took some solace in the fact it might cover our tracks. Then there came the awful thought that it would wash some of the muck from my coat and expose the distinctive blue fabric. I kept checking, sure that at any moment I would be plainly discernible. Thankfully, the mud stuck fast; we just became more slick.

At last, we came to a great ragged section of rock, protruding from the mud like some crude temple monument. We scrambled round to the far side of it, where we would be concealed from the Germans. Soaked and exhausted, we nestled under an overhang, out of the rain, panting for breath but exhilarated. Holmes produced a metal hip flask from his pocket and I sipped luscious, fiery brandy. It thawed something of the cold terror inside.

"Better?" Holmes asked me, keeping his tone low.

"Better," I agreed, though when I handed back the brandy my hands were obviously shaking.

He made no comment, took a swig of brandy, and settled back against the rock beside me. We surveyed the desolation, mile after mile of it with no trace of tree or building, no solace or aid in sight. The scale of it, arraigned against us, overwhelmed the senses. We sat there, stunned.

Eventually, Holmes broke the silence. "Miss Watson, I apologise," he said. "This is my fault entirely."

"There is really no need, Mr Holmes. I asked to accompany you. I was well aware of the dangers."

"I should have questioned the map. One cannot take things for granted."

"We share the fault equally," I told him.

He smiled at that, consenting with a curt bow. We sat together, watching the birdless grey sky. Then he spoke again.

"There is another matter for which I should apologise, but I am not sure I understand it precisely. When we first met, you strongly resented me."

I actually laughed. It seems so ridiculous. "You want to talk about this now?"

Yet Holmes was in earnest. "We might not have another chance, and I should like to settle things between us while we can." The implication of that twisted inside me: he did not see any way out of our current fix. "I am aware," he continued, less sure of himself now, "that for all I observe, I sometimes fail to see that which is right in front of my face. Facts and details, yes, but the play of emotions can be elusive. I know that you were angry with me when we first met."

That rage kindled inside me, unquenched. "You assumed that a man would be a better guide to the ward."

"I was putting that rude nurse in her place, so she would leave you alone. Besides, the animosity really came later, when you realised who I was. We had never met, and yet you were angry with me."

"Not with you," I told him, guardedly.

He did not register my reluctance and continued to puzzle out the mystery in his usual way. "We had not met before that night in Sister Gloria's office, so there must be someone else. The strength of your animosity suggests a personal connection. You believe I have wronged someone close to you."

"No," I said.

"Then," he persisted, "I have offended them more generally. You received a report from someone you trust as to my conduct or attitudes."

"The only reports I have ever had of you were those printed in *The Strand.* But I really don't want to get into this." Truly, I didn't. I knew then that I had come to respect and even like Sherlock Holmes, for all that he infuriated me.

"It's not just something you read in that magazine," he persisted. "What I did affected you personally."

"It," I said through gritted teeth, "was not about you."

He considered this a moment. "You were angry that I asked Sister Gloria for you in particular. You were angry that I lied, and suggested some connection between us." Finally, the light seemed to dawn. "A connection based on your name. And that of my friend, Dr Watson."

Just the name struck me hard. "I am nothing to do with him," I said bitterly. "I want nothing to do with him. I never have!"

Holmes looked shocked – and hurt. "I am sorry," he said.

I tried to keep my voice steady though my anger was still raw. "All through my childhood, any wit or initiative I might have shown was always met with, 'Elementary, Dr Watson!' The irony is that I long to go into medicine. Everyone, *everyone*, dismisses my ambition on the basis of my name. All thanks to your famous friend."

To my enormous relief, Holmes did not try to remonstrate. We sat for a while. Away in the distance, a trail of dirty brown smoke bisected the grey of the sky. The desolation, the vast empty silence, quelled some of the heat inside.

"I am sorry," I said, at length. "Really, I know it is unfair to take against a stranger."

Holmes smiled. "It is I who must apologise. A thoughtless action on my part and I caused you great offence, awakening old sores. I am truly sorry."

I wiped my eyes on the back of my hand, then realised too late that I had just smeared mud across my face. "Oh, heavens."

Holmes fished in his pockets and produced a handkerchief that had the temerity to be spotless. I took it from him, and immediately ruined it with mud. It was now perfectly useless for my face and with a sigh I handed it back. Holmes neatly refolded it and placed it back in his pocket, as if it were perfectly clean. That made me laugh. How ridiculous to laugh and cry all at once.

"Sorry," I told him. "What a mess you must think me. Another irrational specimen of the weaker sex."

Holmes tutted. "You should not be surprised by the force of your feelings. We are deeply affected by our early experience: it shapes our very being. This Frenchman, Proust, writes about the little cake whose flavour conjures a whole world of his past. I suspect this is something similar."

"You're saying I'm being logical," I said.

"Why not? That association with my friend diminished your every achievement and success. Of course you resented it – and him, and thus me. And of course you determined to prove your tormentors wrong. You have led an extraordinary life in just a few short years, Miss Watson. If I may, John Watson would be honoured by any possible connection."

My cheeks flushed. "That is kind of you to say, Mr Holmes, but hardly true."

"Perhaps when we are back in England I might introduce the two of you. He would surely like to hear your account of this present, curious case. You could share with him all the various ways in which I have been mistaken."

I shuddered at that. We were out there in the middle of No Man's Land, a great distance from our own lines and with Germans in active pursuit of us. They sky seemed darker and more hostile, and this time I could not dispel the storm simply by counting. The thought of home, of catching up with friends and telling stories, was simply too much. I hoped that in thinking of the future, Holmes had not cursed our luck.

Keen to change the subject, I edged forward round the overhang of rock to look back the way we had come. The smoke had gone, so I could no longer trace the position of the ambulance. Perhaps the rain had put out the fire.

I turned back to Holmes. "There's no sign of the Germans."

"They know better than to stand in the open for too long," said Holmes. "They will be lying in wait."

Again, I felt that dread creeping over me. "Then what can we do?"

Holmes beamed at me. "We use our intelligence. Let us start from what we know."

"We're in big trouble," I said.

Holmes smiled. "The odds are indeed stacked against us. Do you not find it curious that they have gone to so much effort? All these men, this whole search party, for two civilians driving an ambulance. And why insist that we are not to be taken as prisoners?"

"They think we're spies," I suggested.

"I rather think they know exactly who we are," said Holmes. "Or rather, whoever gave them their orders knows what we are about. These men were lying in ambush."

I tried to follow his reasoning. "But that isn't possible. It would mean the people placing the betting slips had told the Germans we were coming."

Holmes nodded gravely. "I rather think it would."

"Impossible," I said.

"Not at all. We already know there is a form of daily communication between the two sides. We observed something of it two days ago, when we were on the front line." I could not think to what he was referring. Holmes shook his head wearily at his slow-witted pupil. "You will recall the trading of insults?"

"What? You're not serious."

"I merely state the facts. You said it wasn't possible to communicate across the line, but I demonstrate that it is commonplace. We were told the men traded insults at least once a day. Each such bout goes on for some time, during which they deploy a creative range of analogies and vocabulary. It would be simple enough to include a few pre-agreed coded phrases. Yes, the more I consider it, the more it fits. We know a conspirator was near the place where we saw these insults traded, because it is close to the dugout where Ogle-Thompson and Boyce both received their betting slips."

"Then it's easy," I said. "We find the men who shout insults and arrest them."

"I suspect the conspirators are a little more cunning than that," said Holmes. "There were men who whispered suggestions to the ones who shouted. It would only need one of those to be in on the plot, and they might not be there all the time. We could arrest a dozen men and find our culprit had slipped through our fingers – but now he would know we are on to him."

"He already knows we're on to him," I said. "That's rather how we've ended up here."

Holmes ignored me, distracted by his own thoughts. "The intriguing factor is who precisely the conspirators are speaking to."

"The Germans," I said.

Holmes looked at me witheringly. "I meant more precisely than that. Something about this whole business troubles me greatly, Miss Watson. The betting slips, the efforts to get you and me out here, the lines of communication implied... It is a sizeable operation, all told. Yet what has been its effect, beyond a little ill-feeling between officers and men?"

"The death of Captain Ogle-Thompson, at least," I reminded him.

"Tragic though that is," he chided, "it is not of great statistical note, given the daily tallies of loss. That cost has not materially altered and the Germans have made no great advances. The wretched stalemate continues."

"Then their convoluted scheme doesn't work," I said. "Or it hasn't yet kicked into gear and there's more to come."

Holmes considered. "I think there is definitely more. Miss Watson, we have to uncover what is really at stake here. I must ask that you trust me."

"Yes, of course."

"And you will have to be brave."

I didn't like the sound of that. "All right. We can't hang about out here all afternoon, anyway."

Holmes brushed mud from his fingers, then took from his pocket the crumpled, stained map that had been used to deceive us. He looked around quickly, confirming his bearings, then pointed off across the unprepossessing terrain.

"We're not making for the road or the hill," I said – not a question, just a statement of fact.

"That's where they're looking for us," said Holmes. "I mean to confound them."

"So where are we heading?"

"If we hold this course, I am confident we shall reach the trenches. That is, if we are not shot or blown up first." His eyes were bright with excitement, relishing the prospect of such extraordinary danger. I well understood our meagre chances, but what other choice did we have? More than that, I would not allow Holmes to think I was daunted.

"After you, then," I said. He bowed, politely, and we set off at once.

We crawled across that nightmare landscape for what must have been half a day. It rained and we were both drenched. Then we had to press on, sodden and heavy, and liable to catch a chill. My fingers were bloody but I could feel nothing but the awful cold. With leaden limbs and thoughts, I lost all sense of time, of distance, of even myself.

At last, when I thought I could drag myself no further, Holmes came to a stop. But we had not reached our goal. He showed me the way ahead, and the knotted, gnarly barbed wire. It might once have been arranged in neat lines, strung between thick fence posts as a border, but since then the ground had been torn asunder, the posts obliterated and the wire scattered all about in a tangle. As a result, we would need to pass through several overlapping coils of wire.

Holmes dared to kneel up to assess the immediate vicinity, but could see no better route than just to continue as we were. We approached the first wire with caution. The barbs were scabbed with brownish rust, and yet still sharp to the touch. I stopped Holmes probing too closely with his bare finger, warning him of infections that I had seen kill men in the hospital. He withdrew the muddied handkerchief he had offered me before and tied it tightly round his right hand. With this measly protection, he began to crawl under the first line of wire. Where it snagged his clothes, he used his one bandaged hand to extract himself. It took an age, but he got through.

Then it was my turn to join him. With his bandaged hand he lifted part of the wire to make more of a gap I could crawl through, but the barbs still caught against my coat and I heard it tear. Holmes told me to stop and plucked the wire away from me. We got through it, and proceeded to the next coiling wire. That proved more difficult, and I cut my ear and face. I assured Holmes I was fine, but couldn't help some dark thoughts about having contracted gas gangrene from the human slurry mixed up with the mud, having dealt with some of that on the ward.

We had to cross nine separate lines of wire. Scratched and scraped, our clothes rather ragged, we eventually got through. Each line took an age, and by the time I hauled myself out from under the last one, night had fallen. A few stars peeped through the ominous cloud, and I could only see Holmes as a crude silhouette. I was desperately cold and exhausted by then, and eager to move on swiftly after all that slow going, but Holmes chided me in a whisper.

"The trenches cannot be far now," he said. "We don't want them to shoot us."

I let him lead us carefully onwards. We followed the lip of a great crater, and I told myself the mangled remains glimpsed within it were just a trick of the limited light.

A little further, and something suddenly dashed at Holmes. He recoiled and swung his arm round to fight it off, but the huge rat did not care for a meal that resisted and scurried away into the dark. Holmes turned to check, without a word, that I was all right. My heart was in my mouth but I nodded.

On we went. It struck me that rats must mean we were getting close to the trenches, and that the soldiers on guard there might mistake any sight or sound of us for such vermin. After so much effort to cross that great expanse, I did not wish to be in sight of the end and then get shot by our own side.

Holmes seemed to have similar thoughts and we went ever more carefully. Somewhere, far off, I heard men's voices, though too distant to discern what was said. Then came the transcendent smell of cooking, the pop of fat in a pan. I had eaten nothing since breakfast and was almost mad with hunger. Had it not been for Holmes in front of me, I might have dashed forward – and been shot. We crawled on, that last leg of our journey a torture.

Finally – *finally* – Holmes shuffled his legs round in front of him and then abruptly vanished from view. I lay where I was, listening, but could only hear the men cooking and talking, somewhere off to my right. Then Holmes's face appeared, and a hand beckoning me forward. I was too exhausted to climb, so tumbled down over the side of the trench in an untidy heap.

There, on the half-covered duckboards, I let myself believe what had seemed so impossible: that we had survived our trek across No Man's Land. Relief flooded through me, but also desperate fear, the tide I'd held back while out there in the open.

Stunned with exhaustion, it took me a moment to register Holmes. He had peeled off the bandage around his hand and now used it to scrape some of the mud from his face. Then he yanked off his tattered, muddy greatcoat, revealing the dark suit beneath. His clothes were spattered from our journey, but in comparison to his coat he looked almost clean. He took pains to straighten his tie. I couldn't make sense of his need to look presentable – after all, who did he need to impress?

There was a commotion behind him. Men shouted gruffly, and then a herd of them came rushing out of the dark. They looked so peculiar and wrong, in their long, dark coats and spiked helmets. I wanted to tell them they were in the wrong trench.

Holmes coolly raised his hands. "*Wir ergeben uns,*" he told them with calm authority. "*Wir ergeben uns!*" he insisted, as they pointed their guns in his face.

I did not know much German, but I knew enough to understand. Somehow, we had ended up in the German trenches, and Holmes had just surrendered.

Chapter Fifteen

They shouted at Holmes, and they shouted at me where I lay crumpled in a heap. Then two German soldiers hauled me roughly to my feet and shouted at me some more. I could not understand what they were saying, but even if they'd spoken in English I was in no state to reply. It was all numb horror. I can picture their faces vividly, pressed close, pinched and thin with hunger, wild-eyed as they yelled at me. We were jostled and shoved and then there were more guns in our faces. More soldiers ran in to see what was happening and they were soon shouting, too.

Holmes responded calmly to their questions, in what seemed to be good German. They argued with him, shouted at him, pushed him around – but his firm, polite tone cut through. Soon they were conversing with him, and it began to seem as if they would not shoot us out of hand. Yet we were hardly out of danger.

I had, of course, heard all the claims about German soldiers, their savagery and ill manners and what they would do to an English girl if they got her in their clutches. They were certainly intimidating and I feared for my life and virtue. Yet as Holmes spoke with them I sensed something else: they were also nervously excited, even silly, because of this departure from the dull, cold norm. Our own men had reacted in much the same way to two strange civilians dropping in on them, but what struck me now were the differences from our own side. For one thing, the German soldiers were so young, almost boys playing dress-up. Their coats and clothes seemed too big for them, like on the first day of a new school term. Some sported extravagant moustaches, I'm sure in a bid to look older. I had an urge to reach out and pull one, to see if it were stuck on. None of it felt real – but then how could it be? I was standing with Sherlock Holmes in the German trenches.

Holmes glanced my way with a look of abject apology, but there was no way to tell him that I attributed no blame. Even he, with his extraordinary faculties, had got turned about in that rugged, ruptured terrain. Again, I saw that doubt in his eyes, that fear of his own frailty. I would not compound that by adding guilt for me, and resolved to be courageous, come what may.

That got me through the ordeal of men pawing over me, ostensibly in search of concealed weapons. They were less eager and rough with Holmes, but I saw the look of pain on his face when they took his pocket book and magnifying glass, and a number of other small items. The hip flask was quickly sniffed and then drained by the soldier who found it.

After more jostling and questions, the soldiers suddenly piped down. An older man had arrived, clearly their superior. Clean shaven, muscular and devastatingly handsome, he looked me over with bright, grey eyes then addressed Holmes in a rich, mellow voice like tobacco. Holmes responded in the same formal but mannered tone, and I heard his name in the midst of the foreign syllables, and then my own name, too.

Just for an instant, the German officer's cool expression faltered and he stared at Holmes in wonder. Some of the soldiers laughed scornfully and began to remonstrate, but the officer made the slightest gesture with his hand and they immediately fell silent.

"Sherlock Holmes, *der Detektiv*," said the officer, to make sure he correctly understood what he had been told. Holmes nodded, repeating in good German who we were. Now the officer smiled.

There was some conversation between him and Holmes, and then the officer gave orders. Holmes and I were led away. One soldier took my arm roughly and I yelped in pain. The officer interceded, with a curt bow of apology to me. I almost said, "Thank you," then remembered that this was the enemy.

We were escorted through the trenches. Men stopped to gawp at us as we passed. As with our own lines, the front was made up of ragged, rough-hewn passageways, some half-collapsed and in desperate need of repair. Dirty, thin figures watched from nooks and shadows, and there were swollen, confident rats.

The further we got from the front, the better propped the walls. I glimpsed dugouts that looked almost homely. The trenches weren't better than ours, or even quite the same, but then I had only visited our front line briefly and was hardly an expert. I think the Germans stacked sandbags in a different manner, and I saw more use of wooden fences to support the walls. It was just different enough to be unsettling; I felt like Alice, venturing through a twisted, looking-glass land.

Then we stepped up onto concrete, a pavement through the trenches that gave way to huts. Men sang and cooked and conversed, all quite amiably, until they saw our strange party passing through. One man shouted something at me and the men around him laughed. The officer escorting us pretended not to hear.

During all this, Holmes remained silent and did not even glance my way. He seemed alert and vigilant, absorbing details round us. I imagined him compiling a model of it all inside his head, assessing every means of escape. But his deep concentration made plain the difficulty we would face in breaking out of this dense, crowded labyrinth.

We arrived at a hut and were duly led inside. It was a simple box, a garden shed with a muddy floor, but there was a table, chairs and a stove, a chimney fashioned from scavenged metal parts leading up to a gap in the ceiling. The handsome officer barked commands and Holmes gestured to one of the chairs behind the table, inviting me to sit. Then he sat beside me, as the Germans stood menacingly over us. The officer gave more instructions and some of the men hurried out. He took the seat opposite us and sat patiently, taking his time to remove his leather gloves. The point was elegantly made: we were in his domain now and entirely in his power.

A soldier hurried in, and to my surprise brought two bowls of steaming broth that he placed before us. Its rich, meaty aroma made my insides turn over and I had to bite my lip. The soldier fished spoons from his pocket and wiped them hurriedly on his coat before sliding them across the table towards us. I looked to Holmes, who kept his eyes on the officer. The officer made us wait and then nodded. Ravenous, I tucked in.

I can still taste that blessed meal. The meat was old and hard, swimming with onion and raw garlic in a thin, watery soup. I wolfed down every last morsel. Holmes, too, ate hungrily – though with perhaps more decorum. The officer and his men watched us with no little amusement. I can well imagine them thinking what desperate wretches the English proved to be.

Another man joined us, taking the seat next to the officer and opposite to us. He was thin and sallow, his nose and cheeks flushed scarlet and his long, untidy moustache not hiding the perilous state of his teeth. His eyes were the yellow-orange of gas lamps, and they observed my every movement as I ate my paltry, welcome meal, without once straying to Holmes. It was supremely unnerving and yet I had resolved to be brave. With conscious effort, I continued to eat until I had finished every last morsel.

When Holmes had finished too, a soldier took our bowls. The officer began to speak. Holmes clearly understood him but the man opposite me was also there to translate. He spoke English with a peculiar accent like some fawning lord in a farce on stage, which I realised was him trying to sound like one of us.

"The law will be that you are some prisoners of war, old chap."

The officer spoke some more. I saw Holmes flinch. The translator seemed to enjoy that.

"Or otherwise this is the law: if you'll be a spy, you are shot."

The officer now summoned one of the standing soldiers, who unloaded onto the table before us the various things taken from Holmes's pockets. There was his magnifying glass, his pocket book, a penknife and the twist of wire. His hip flask failed to appear.

"Here then," leered the translator, running a hand over the assortment of objects. "You must show why you are here."

Holmes asked a question in German. The officer responded and Holmes answered him at length. I caught my name again, and "*das Krankenhaus*", which I at least knew meant "hospital". Holmes spoke fluently and fast, a babble of plosive syllables washing over me. Evidently, he told them something of our background. The officer asked some questions and Holmes answered, but the general did not seem satisfied. The officer said something, again using the word "*Detektiv*" but this time in a mocking tone. Holmes only smiled sagely.

Then he turned to the translator, who stiffened in his chair as Holmes quickly looked him over. There were things I could have told you by observing that man. That he drank too much was evident from the flush of his face. He was not a healthy figure, and though his clothes were clean – indeed, barely spattered with mud at all – he had an untidy air about him and terrible, black-yellow teeth. I could not imagine this man showing much prowess as a soldier, yet he held some moderate rank. The implication was that he had risen via privilege rather than merit, which might have explained my sense that the ordinary soldiers did not like him.

Holmes, of course, observed far more than I, and he shared his deductions at some length in his easy, conversational German. I didn't need to understand his words: the reaction from the men opposite was gratifying in itself. The translator looked more and more horrified, while the officer to his side and the men behind were delighted. I realised how clever Holmes had been: by picking on this unpopular character, he created a bond between himself and the others. We could only hope that this made them less likely to shoot us.

I must admit I felt sorry for the poor translator as Holmes continued to pick him apart for the amusement of the men. And then Holmes turned to the handsome officer and made some short observations about *him* – which silenced them all. For a dreadful moment, whatever Holmes had said hung in the air between us. The officer suddenly slammed his hands down on the table, making us all jump. But then he let out a harsh bark of laughter. Much relieved, the soldiers and translator joined in. Holmes went on, making observations about each of the men in turn, and winning them all over. I could not follow much of it, but there were references to places and people, and I am sure Holmes did for them what he had done for the men in the dugout, connecting them with their homes. It was extraordinary to witness: without understanding a word, I saw all too well what he was doing.

Yes, he was in control here – and that gave me pause for thought. Holmes must have had at least a working knowledge of German customs and geography to be able to make these connections. I was reminded of the way, two days before, he had read over the list of names before we visited the unit, committed them to memory so that he could perform his tricks on the men in question apparently without any effort. Now it struck me that he must have read up on Germany as well to work his conjuring here. But if so, then surely he had planned to cross No Man's Land all along. I felt a cold fury then, and wanted to confront him – but there was no way to do so in that little shed full of Germans.

They were getting on so famously with Holmes by now that the officer gave an order and soon someone ran in with a bottle and some mismatched glasses. The officer snapped off the top and splashed out measures of a clear but viscous liquid. He passed the first glass to Holmes, who slid it over to me and then accepted the second glass for himself. I was assailed by the strong, syrupy stink of aniseed. "Schnapps," said the officer in a warning tone; I now know the word means "strong drink". I wanted to be on my guard, of course, but I was also determined not to show any hint of fear to the Germans. To their amazement, I downed my glass in one. It was like drinking pure fire and I almost choked, but it was exactly the right thing with these men. Some of them applauded.

We were now apparently all on friendly terms. The officer passed the bottle to the soldiers, who took turns to glug it down.

Excited, enjoying themselves, they asked Holmes questions and he amazed them with his answers. Then Holmes said something else, and the officer looked uncertain. Again there was an awkward moment, but Holmes glanced up at the soldiers. Warmed by the schnapps, they began to laugh and jeer, clapping their hands and encouraging the officer to take part in whatever had been suggested.

I realised what Holmes must have asked for just before the officer stood up and began to empty his pockets. There were the usual items – a photograph of a woman who might have been his mother, another of the officer with a younger man, a few personal effects. And then he produced something he didn't recognise: a square card printed on one side.

It was not a column of figures like the betting slips; instead, the card was printed with rows of figures and words. It looked, from what I saw of it, more like a typewritten receipt, the kind of chit issued with the supplies we received at the hospital. Yet the effect on the officer was exactly as with Captain Boyce in the dugout. He recognised it at once and stared with incredulous horror. The soldiers with us looked over the card and saw nothing at all of significance. The translator had no idea what it meant, either.

Holmes spoke a few more words of German, and I caught the teasing tone. The officer stared at him in shock. The men began to laugh, realising some new trick had been performed. Holmes held his hand out and the officer passed him the card. Then Holmes, boldly, lifted his own pocket book from the table and slipped the card inside it. The implication was clear: it suggested to all those watching that the card had originally come from the pocket book. There was something more subtle going on, too. Without anyone quite noticing what he had just done, Holmes reclaimed his possessions. One after another, he took the pocket book, the magnifying glass and the other bits and pieces, and slipped them into his suit.

That done, Holmes broke the spell. He said something, a single sentence, that made the men blanch. The officer considered, then nodded, and got to his feet. He took his time, meaning that the translator had a chance to stand up first, showing his subservience. I wasn't sure if I should stand too, but Holmes remained seated so I followed his lead. There was some complex play of power going on that I didn't quite understand. It was evident in the cross, curt orders that the officer now barked at his men – where there was no question of who dominated whom. They hurried out and the translator followed. We were left with just the officer, who said something more to Holmes, perhaps an instruction or warning. Then the officer left, closing the door of the shed behind him. I heard the key turn in the door.

Holmes was immediately out of his seat. He stalked silently to the door and examined the lock, the edges of the door and the panels of wood. I noted that he didn't touch anything, just examined it closely. Then, as if his suspicions were confirmed, he came back to the table and retook his seat.

"Even if we could get out," I told him in a whisper, "there is the whole German army to get past before we could escape."

He smiled. "Indeed. I only wished to establish if there are men outside the door to eavesdrop."

"And are there?"

He smiled again. "Impossible to say. Let us suppose that there are. My guess is that they cannot overhear us if we speak at this level. Hauptmann – or Captain – Weich will return soon enough, so tell me: you observed what took place here and I think you followed most of it, even without speaking the language. What do you still wish to know?"

"You brought us here on purpose," I said coldly.

He seemed surprised by that. "I thought I had explained. The men pursuing us out in the open had orders to shoot us on sight. We stood little chance of getting back to our own lines without being seen, therefore the only option was to head in the other direction. I took us a little into No Man's Land first before we veered round, just in case the men pursuing us were only the first vanguard. That seemed provident, I thought."

Oh, he seemed very pleased with this particular cunning. "You could not have known," I said, "that once we reached the German trenches the soldiers would not shoot us anyway."

Holmes looked uneasy. "There are rules about the treatment of prisoners. That is what made the order to shoot us so singular. I calculated that the men who ran us off the road were part of the conspiracy, and that they constitute a minority of all those at the front – in the same way as seems to be the case on our own side."

I was angry now. "You gambled with our lives," I told him.

"A calculated risk," he said.

"And how long has it been since you first made that calculation?"

It was extremely satisfying to see Sherlock Holmes squirm. He shifted uneasily in his seat, and stroked his jaw as if to encourage himself to speak. Yet he could not find the words.

"We could have ventured further into No Man's Land and then veered round towards our own lines," I said, "but you chose instead to come here. Then there is how well you entranced those men just now, making connections to their lives back home. With our own men, you had to prepare a little – committing their names to memory. You had done something similar this time, hadn't you? Some research into German geography and customs. Then there is the small matter of the map. Were you ever really deceived?"

His nostrils flared and there was colour in his cheeks and ears. I do not think Holmes was used to being cornered. He was irritated, yes, but as much angry at himself because he had been caught.

"I thought something was afoot," he told me. "The general did not call for me – or for you, either – to instruct us in person. He dared to send his orders by the ordinary post, though we knew there was a conspiracy somewhere among his own people. I admit, the front line on the map did not trouble me: I suspected some kind of trap, but I thought it might prove fortuitous as it required our enemies to show their hand. Otherwise, I had considered the value of crossing the lines and prepared a little, as you say. But I did not see a way to make such a crossing possible until after we'd been attacked. And you must see what we have gained. We now know that betting slips are distributed among German officers. Captain Weich was in receipt of one, as you saw. This might explain why things remain at a stalemate. If both sides are plagued by this conspiracy, neither one advances."

"Maybe," I told him, "but that doesn't tell us why this is happening. And it doesn't mean you were right. We could easily have been killed."

"I apologise," he told me. "You deduce entirely correctly. I made a mistake."

"You used me," I said. "You thought we would be protected by the red cross."

Holmes slowly nodded. "I thought they would merely take us prisoner."

"You underestimated the people behind this conspiracy," I said. "They have seen this war and its awful suffering and they have conspired to make it worse. They are utterly ruthless. This is not a game."

Holmes nodded, accepting defeat. Yet what good did that do me, given our circumstances? I knew all too well that I needed Holmes, now more than ever. However much I hated him for using me so abominably, and his reckless self-belief in the face of such atrocious danger, we had to see this thing through.

"Who are they?" I said more calmly. "The people doing this. You must have some idea."

He sat back in his seat, brooding for a moment. "I don't know," he told me.

"They must be fanatics. The war has driven them insane." I didn't really believe that, but I knew I needed to prompt him.

"They are too organised for insanity," said Holmes.

"But to inflict further misery!"

Holmes nodded gravely. "It is incredible, yes. And despicable. But let us assume that the evident skill and ruthlessness involved runs on logical grounds. There are certainly those who could benefit from making things worse for the Germans and ourselves at the same time."

"You mean some third party, an enemy of both sides," I said. "But who? The Bolsheviks? Perhaps socialists in our own countries, inspired by the Bolshevik example…"

Holmes held up a hand. "There are a number of candidates but as yet we can only speculate as to their identity. That is, until they make themselves known."

I laughed. "You think they'll just step forward?"

He held my gaze. "I rather think they have to. We threaten to expose their whole operation. I just told Captain Weich to fetch a senior officer as we have information of the highest importance to share."

"What? But that would be aiding the enemy! And why? To force these people to try another attempt on our lives? Holmes, we're in no position to defend ourselves!"

Holmes seemed annoyed that I felt this to be of concern. "It is," he told me, "a calculated risk."

Chapter Sixteen

I couldn't believe him. "You mean we just sit here and wait to be murdered?"

Holmes stroked those long fingers over his chin. "What else would you have me do? At last we will know who they are."

"That knowledge will not prove of much use if we're dead."

"Really, Miss Watson, you disappoint me. I thought you would relish a little adversity in pursuit of a greater good."

"I relish finding and stopping these people. But if they kill us, they can continue their scheme. Even if they do not kill us, we may well be executed as spies. And if we are not, I fail to see how we can ever get back to our own side and expose the conspiracy there!"

Holmes frowned. "We can expose the conspiracy here, at least."

"Mr Holmes!" I exploded, then clamped a hand over my mouth – all too aware of the whole German army just outside the door. "Mr Holmes," I said again in a harsh whisper, "I do not wish to help *them*."

He seemed to take the point. "Do not misunderstand me – or my loyalties, Miss Watson. I assure you, we are doing our duty in this business."

His protestations hardly convinced me. I would have said more but Holmes suddenly tensed, holding up a finger to shush me. We both listened: I could not hear anything, but Holmes evidently did. Quickly, he took his seat at the table and motioned for me to do the same. Then came the sound of the key in the door, and Holmes sprawled languidly back in his chair, adopting a pose of insouciant boredom.

In an instant, the door was flung open and Captain Weich strode in, a determined look in his eye. Holmes got stiffly to his feet, so I did the same. He and Weich exchanged a few words, but now with little sign of the friendliness from before. The captain seemed agitated, even nervous, and when Holmes said something in a questioning tone, Weich snapped angrily back at him. Holmes caught my eye and I saw his look of alarm before he turned back to Weich with a smile. He bowed, placatingly, surrendering to the captain.

Something had changed, and not in our favour. There was no senior officer, as Holmes had requested. Weich issued a command and Holmes led me smartly out of the hut. Outside, in the gathering gloom, we found a line of soldiers waiting. Many of them were the same men Holmes had charmed and entertained with his tricks. Each man had a gun in his hand and one at least could not meet my eye.

I felt cold terror. What else could we have expected by plunging right into the lair of the enemy? But I would not have shown them my fear for all the world. Chin up, shoulders down, my back straight as a rod, I met them as an English lady. Mother would have been proud. Indeed, Holmes seemed rather taken by my defiant air. With an ironic smile, he crooked his elbow and I demurely took his arm. The captain led us away. We promenaded after him.

The soldiers did not lead us back the way we had come, towards the front, but away, ever further "inland" as I thought of it. Every step, then, took us further from our own lines and people, and reduced the prospect of escape. Yet I did as Holmes, watching and listening hawk-like, taking in every detail that might yet be turned to our advantage.

We followed a course between huts of various sizes, sometimes tacking left and sometimes steering right. Yet each turn was perpendicular, the whole arrangement a perfect grid, the concrete paths between the buildings running straight. Some of the buildings were marked with numbers and letters – DD34, DF32. It did not take much thought to decipher the system as positions on the grid. The double-digit numbers fell as we moved further from the trenches, the double letters tracking our course north-eastwards.

Other than that, I could see no way we might retrace our steps. The avenues were sporadically populated, in some places crowded with soldiers. They came out of their huts to watch us pass. Just as in our own trenches, anything out of the ordinary here caused something of a stir. We would never slip past so many men unnoticed. They watched us with open scorn.

A cloud settled over my heart. But until we came to the factory, I did not expect to die.

The Germans referred to it as "*die Fabrik*", which Holmes translated for me as "factory" – only to be rudely shoved by the soldier beside him, as we were not permitted to talk.

Looming from the darkness stood a long, windowless, brick oblong. Defences had been added to the basic structure, rather than being part of the original design – which suggested that it had been commandeered rather than built by the German army. Despite being a single storey, it was somehow imposing, disquieting in a way I couldn't identify. We made our way towards a wide concrete ramp leading up to open double doors. Pallid, fizzing light from inside cast long shadows back at us, picking out marks in the surface of the ramp, dotted in parallel lines. Nearer, and I could see the marks were squat tear shapes in pairs. They were the hoofprints of an animal. My first thought was sheep, but why pen sheep in such an austere building? Then I realised the grim truth: the hoofprints were those of a pig, leading into this abattoir.

As we crossed the threshold, I am sure I could smell the unmistakeable, iron-rich tang of blood, ingrained in the very walls and floor. They had been scrubbed so much that they shone – the wan light from a few bare electric bulbs showed the brick and concrete gleaming. Yet, like Lady Macbeth's obsession over her hands, that very spotlessness betrayed guilt.

Our footsteps sounded loudly in the enclosed space. Otherwise there was silence – the walls must have been very thick, and even kept out the pervasive rumble of war. I still had my arm in the crook of Holmes's elbow, until he gently let me go. It felt like losing my mooring, but I soon saw why he had done so. The corridor tapered as we went on, requiring us to proceed in single file, all the easier to slaughter.

Holmes went first and I followed him. That seems so strange now – the fact I went willingly and did not resist. Of course, there were the soldiers behind and in front of us, so it would have done little good. Yet many of our own bravest men have faced certain death and decided to at least go out fighting. Perhaps if we had still been out in the open, even among the huts, I might have attempted to run. Somehow, the narrow confines of that corridor made it seem impossible to go against the flow. Perhaps the silence added to the dislocated feeling. Just as in a dream, I had no power for anything but to continue.

Then we came to a room. It didn't have a light of its own, just the pallid glow from the bulbs behind us. Stepping into it from the corridor, there was space to stand beside Holmes, but I couldn't see how big a room it was. Another step and I felt giddy, but in fact the floor sloped to our left, down to a gulley in the floor. It was, I realised, a drain. Above it, at head height, ran a series of strong metal bars, and from these swung ominous s-shapes of rough and rusted steel. They were butcher's hooks.

I faltered now, unsteady, and Holmes swiftly took my arm. He started to say something but a German soldier barked right in our faces.

"*Seid ruhig!*"

Then two men pressed forward, wielding long strips of material. Before I'd quite taken in what was happening, they were pulling the strips tight over our eyes.

"I don't want a blindfold," Holmes said, politely – and I heard the grunt when they hit him.

My own blindfold was rough and greasy, and painfully tight against my skin. I fought the reflex to gag, but my whole body was quaking. I did not want to die and certainly not like this. The thing that got me through was my training. Whatever the enemy might do to us, we'd been told, we were to hold up our heads and show them what we were made of. It was a small resistance; it was all I could do.

They jostled and shoved us, and of course I tripped because I could not see a thing and the floor was on a slope. They might have done that deliberately. Before I crashed to the floor, strong arms caught and righted me, and pushed me further along. We were moved – I had a sense of Holmes still beside me – *across* the slope of the floor and then up onto a step. Blind, I bumped into the wall in front of me. We were held in position, facing it. I felt a surge of indignation that they meant to shoot us both in the back!

I stood there, waiting for the end, thinking of my mother and how distraught she would be that I couldn't have found a more dignified manner in which to die. Then something scraped, just in front of my nose. I jumped, and yet didn't bash into the wall. Even through the blindfold, there was suddenly light – and a good deal of noise. The wall had opened in front of us.

We were assailed with bustle and activity: voices in German, the clatter of typewriters and machinery. Before I could take any of it in, let alone try to decipher individual sounds, strong hands took my upper arm and dragged me forward. I stumbled as we stepped down onto wooden boards and the hand on my arm closed tight to stop me falling – or escaping. Seething with pain and frustration, I resisted just enough that this brute had to exert some effort as he dragged me on.

I could not see through the tight blindfold, but much could be discerned just from sound. After the close confines of the corridor, we were in a wide-open space. As we moved down what I guessed to be a central aisle, the sounds of urgent business came from at least two rows of desks on either side. There were women's voices among those of the men, and I longed to see if they held equal standing. I heard a voluminous flapping of paper, the sound distinctive given that I had been at the Chateau: it was someone struggling with a large map.

That explained why they could not allow us to see. This was a nerve centre in the German war machine, an office for planning and analysis, urgently responding to our own troops' every move. The Germans called it a "factory"; it was where they manufactured war.

I should have thought to count my steps to measure the length of that room. It seemed to stretch on some way, far longer than the dining hall back at the Chateau. I imagined it snaking away into the distance, a vast operation.

But then my escort halted, so abruptly that I twisted my ankle. Oh, I hated him by then. We paused a moment, then I heard the squeak of a door and we were led into a small room. My escort manoeuvred me in and then round to the left, behind the door we'd just come through. There were other sounds I couldn't identify, the movement of wood and fabric. Then the door slammed shut like a thunderclap. I cursed myself for yelping. Someone moved roughly round behind me and I tensed against more violence. They yanked hard at the back of my head, but only to whip off the blindfold.

I stood beside Holmes, both dazzled and blinking, in a comfortably furnished office warmly lit by a standing lamp with a pale green shade. Matching curtains had been drawn, I assume over windows that looked out on either the planning room we'd just passed through or the world outside. There was a rug on the floor and flowers in a vase on the desk, cushions on the leather settee, and photographs of a family with children, plus a portrait of the Kaiser. I gaped at it all in amazement, the most comfortable space I'd been in for perhaps a year.

Behind the desk sat a middle-aged man in high-ranking uniform, staring in deep contemplation. His wide face and large, round eyes put me in mind of Mr Toad. I was also troubled by the fleshy pink of his long, delicate fingers, and the sense that he went to some trouble to keep them so very clean.

The only other person in the room was Captain Weich, who must have been the brute who had dragged me, and who had removed our blindfolds. He stood to attention, waiting for the toad-like man to grace us with his notice, and clearly used to having to wait. After a suitable interval to put us in our place, the toad's eyes slowly blinked and he looked up at us as if waking from a pleasant dream.

"Mister Holmes," he said cordially in English. "My name is Meyer. You are most very welcome." He offered Holmes the single chair in front of the desk. There was no like offer to me – I might as well have been invisible, and it made my jaw clench. Holmes, however, remembered his manners and ushered me to the leather settee. Only when I was seated did he take the proffered chair.

"Herr Generalmajor," said Holmes, having read the man's insignia. He proceeded to speak in fluent German. Generalmajor Meyer did not stop him, but he did not seem pleased to be spoken to in such informal terms. Colour flared in his cheeks and his fingers clenched into fists. And yet he listened. Holmes spoke conversationally and calmly, and the man was hooked.

Then Holmes withdrew his pocket book, and extracted items I recognised: the betting slips he had found in our own trenches, and the card he had taken from Weich. Holmes turned to Weich at this juncture, who confirmed haltingly that the card had been in his pocket. Now Holmes told them what we knew: that the source of these cards and the conspiracy affected both sides. I didn't need to understand every word: I could tell what he told them from the astonishment on the men's faces.

There followed some discussion, and though the major general was angry, it was not directed at Holmes. He made notes in an elegant notebook as Holmes answered his questions, then asked some questions of Weich. At one point, Holmes mentioned my name. My heart swelled as both Meyer and Captain Weich turned to regard me. Holmes spoke some more, and I took pride in his acknowledging my role. I bowed my head, less from modesty and more to hide the grin on my face.

The men were soon on to more important matters that acknowledging that I existed. The major general issued Weich with orders. Holmes got up from his chair, and I followed his example. Weich reapplied our blindfolds and then led us from the room.

I could see nothing of the staff working at the rows of desks in the long hall, but I heard several women among the hushed, busy voices. I tried to take in any detail, in the hope of somehow reporting it back to General Fitzgerald, but hardly had the chance. Weich did not lead us back the way we had come but through another door and into a quieter corridor.

"Again, I owe you an apology, Miss Watson," Holmes said as we walked. "That *experience* was entirely down to my own blessed arrogance."

He, too, had thought we were about to be shot in the back. "Honestly, I'm fine," I told him, glad he could not see me trembling.

"I admire your courage. Yet I am mortified by the thought of how close I brought you to destruction, and in such a place as that. I am truly sorry."

"Thank you," I told him – and really, I was grateful.

Weich led Holmes and me through another door and out into the open. There, we were permitted to remove our blindfolds, because there was little to see. It was blackest night and bracingly cold in what seemed to be a parade ground. I wrapped my coat around myself, for all the good it did me.

At a signal from Weich, a rather elegant, open-topped car pulled up beside us, the driver no more than a boy. This grand vehicle was surely the preserve of the major general, and that we might use it was another sign of his faith in our story. I couldn't understand what Holmes thought he was up to in all this. We should not have been helping the Germans!

Weich addressed the boy driver as Dieter and gave him curt instructions, then gallantly opened the back door for me. I had no choice, so stepped up into the richly upholstered back seat, moving over to make room for Holmes behind me. But as I sat myself down, Weich curtly slammed the door.

Holmes was at my elbow, on the far side of the car. "They assure me you will be well cared for, and comfortable for the rest of the war."

"What?" I exploded, trying to get to my feet. But Weich gave an order and the car started off so quickly I was knocked back in my seat. "You can't decide that without me!" I shouted.

"I already have!" called Holmes, already at some distance. We scrunched over gravel, the horn sounding so that soldiers scurried out of our path. I righted myself just in time to see Holmes and Weich duck back through the door of that long brick slaughterhouse. Holmes did not spare me a glance.

Chapter Seventeen

❦

I boiled with fury, indignation and complete humiliation. But to cry, in front of the Germans, would have compounded my shame. I sat back in the seat of the car, staring ahead, trying to appear nonchalant, or at least numb. Inside, I was crumbling and could hardly breathe. Just as well – or I might well have screamed.

A prisoner of war! And I'd not even been captured by the enemy, just handed over to them, surplus to requirements. The gross injustice! The agonising betrayal!

I was too upset to take much note of the journey, or the route followed by the car. It all passed in a blur. Anyway, what would have been the point? There was no chance to escape, or to find my way to Holmes and beg that he reconsider. I was in the midst of the whole German army, utterly friendless, alone.

After some way, I do not know how long, we pulled up at a series of drab, square buildings. The driver, Dieter, jumped out and gesticulated at me crossly. I realised the boy meant me to get out and go with him, and was making a point of not opening the door for me. To underline my position, he lay one hand on the pistol in a pouch at his side. I did as I was bidden but with my head raised and back straight, to show my defiance. Admittedly, that did not make it easy to work the clasp on the door.

With as much dignity as I could muster, we tramped across mud and round the back of one of the buildings, Dieter keeping a close eye on me. Another soldier passed and they exchanged a few short words that I am sure were not complimentary in my regard. It might have been meant to intimidate, but I made a show of ignoring them. Perhaps it was unwise to be so contemptuous. Riled, the men could well have turned nasty. Still, Holmes had told me I would be well cared for and I could prove him wrong.

As it was, the man passed on and Dieter led me through a back door into a plainly furnished office, soldiers behind a high desk as you might find in a police station. Dieter, who seemed well known as an errand boy, explained who I was and the soldiers looked me over with hungry fascination. I feared there might be some unpleasantness, but Dieter mentioned "Generalmajor Meyer", which quickly tempered their spirits. One man reached for a book to register my arrival – without asking me to confirm my name or details.

Had anyone been kind to me, I might well have wept, so I was glad of their disdain. Yet I also resented the fact that they did not consider me to present any risk. A male prisoner would have warranted several guards, not the single, bored soldier who escorted me down a dank corridor, a series of doors marked with numbers in precise, painted numerals. Perhaps I should have taken advantage of the man's indifference and tried to run, but I knew I would never get far.

I had been assigned room 4, which the bored man unlocked. The heavy door scraped open inwards and crashed hard against the wall, so loudly that I jumped. The soldier said something, then jabbed with a finger, indicating that I should enter. I swept imperiously into my cell.

The room was cold and narrow, with a barred slit of a window right up by the ceiling. A shelf extended from the wall as a bed, a scrap of linen across it. An open hole in the corner would have to serve as a toilet. The floor was bare, uneven flagstones. Otherwise, that was it.

I had hardly taken in this impoverished sight when the door clanged shut behind me. Hurrying to it, I banged with my fists and begged for water or anything to eat. There was no response. I went over to the shelf and perched on one end. It bowed distressingly under my meagre weight, and offered little comfort. The wind whispered through the slit of the window. Far off, I could hear shouted words of German, the thrum of engines, the endless rumble of war. It might have been miles away.

So, Holmes had been wrong about their care. I took no delight in that. Already alone but now unobserved, I allowed myself to weep.

Yet they allowed me little time for self-pity. A bare few minutes passed before the door opened again. Dieter had returned, with a short, stocky woman in a simple, black outfit, pushing a trolley loaded with supplies.

I didn't recognise her uniform but could see at once that she was a nurse. The trolley was much like the ones I had spent months trundling round. She also had the brisk, no-nonsense manner, and the sturdiness that comes from lifting patients – even the slightest-looking men prove to be heavy. There was something unyielding about her generally, her eyes like flints as she assessed me. Then she got on with the task at hand, scrubbing the dry blood and muck from my face and hands with a tepid flannel, while Dieter wavered at the door. The nurse checked my various cuts and bumps, took my pulse at the neck, and then used the flame from a cigarette lighter to check that my pupils contracted. There were more tests, the standard medical fare. Yet it slowly dawned on me that she treated me as though I were ill.

"I'm fine," I shivered. "Just cold."

She took my icy hands in hers and rubbed them, gruffly. "*Ja*, cold."

"You speak English," I said, relieved.

She nodded and continued to prod me. Behind her, the boy still hovered at the door. "I speak English also," he told me. "Fish and chips. What-ho."

The nurse snorted at such foolishness and the boy fell silent, cowed by this bullish female. "You are a nurse," she told me.

"Not quite," I said.

"You wear a nurse's clothes," she tutted.

"I'm a VAD, a volunteer. I drive an ambulance, help out where I can. But I've had a little medical training and one learns a few things on the job." Then I bit my lip, embarrassed to be rattling on and not sure what I might be permitted to say. The nurse saw and shook her head wearily, then pushed a thermometer into my mouth.

"You do not need to tell me," she chided, as she counted seconds on her nursing fob watch. "But you have some medical knowledge and will understand." With the thermometer under my tongue, I couldn't ask what I was meant to understand. She counted the seconds in silence, though I saw her lips moving. I waited, the glass vial hard and awkward against my teeth.

At last, the nurse fished it out – and then she came right up close, peering into my throat.

"Say 'Ah'," she instructed. I did as I was bidden and she did not look happy at all. She held up the thermometer to examine my reading. "One hundred and two degrees," she said.

"What? No!"

She waved the thermometer in my face so I could see. Yes, the reading was just past one hundred. Instinctively, I put a hand to my forehead. My temples felt clammy and hot.

"A fever," concluded the nurse.

"I felt fine," I said, but the wind had been taken right out of me. That dizzy whirl of emotions I'd been feeling for some time had surely been other symptoms.

"You were exposed to the elements," said the nurse. "There are also diseases. What can you expect from such insanitary conditions?" She said it as though blaming me for the state of the trenches.

"I was wet through for a while," I said meekly.

She ran a coarse hand over my shoulder and down my arm, then examined her fingertips with some distaste. "I think take everything off."

When I didn't immediately obey, she grabbed the tattered lapels of my coat and began to haul it off me. I attempted in vain to resist by crossing my arms, but she was a strong woman and simply shoved aside my protests. Then she was at the clasps of my apron. I had not seen until then how ragged I'd become, how threadbare and dirty my clothes. The long skirt of my uniform was horribly torn where I'd gone through the barbed wire. One rent exposed a bright white flash of my under-things.

The boy at the door stared in slack-jawed horror at the prospect of what was to come. His cheeks and ears burned pink.

"Please," I said, nodding my head in his direction.

The nurse was already unfastening my uniform. She looked

up, annoyed, and acknowledged the boy. "Honestly, Dieter," she said, then proceeded with some terse words in German. He looked rather pitiful, shrinking back like a scolded puppy. He hurried clumsily out through the door.

The nurse yanked and pulled to peel the dress from my body. With the door of the cell still wide open, I stood in my torn and tatty long underclothes. I shivered, feverish, and saw the damaged inflicted by our long journey across No Man's Land. Bruises bloomed along my exposed arms and lower legs. There were gashes, grazes, and some of the injuries still bled. In all, I ached intensely.

The nurse bundled the ragged remains of my dress and apron and tossed them into the corner. Then she noticed the door standing open. "Dieter!" she hollered. "*Die Tür!*"

Sheepishly, head bowed to avoid the unspeakable sight of me, Dieter shuffled round from the corridor and reached for the door without looking, slamming it shut. The impact echoed through the cell.

"Men," said the nurse, exasperated.

"Boys," I said, and she smiled.

From the bottom of the trolley she took a folded grey blanket which she unfurled and draped round my shoulders. The coarse material scratched at my sore skin but offered little warmth. She told me to sit, and I perched on the shelf-bed while she went through the other items on the trolley. There were various bottles of medicine and a box that she opened to reveal neat rows of glass ampoules. Then she selected a syringe.

It was curious to watch her, for all that my head was reeling. The syringe was smaller than the ones we used in the hospital, with a curled metal part to the plunger. Yet the ampoules looked comfortingly familiar, and had the same foil seals which you pierced with the tip of the syringe. The nurse saw me looking and lifted out one of the ampoules so that I could see.

The glass capsule was cool to the touch. The printed label was, of course, in German, but I assumed it was some form of analgesic of the sort we used all the time on the ward. Satisfied, I tried to pass it back, but the nurse had already taken another ampoule and was inserting the syringe.

The ampoule in her hand looked exactly the same as the one in mine – except that it did not bear a label. I saw that in the moment just before she closed her hand around it.

She eased up the plunger, filling the syringe with clear liquid. Then she pressed the plunger to squeeze out the air, a few drops of liquid flicking out. Our nurses would often tap the syringe, or hold it up to check for air bubbles. This nurse, I noticed, kept it well out of reach of her face. It was the tiniest detail; it felt utterly wrong.

The nurse now turned on me and I stood gingerly. She was between me and the door – and where could I even run to? But when she brought the syringe up towards my arm, I twisted quickly out of the way.

In an instant, her other hand lashed out and grabbed my throat. She stabbed at me with the syringe, but I knocked it from her hand. The syringe clattered to the floor – but didn't break. I tried to stamp on it but only managed to kick it across the stone floor. The nurse cursed in German and let go of my neck to punch me in the face.

Stunned, I fell back, blood spouting from my nose and colours dancing in front of me. I hit the wall and rebounded, and used that to launch myself at her. She punched me again but then I was on her, my nails clawing at her face and neck the way I had been trained by the WVR. "Be quick! Be brutal!" they had told us. "Be the one who walks away." The nurse grappled with me and managed to pin my arms. I kneed her, kicked her, and smashed my forehead into her chin.

She fell back into the trolley, sending it clattering, but reached for an upended tray and grabbed one of the scalpels. The blade flashed and I leapt out of the way, colliding again with the wall. Twisting, I ducked another slash of the blade – though it nicked my corset and cut cleanly through.

I tried to hit her but she backed out of reach, and then came at me again with the scalpel. Dodging the blow, I retreated – until I hit the wall. The nurse advanced on me, pure malevolence on her face.

"You're part of this conspiracy," I told her, spitting blood.

She said nothing, just leered at me.

"But you're a nurse," I persisted. "How can you, of all people, be involved in something that makes suffering worse?"

"It will be better in the end," she said. "A better world for us all. All those who survive."

She slashed with the scalpel. I threw myself to the right, just as the door swung open to my left. The nurse was between me and the door, blocking my escape. But in the doorway stood Dieter.

"*Was ist–*" the boy started to say, taking in the extraordinary scene. The nurse took the scalpel to his throat.

I shouted. Dieter looked at me in astonishment, a plume of blood welling from a long slit in his neck. He tried to say something and the slit bubbled and gaped. The nurse tore at him again, jabbing the scalpel into his chest.

I pounced on her and we fell against the trolley. She still gripped the scalpel but I held her tight. For all that she twisted and kicked, she couldn't prise me away. Dieter tottered backwards out the door, clawing in vain at his blood-soaked neck. I never saw him again.

Enraged, I clung to the nurse for dear life. She elbowed me hard in the stomach but I kept my grip. Then she smashed me against the wall and elbowed me again. My grip loosened, and she threw me at the wall once more, this time with such force that I cracked my head.

Then I was falling, my legs having given out. As I fell, there was a flash of steel close by. I raised my hands to parry the scalpel and it cut a rent up my arm. Seething with pain, I hit the cold, hard flagstones. The nurse stood over me, and I tried to scrabble away but my legs would not respond. As she came at me again, I looked desperately round – and saw the syringe lying to one side. She seized me by the hair and in her other hand raised the scalpel. But by then I had the syringe, which I stabbed into her leg.

Nothing happened. The nurse stood over me, scalpel raised above her head, my hair coiled tight in her other fist. I looked up at her and that expression of cold fury. There was the strangest silence. I heard shouts and running footsteps. Then the scalpel dropped from her hand.

I tried to dodge, but it missed me anyway and clattered across the stone floor. Before I could reach for it, the nurse had fallen on top of me.

Her hands were on me, trying to cling on. I scrabbled and kicked, and hauled myself partially out from underneath her. She sprawled heavily across my legs, and looked up at me with scorn.

"You," she spat. "You're a nurse. How can you…" But the breath escaped her and she was a dead weight on top of me.

Then the soldiers rushed in.

Chapter Eighteen

It was all too horribly easy to see things as the German soldiers must have: that I had savagely murdered an innocent woman and a sixteen-year-old boy. "Dieter!" they yelled at me. "Dieter!"

Choking on his own blood, poor Dieter had staggered down the corridor to raise the alarm before he collapsed. Despite the severity of his wounds, he did not die quickly or easily, and I saw how that haunted the men. The thought still haunts me now.

It took three German soldiers to untangle the body of the nurse from me and then lug her away. Too late, I realised her eyes were still open, staring – but there was no chance to close them. My last sight of that woman was of her baleful, accusatory eyes as she was bundled away by clumsy, heavy-footed soldiers. I did not even know her name.

They left me where I lay. No one helped me to my feet or tended to my wounds. I clutched my bleeding arm and watched them gather up the trolley and its spilled contents, including the syringe. When I tried to stop them taking the unmarked ampoule, they shoved me back so roughly against the wall that I hit my head. I quickly raised my hands in surrender but one man then kicked me and yelled abuse. The others hauled him out hurriedly, as if *I* were the one who was dangerous.

Keeping their distance, they cleared the last of the detritus. It was no use my trying to appeal to them. If they spoke any English at all, they ignored my entreaties. They couldn't get out of the cell soon enough, slamming the door behind them. I crawled over to bang on it and shout my innocence, but the key turned in the lock and I heard them march away. Hollow, exhausted, I lay against the cold metal of the door, feeling just as cold and hard inside.

It's a strange thing to be a pariah. Those men, with their guns and army, were terrified of me. It was not simply that they thought I had killed the nurse and Dieter; they were scared for themselves. They had made a gross mistake, dismissing my potential as a threat on the basis of my sex. As a result, I had committed this atrocity and they might well face charges.

Alone, I tortured myself with visions of them planning their next move. They would want to be rid of me entirely, and the easiest way to do that was to have me shot.

My only hope was that the men would want to get rid of me by referring the matter upwards, and then I might put my case to Captain Weich or the major general, or some other authority. But the more I picked over it in my mind, the less likely this prospect appeared. In doing so, the men would have to answer for their own actions in not guarding me properly. How much easier it would be for all concerned if I disappeared, or met with some accident, one more unfortunate loss in the ongoing conflict. It was all so clear to me: the brutal logic of it, the absence of any alternative. I could defend myself against one murderous woman but not a whole unit of soldiers.

They had at least left me the coarse blanket. I retrieved it from the floor and wrapped it around my aching, bleeding body, but could not keep out the cold. I perched upon the shelf-bed but couldn't keep my eyes from the empty space where the nurse had died, as if the bare flagstones might reveal some clue to explain what she had done. There was a little blood on the flagstones – less than on the wall by the door – but nothing else that might count as evidence. I puzzled over the dead woman's words, re-staging our conversation before the fight. Then I reanalysed every part of that, too. Over and over I went, desperate to glean some new detail or insight. But try as I might, there was nothing. The curse of my new-found skills in deduction was that I could see it was utterly hopeless.

Despite my dread, I slept, exhausted by the horror of all that had befallen me and whatever was to come. In fitful dreams, I floundered in endless mud from which protruded wan, long-fingered hands, grasping and grabbing at me, pulling me down into the soft, black earth. I didn't resist; I welcomed the endless dark.

A polite rap on the door woke me from the quagmire. I hurriedly sat up and adjusted the blanket around me, scraping the hair out of my face, a wretched, useless attempt to make myself somehow presentable. It was all I could do to brace myself for the coming ordeal. The door was unlocked and clanged open. The soldier who'd opened it then backed away, allowing Sherlock Holmes to step lightly inside.

I had never been so glad to see anyone and rushed to embrace him. Holmes went utterly rigid, like an embarrassed child. I hugged him all the more because of that, angry with him for abandoning me, grateful he had returned. Soon he grew impatient.

"Miss Watson, we do not have time."

Against my better judgement, I let him go and retreated to the shelf. He stood over me with a sorrowful expression. I was painfully aware what a state I must look in my bloody, torn underclothes and blanket.

"Tell me everything," he said sternly. "Omit no detail, however small."

I recounted the events since I had last seen him – the car, the man who had spoken to Dieter outside, the response of the soldiers at the desk, and then everything that had happened with the nurse. "She put a thermometer under my tongue," I said. "And then she showed me the reading. One hundred and two degrees!"

Holmes put cool fingers to my forehead, and then felt under my jaw for swollen glands. He evidently found nothing of concern. "I take it she didn't show you the reading straight away. Some small distraction, some pause, allowed her to grip the bulb of the thermometer in her hand. Or perhaps she had some excuse to make a flame. Did she light a cigarette?"

I couldn't remember clearly enough, it had all been a blur – which did not endear me to Holmes. "I'm sure she faked it," I said. "But she showed me the reading and got me to confirm it in front of Dieter, the boy. Then she said I had to take off my clothes, which gave her the excuse to dismiss him from the room. Free from prying eyes, she could then kill me with an injection. If things had gone to plan, Dieter would have told the soldiers that I'd checked my own temperature and said myself that I was gravely ill."

Holmes's eyes narrowed. "But things did not go to plan. What did you do?"

I told him about the unmarked ampoule and was rewarded with a smile. "That was very good," he said. "It will save your life twice over, as we can use that ampoule as evidence of the attempt made on your life."

"I'm afraid they took it with them when they cleared the room."

Holmes looked drawn and tired, an old man assailed from all sides. "Then it may well have been disposed of. I cannot think that the nurse worked alone. We are not out of this yet."

"Yes, I know," I told him, annoyed that he felt the need to explain. "You might ask the soldiers if they still have it," I suggested. "They will not listen to me."

Holmes seemed surprised and then laughed. "My dear Miss Watson, you have missed out on developments. I am in no position to command. Pray, observe the door."

It had shut behind him but I'd not thought anything of it. Now I saw that we were both locked in. "But why?" I protested. "You had nothing to do with this!" Then the truth hit me. "They think we are both spies, because of what I have done!" I flushed with rage and embarrassment. "I have ruined your investigation."

Holmes only shook his head. "In many ways you have done me a favour. The major general was all set to send me to Berlin! He would not listen that I could be of more use here, exposing the conspirators. Now that looks as though I wanted to stay because you and I had something planned. I tried to explain, I told him what we have discovered, all to no avail."

"You told him everything?" I said, mortally offended. Generalmajor Meyer was, despite everything, still the enemy.

"I told him enough," said Holmes glumly. "I thought in doing so the conspirators would try to silence me. I had not anticipated that they would start with you." Then his eyes glimmered with sardonic humour. "You have ruined my perfectly composed strategy."

"They thought me the easier target," I said.

He smiled. "And they were wrong."

"You were wrong, too," I told him. "For sending me away – without even consulting me!"

He shifted uncomfortably and would not meet my eye. "I thought only of your welfare. I thought I could keep you safe."

"You were wrong," I told him, and he bowed his head.

"Not for the first time, Miss Watson, I apologise."

"What will happen to us now?" I asked.

Holmes brooded a moment. "There are too many factors involved to make a reliable prediction. I'm afraid I do not know."

Captain Weich came for us later, accompanied by a whole squad of soldiers with pistols in their hands. One man brought in a misshapen, woolly mass that he flung at me. I pulled the crudely knitted sweater over my head and aching body. It reached down almost to my knees and I had to roll up the sleeves, but though I must have looked quite peculiar I was grateful to feel a little more decent and, more importantly, warm. They also had my shoes, now without their laces. Holmes asked a question and then translated the answer for me: my VAD uniform had been in such a wretched state that it had been taken out and burnt.

We were led to another room in the same building, this time comfortably, not least in comparison to the cell. The toad-faced major general glowered behind a desk, regarding us with cold fury. Holmes and I were not permitted to sit. Our escort of soldiers waited outside, except for Weich and one other man, who took a position by the door. He kept hold of his gun.

We were clearly an embarrassment to them, but I noticed that the major general now at least acknowledged my existence. As with the soldiers, he clearly regretted not taking me more seriously before – and resented me all the more for this, as if it were my fault. I am sure it did not help that I looked such a blessed shambles in my knitted sweater and underclothes. Meyer's jaw clenched with distaste as he prepared to harangue us, yet Holmes took the initiative and spoke first.

"My dear gentlemen," he said. "Now you have evidence that there are those in your own ranks working against you. That nurse tried to poison Miss Watson, and would have done so if not for the intervention of that courageous young man."

It wasn't quite the truth, but I could see what he had done, playing to their emotions. In all the unfolding horror, they would want to believe that Dieter had died in the brave pursuit of duty.

"An autopsy will show that the nurse was poisoned," Holmes continued. "There is also the ampoule that your men took from the cell. You will find that it is of exactly the same type as the other glass capsules in the box on the trolley, except for the notable difference that it is unmarked. There is no possible way that Miss Watson or myself could have brought that ampoule with us. It would hardly have survived the journey, and anyway, we could not have known the kind of capsules that your people use. That it matches them is uniquely telling."

"No ampoule was found," snapped the major general. "There is no evidence at all."

Holmes continued, undaunted. "That is also telling. Then there is the nurse herself."

"Valerie Schneider," said Captan Weich, bitterly. I felt a pang at that: with a name she became a person.

"Then you have her history," said Holmes. "And you will be able to tell me who sent her to attend on Miss Watson." Weich and Meyer conferred and it was clear neither of them knew. "You see the significance, of course," Holmes told them. "She arrived remarkably quickly after Miss Watson reached the cell. You will be able to verify if she was stationed somewhere close already. If not, that is also suggestive."

With a nod from the major general, the captain said something to the soldier at the door, who hurried out.

"It will exonerate Miss Watson," said Holmes. "Now, perhaps we can get back to business."

The major general did not look any more happy. "Mr Holmes," he said. "We do not believe you, necessarily. You have given us something we can investigate and then we shall see. It is for the time being, provisionally, a stay of execution." He looked contemptuously up at me as he said this.

"Of course," said Holmes, as if agreeing some minor point of order. "Now, the conspiracy we have talked about…"

"There will be a full inquiry," said Meyer. "High Command take your warnings to heart."

"Then they recognise a problem of officers suffering breakdowns?" said Holmes.

The major general glowered at him. "I cannot confirm or deny such a thing, and certainly not to an English…" He stopped, considered his words. "…detective," he concluded.

"It is wise to be wary," Holmes told him. "And to work from the evidence. 'Sceptical, not cynical,' as a shrewd friend once put it."

"You are a prisoner here," Meyer told Holmes. "You have no standing or authority." He paused, to see if Holmes would argue. When he did not, the major general seemed satisfied. "Even so, I should be interested to hear your suggestions for how we now proceed."

Holmes responded with a cat-like grin. "My modest proposal," he said, "is to use what we know. I had thought these people would attack *me*. Why did they attack Miss Watson instead? I flatter myself that I present a more direct threat to their conspiracy. However, I was always in company, whereas Miss Watson was placed in that cell on her own. Therefore, logically, we might entice these people to come forward once more if you put me in solitary confinement."

The major general warmed to the proposition. "A trap!" he said, clapping his hands.

"But you wouldn't actually be on your own," I said.

"But of course," countered Holmes. "It must be entirely convincing."

The major general nodded. "What did you have in mind?"

"You might leave me in this very room," said Holmes. "That is simple enough to contrive. Perhaps, Herr Generalmajor, you could be called away on urgent business. Then, a little later so it does not seem as though we are all working together, Captain Weich might take Miss Watson to find some more suitable clothes. I am an unarmed old man, so Weich will think it safe to leave me behind, as long as there is a guard on the door to prevent me from escaping. That guard should be someone you trust implicitly – but do not let them in on the plan. The less they know, the less they can give away, even unconsciously. Then we shall see who decides to come visit me."

"Maybe," mused Meyer, though I could see he was taken by the idea. "How do we let these villains know you will be on your own?"

"You might mention it in passing to anyone you encounter," said Holmes. "Though my suspicion is that someone will already be watching. They know I must be dealt with."

"They want to kill you," I said.

"Indeed," said Holmes. "And they will be determined. They failed to kill you and they cannot fail again."

"And you're just going to let them walk in!"

Holmes turned to Meyer. "I am taking a risk for the sake of exposing this conspiracy," he said. "But perhaps you might show some faith me in, sir, by allowing me the use of a pistol."

The major general turned puce. "That," he said, "is asking a great deal."

"Yes," Holmes told him levelly. They stared at one another for a long moment. Then the major general shook his head.

"It is asking too much. We must think of something else."

Holmes only looked quizzical. "This is our best chance of learning the truth. I propose to continue, with or without a pistol."

I wanted to protest, but there came a knock on the door. "*Ja!*" barked the major general. The door opened and in came the soldier that Captain Weich had earlier instructed away. He reported in German but Holmes translated for my benefit: no unmarked ampoule had been found. The evidence, he concluded, must have been destroyed.

Meyer studied my reaction to this disappointment, weighing up his next move. I understood the options all too plainly: the only way Holmes could prove my innocence and save us both from being shot was to produce the conspirators. Whatever the risks, we had to follow his plan.

The major general soon enough reached the same conclusion. He spoke a few words to the solider and then left the room, leaving Weich and the soldier to watch over Holmes and me. Holmes took a chair just inside the door, stretching his legs out and making himself quite at home. The captain and I stood awkwardly, the soldier watching us. After a time, I shivered. Captain Weich played his part well – noticing, as if for the first time, that I was in an oversized, ragged jumper and little else. He spoke to the soldier, and then snapped his fingers to get my attention. With a last look to Holmes, I followed the captain and soldier through the door. Holmes didn't even look up at us, apparently lost in his thoughts.

Out in the empty corridor, Weich gave the soldier instructions. There was no one else to hear what he said, at least as far as I could tell without looking round too closely. Everything seemed silent and ordinary. It all felt horribly wrong.

We left the soldier on duty outside the door, Weich escorting me smartly down the corridor. We did not dare look at one another and both stared fixedly ahead, trying to look impassive, to give nothing away. We turned a corner and joined another corridor, where there were more soldiers. They were, of course, surprised to see me – given what I was wearing and what they must have heard I had done – but Weich's commanding presence at my side was enough to assuage their concerns. If he was taking me somewhere, I could see them thinking, then it must be all right. He nodded a greeting and exchanged a few words in German, telling them where he was taking me.

There were more soldiers further down the corridor. Weich greeted them, as well, and knew everyone's names. He was on good terms with them and I could see he was well liked and respected. Again, I felt that inner conflict about this good and handsome man who was also my enemy. He also played his part a little too well, all too easily making conversation and mentioning Holmes had been left on his own.

At the end of the corridor, three men stopped to let us pass. One of them, a red-haired, ratty-looking man, gazed down his long beak of a nose at me with unsettling interest, a cold glint in his eye. I hitched up the collar of my jumper to show less of my bare neck. Weich thanked the men for stopping and we went on, but after a few steps I glanced back at them – just as they turned the corner and were lost from view. Weich turned to see what the matter was and I couldn't at first explain. There had just been something strange about the three of them, and that cruel look from the red-haired man.

With a sudden start I realised I had seen him before, and the cold scrutiny of his unseeing glass eye. He had been one of the search party who forced our ambulance off the road!

I started running, back the way we had come. Holmes might defend himself from one attacker, but this was three armed soldiers!

Weich caught up with me as we rounded the corner and I saw the men up ahead, already with the sentry – who had started to open the door. The sentry saw us and one of the men turned, raising his gun. The red-haired man pushed past the sentry and went through the door.

"Holmes!" I shouted – but too late. There came the sound of a gunshot.

A second shot sounded, deafeningly loud right beside me, and with a whiff of cordite. Weich shot the armed soldier in the leg and he toppled back, into the other conspirator. By the time we had reached them, the sentry had his gun on them and they raised their hands.

Without a thought for my own safety, I dashed into the room – and almost fell over the red-haired man, kneeling on the floor and nursing his wrist. Holmes stood over him with the man's own pistol, which he now surrendered to Weich.

"You know," Holmes said pleasantly to me, "I think that went rather well."

Chapter Nineteen

C aptain Weich held the three conspirators at gunpoint. The sentry stood with him in the corridor, and more soldiers hurried to join them. It caused quite a stir: these three villains were clearly well known and liked. The red-headed man with the false eye, one Oberleutnant Reinhardt, had been friend and mentor to many of the ordinary soldiers. Some of them now called out to him but they got no reply. The conspirators kept their heads down and did not say a word.

Holmes maintained a discreet distance, leaving the business of guarding the conspirators to the captain and his men. Yet I saw his quick eyes watching the three villains, taking in every last detail. I joined him, and endeavoured to observe what he could. The truth was, they looked no different from the other soldiers: the same grey, woollen uniforms, the same nervous, hungry look about them. I could see the soldiers wrestling with the same thought: that these men were of their own kind. They repeated Reinhardt's name to one another in abject disbelief.

Then in marched the major general and proceeded to upbraid the three men, his face so red and swollen I almost thought he might burst. The watching soldiers backed off, some making themselves scarce. Holmes, still out of the way, said something softly in German and Meyer whirled round. Undaunted, Holmes continued with his suggestion and the major general slowly nodded.

He gave an order, and Weich and the sentry led the three men away. A crowd of soldiers followed, and Holmes and I trailed in their wake. Meyer joined us and spoke to Holmes in hushed but urgent tones. Whatever Holmes had said, it quelled Meyer's fury – but I couldn't guess what new ploy Holmes had in mind.

We followed the men to a hallway where more soldiers gathered, some eating meagre dinner. The sight of the three conspirators got quite a reaction, men getting to their feet, some jeering. Evidently they, too, shared a bond with the three prisoners. Again, the name "Reinhardt!" was repeated in dismay. Oberleutnant Reinhardt drank it in, grinning defiantly at Weich.

Meyer pushed forward so that the men in the room could see him. The noise quelled but I could see they were not in the least bit mollified. Some watched me and Holmes with open hostility, no doubt wondering why on earth their superiors had sided with two British spies against their own kind. The major general addressed the soldiers, and though I couldn't understand him, his headmasterly tone misjudged the mood of those around us. It was a precarious moment, and yet he mentioned the name Dieter and it had a powerful effect. At least some of the men now looked on the three conspirators anew.

Then the major general pointed back at me and Holmes. "Herr Holmes," he announced as if expecting some applause. The men only stared, some apparently outraged. Holmes stepped forward into that heavy silence and I was all too conscious of now being alone, barely dressed, surrounded by German soldiers in a dangerous temper. Yet their eyes were on Holmes as he joined Meyer. Then Reinhardt spat at the floor in front of Holmes.

There was a collective gasp, but many of the men watching were roused by this act of intransigence. They had, after all, endured years battling the English. The tension in the air was palpable. How very easily the men might have turned on the officers right then and there.

But Holmes said nothing and deferred to the major general. Meyer spoke, and as he did so Holmes produced from his own pocket the card he had taken from Captain Weich. He held it up so everyone could see as the major general explained what it was, how it had been planted on the captain, and what it had been intended to do. Reinhardt said something gruffly, and Holmes turned to him in surprise.

I followed the gist of what then passed between them, though Holmes later provided a more detailed summary. Reinhardt denied ever seeing such a card before and then taunted Holmes that he could never prove otherwise.

"Your confession would make things easier," admitted Holmes. "But if you won't help us willingly... Herr Generalmajor, do you have the knife?"

I remember how mildly he said it, and also the electric effect of his words on the room. Someone shouted to protest but was quickly shushed, because they all wanted to see what would follow. To my astonishment and theirs, the major general produced a slender dagger, its polished blade gleaming silver. It was an ornamental piece, antique and exquisite – but also very sharp. Meyer turned it about in the air with a flourish, so all the men could see, and then offered it to Holmes. Holmes affected not to see, his eyes fixed on Reinhardt.

"The left side, I think," he said.

With bated breath, we watched the major general advance on the prisoner. Reinhardt tried to back away, but the wall was behind him and Weich had a gun on him. The red-haired man also did not want to look cowardly in front of this crowd: that would have cost him their favour. Mustering his dignity, he stood firm.

Meyer stalked up to him, lingering with the knife. Then he suddenly yanked at the man's woollen tunic, pulling it open. As one, the men watching gasped and shouted in response to the scandalous sight: the tunic was lined with glistening raw silk. The delicate sheen seemed especially incongruous next to the rough, woollen uniform. Some of the men started to laugh. Yet the silk provoked outrage in Meyer, who slashed at it with the dagger.

The blade cut a long gash through the soft material. Meyer struck again, and a third time – and this time struck something hard. The major general picked and prodded with the dagger, and out spilled a selection of cards. They scattered across the floor, some reaching as far as the boots of watching soldiers, who hunched down to examine them.

"I am sure," said Holmes, addressing the room, "that a cursory inspection will show they are of the same kind as we found planted on Captain Weich." The men with the cards confirmed this, showing them to the soldiers round them. "You might also note, gentlemen, that I have never been in closer proximity to Oberleutnant Reinhardt than I am at this present moment – a good three feet apart. Several witnesses can confirm that. My colleague Miss Watson, I understand, passed Reinhardt in the corridor briefly, and it is just about conceivable that in doing so she might have placed these cards into this man's pocket. Secreting them into the *lining* would not be so conceivable, not least because that lining should not be there at all. That lining and those cards are therefore Reinhardt's own work."

"How many of these damned things have you given out?" the major general seethed – or its equivalent in German. Reinhardt did not respond. He continued to glare at Holmes, his false eye catching the light.

"You slip these cards into the pockets of particular officers," said Holmes in German, his voice raised so that all the soldiers in the room would hear. "The detail on the cards will mean little to the ordinary soldier, but an officer understands that it is a coded report of the latest casualties, and paints a very sombre picture. It is a lie, the numbers exaggerated to suggest things are worse than they really are. The purpose is to undermine the officer, to drive them to despair. I can see the men already recognise something of this. Many have seen one officer or another losing their grip, and have not been able to comprehend why, when officers and men all face the same conditions. That is very much the point. Reinhardt and his fellows target only the officers, and thus drive a wedge between them and the ordinary soldiers."

"But why?" someone shouted from the back of the room.

Reinhardt grinned lasciviously at Holmes. "You're so clever, you can tell the men how we seek to help them."

There was now quite a commotion among the watching soldiers. Meyer called for silence, with only limited success. Holmes did not seem in the least put out.

"I can tell you," he said, "what you might claim to be your motive. Your example is the eastern front, where horrendous conditions and the vast numbers killed have led to revolution and the fall of the Tsar.

You tell yourselves that you are working to liberate the ordinary soldier, the working man, whatever it might be."

"That's right," growled Reinhardt. He turned to the men. "You know I'm one of yours. What I've done has only been for all of us." He nodded disdainfully at Weich and Meyer and Holmes. "But not for the likes of these."

He had them, the core of these men. They had lived so long in the squalor of the trenches, endured mud and hunger and constant risk of death. We all longed for the end of the conflict, after all. Now this man seemed to offer them a chance.

But Holmes laughed. "Is that what you tell yourself when you talk to your comrades in the British trenches?"

Reinhardt blanched – but did not answer.

"I cracked your code," said Holmes. "You hide coded words and phrases in the insults you shout across the lines. Ah, you see – the ordinary soldier can recognise it now. They know they have been used. Because you never shouted insults, did you, Reinhardt? But all too often you suggested what might be said."

It was true: some of the men did seem to recognise what Holmes had said – but not nearly enough of them. The majority still felt a bond with Reinhardt. I suspected their pride may have been part of it; they did not want to believe they had been duped.

"We traded information," said Reinhardt. "Our comrades among the British warned us of impending attacks. We used that information to benefit the men."

"I see," said Holmes darkly. "And who here has received such a warning? Which of you knew to be ready – or to be out of the way – because Reinhardt or his people said so?" There was an awful silence. "Any one of you?" snapped Holmes. "A single example. Anyone that you *know of* who has been aided by this man?"

No one came forward. They were dumbstruck in horror. I saw the blood drain from Reinhardt's face, and the looks of his two fellow conspirators.

"No," said Holmes. "The saddest thing is that you *could have* used that information to help the ordinary soldier. But you have kept only yourselves out of danger. That was hardly in the spirit of comradeship with your brother man! I should say it was *cowardly*!"

Reinhardt launched himself at Holmes, without thought of Weich or the gun. But it wasn't Weich who saved Holmes. Instead, the soldiers pushed forward and grabbed Reinhardt. They punched and kicked, and restrained him. Oh, they would have done much more if Holmes had not called them to a halt. Reinhardt hung in their arms, seething and howling, but could not break free. He knew, as we all did, that he had lost the soldiers now. They could see all too well what he was.

"I am not a coward," he told them, rather pitifully.

Holmes addressed the men. "It is worse than that," he said. "Reinhardt took this terrible war and sought to increase the suffering, in the hope that such desperate misery would provoke a revolution. There has been a terrible cost, inflicted upon officers and soldiers alike. In that, you are united."

They dragged Reinhardt and his two comrades away. Holmes offered to help question them to find out who else was involved in their conspiracy, but the major general felt this should be left to the military authorities, assuring Holmes that there would be a full investigation before the men faced the firing squad.

I thought that meant we could not pursue the matter further, but plenty of soldiers came forward with the names of Reinhardt's associates. Now the plot had been exposed, the soldiers could see how they had been manipulated and were keen to fight back. There were soon more arrests. "Clearing up," the major general called it, with odious satisfaction. I hated how much he enjoyed it.

He treated Holmes as a hero, the saviour of the hour. We were taken to the major general's office with a number of senior officers and given warm champagne. I felt rather sick and couldn't bring myself to drink it, skulking at the back of the room out of Meyer's line of sight. The officers toasted Holmes and made speeches, and he looked ever less comfortable. When it came to his turn to reply, Holmes thanked them in just a few modest words. This made the major general laugh.

Officers wanted to show Holmes and I how well they spoke English, and asked Holmes if he thought the Bolsheviks had organised the plot themselves, or if it had been dreamt up by German anarchists inspired by events in Russia. Holmes confessed that he could not be sure without further evidence. The officers talked more on the subject of Russia and how socialism was anathema to the German people. Holmes and I had little choice but to stand there, waiting for it all to be over.

After another toast, the major general fixed his attention on me. "Fräulein Watson," he called me, as if I had now become German. "You will need some more suitable attire to join us in Berlin. I think you could be made agreeable, yes?"

My blood ran cold, and anyone else would have surely read in my expression what I truly thought. Meyer, however, was too pleased with his own idea and had no interest in my opinion. He began to tell me – or, rather, the men around us – about Berlin bars and restaurants where he was welcomed as a friend. Exasperated, I glanced again at Holmes – and the major general noticed.

"Do you not enjoy high dining?" he asked crossly.

Holmes shook his head, but not to disagree: it was as if he needed to clear his senses. He swayed unsteadily, then staggered back a few steps. I rushed forward and took his arm, plucking the glass from his hand before he dropped it. Someone found us a chair and Holmes almost fell towards it. I helped him, turning the chair so he had his back to the officers, and would be less aware of them gawping.

"There we go," I said, setting him down in the seat. "We'll just a have moment to catch our breath."

"The champagne," said Holmes in explanation, his voice high and reedy.

"Yes, yes," said the major general, more for the benefit of everyone else. "And perhaps too much excitement for a day. Please, let him have some air."

As he shooed back the officers, I took Holmes's pulse but it seemed steady and a healthy eighty beats per minute. He didn't seem overly hot or cold, and when I turned his head away from the light, his pupils expanded quite normally. He was neither sweating nor pale, and yet he hung on to me limply, a weak rag doll version of his usual self.

The major general huddled next to me, rather closer than I liked. "It is the greatest fortune that we have a nurse," he said, again playing to the room. "Assure us that Herr Holmes will be well enough for his trip to Berlin."

Again, I bristled at this dread prospect, but the major general's words earned a polite laugh from the officers. Meyer turned to bask in their good favour. When I didn't reply, he looked back at me with alarm.

"Mr Holmes is unwell," was all I could tell him.

"Unwell how?" he demanded.

I didn't answer, not sure what I could say. Then Holmes began to tremble, clutching at his forearm and wrist. I reached to loosen his tie and undo the top button of his shirt, but he jerked violently backwards. The next thing I knew, Holmes was on the floor in convulsions.

Chapter Twenty

It took three of us to restrain Holmes and ensure that he did not do himself any damage. He fought and frothed, his eyes bulging from their sockets. I spoke to him, soothing him, telling him everything would be all right, just as I had been taught. He twisted and strained blindly. His lips were thin and blue, and he struggled for breath. We were losing him.

One thing I knew about convulsions was to ensure that he did not bite through his own tongue. On the ward, the nurses would force a wooden spoon between a man's teeth, but the major general didn't have one. Holding Holmes tight, I begged for anything similar. Meyer gave me his riding crop and it did rather well, flexing with Holmes as he ground his jaws.

By the time I'd done that, doctors rushed in and took over from me. I reported everything I could to them, as I would for British doctors, but I'm not sure how much they understood – or ignored. They repeated the things I had done, checking his pulse and eyes, talking to him calmly, trying to make him more comfortable.

Holmes gradually settled, which I tried not to take as a rebuke of my own care.

Sitting back, I took in something of the room around me. Many of the officers had left, and the few who remained stood awkwardly watching the morbid show. Glasses of barely sipped champagne stood abandoned on the desk, where Meyer regarded them coolly.

"Poison?" he asked me.

"I don't know," I had to admit. "But it wouldn't be the first attempt on our lives."

Meyer held up a finger, cautioning me not to say more with the doctors there. He beckoned Weich and murmured instructions. The captain hurried off, returning promptly with two more soldiers. With great care, they gathered up the glasses and carried them away, presumably to be tested. Meyer watched them go, looking queasy. Sweat beaded on his brow.

I didn't know how much champagne the major general had drunk, and I could have attended him. We have a moral duty to help anyone in need of our care, and it might have been wise out of self-interest, too. With Holmes in such a parlous state, I was at the major general's mercy. Yet I had been chilled by his words about taking me to Berlin, and about finding me suitable clothes, bristling at the very idea of being *agreeable*.

As a result, I made a point of keeping out of his way, and remained on my spot, near to the doctors treating Holmes. When they struggled to lift Holmes onto a stretcher, I was close enough to help. They did not object, so long as I only assisted their efforts and did not get in their way.

Holmes seemed to be rallying, and responded to the doctors' questions in a breathless, reedy voice. The doctors discussed options, and evidently decided that he should be moved. Between us, we got him gingerly to his feet and he clung feebly to me as we walked him out.

We went slowly, fearful of jarring the patient. There were soldiers with us, and I realised we had an escort, their guns held ready in case of an attack. Other soldiers and staff watched us pass in awed silence. They all knew who Holmes was now and what he had done in exposing the conspiracy, and many doffed their caps in respect. I found that deeply unsettling, as if Holmes had already died.

Presently we came to a room that I almost recognised, since it was the equivalent of a dressing station. Curtains divided the bays, and there were wounded men in a few of the beds. The doctors conferred and thought Holmes should have the private room at the end of this little ward. I don't know if they did so out of respect for him, or because he was still considered an enemy. It was not that they conferred any luxury on him: the room was small and barely furnished, the window looking out onto the back wall of a drab little hut. Yet I was grateful for the privacy, given the wretched state of Holmes. We manhandled him into the bed.

He barely stirred as the doctors checked him over. I removed Holmes's shoes and placed them in the cabinet by his bed. His patterned Argyle socks drew some comment from the doctors, and I could see they were trying to raise the spirits of us both. It was the same technique we used on my own ward, especially when things were serious.

Then the doctors had done all they could and they retreated, leaving me alone with Holmes in the quiet room. He lay still, asleep, and I held one of his hands in mine, though there was no sign that he knew I was there.

At some point, Meyer and Weich looked in on us. "There are soldiers outside the door to protect you," Meyer told me, gravely.

"Though I do not think these people will need to try again." He did not sugar coat anything; the doctors did not expect Holmes would survive the night. Meyer scrutinised Holmes for himself, then walked smartly out.

Later, they brought me a plate of stew and dumplings. I had not realised the passage of time, but it was night when I stepped out with my empty plate. The sentries at the door turned to check there was no problem, and a nurse hurried over to take the plate from me. She spoke no English but she was very kind. I returned to Holmes, settling in the chair beside his bed, his hand once more in mine.

It had been another wearying day but I did not mean to fall asleep, and woke with a start, cursing myself. Wiping the hair from my eyes, I looked over at Holmes but could discern no change. I got up to stretch my weary limbs and went over to the door. The soldiers guarding us smiled sympathetically and the nurse looked up from the desk at the far end of the room. Yet I felt utterly alone, and trapped, and distraught. I closed the door and turned back to the bed, which was when Holmes promptly sat up.

I clamped a hand over my mouth so I didn't scream. Holmes beamed at me, beckoning me over. I wanted to throttle him, or at least give him a piece of my mind – and he clearly knew it.

"Recriminations must wait," he whispered. "We must warn our people what we have discovered here, before the Germans can gain the advantage."

I could not think how we might manage such a thing, but Holmes, of course, had a plan.

The door squeaked when I opened it. The two sentries whirled round, rifles raised, and then grinned sheepishly down at me. I pointed at myself and then up to the nurse on duty at her desk, and they nodded their consent to let me pass.

The nurse had a heart-shaped face and wide, expressive eyes. She was also younger than me and rather easy to dominate. I marched sharply up to her and held out a strand of my hair. Of course, she had no idea what I meant by this, but I impatiently gestured some more as though it were obvious. Then I pointed at the shelf to her side, stacked with linen. She still did not understand me but held out her hand, indicating that I could help myself.

I checked quickly over the supplies and selected a square of linen a little larger than a tea towel, which I then draped over my head and used to tie back my hair. That done, I rolled up the sleeves of my jumper and scrubbed my hands in the little sink to one side. Then I pulled on a new apron and grabbed a couple of bandages, but could not see the one item essential to our plan. Frustrated, I held up two fingers at the nurse and mimed "scissors". She found me a pair and ventured something in German. I think she asked if I needed any help. "*Nein danke*," I told her, and turned away.

I held up the bandage and scissors for the sentries to see as I walked back into the private room. Then I was out again, looking quickly round for the next thing I needed. The nurse was still keen to be useful and made her way over, but by then I had spied the bulging linen bag lying off to one side, the end of a grey trouser leg hanging out of it. I dragged this washrag back to the private room, but the nurse now blocked my path. She said something I didn't understand, a question, and all I could think to do was respond with a look of puzzlement. The nurse turned to the two sentries in exasperation, then held out a roll of surgical tape. She can't have thought much of my nursing skills to have forgotten it! I blushed, took the tape from her, and she stepped out of my way. Playing up my embarrassment, I thanked them, bustled into the private room, and quickly closed the door.

Holmes sprang up and we went through the washbag, holding up each item against me to approximate the fit. I tugged off my head scarf and Holmes came at me with the scissors. He put a hand around the blades to deaden the sound of each snip, but it sounded horribly loud as he deftly sliced through my hair. Tangled locks fell about my shoulders, and I gathered them up to stuff into the washbag. It did not take long to shear me but I had no sense of what I looked like. Holmes then stashed the last of the fallen hair in the washbag while I retied the linen sheet around my head. He checked I had it on right, brushed some loose clippings of hair from my forehead, and then scrambled quickly back into bed. Once again, he was the prone, sick man at death's door.

I went back out, returning the scissors to the waiting nurse. She also took the washbag from me and returned it to its spot by the wall. I felt sure that she or one of the sentries would notice it was now lighter, or that my head looked different. They only smiled, awkwardly, wanting to aid me but not wishing to intrude. No one wants to help change dressings or soiled clothes if they can avoid it.

"Good night," I told them as I closed the door one last time.

I turned off the light, then stripped off my head scarf, shoes and the ragged, old jumper. My head felt almost weightless, and it was oddly intimate to stand there in my underwear while Holmes watched from his hospital bed. With any other man I might at least have had second thoughts. Yet Holmes watched indifferently, his focus on our plan. His disdain for women had its occasional plus side.

I pulled on the uniform we had taken from the washbag. I had to dispense with my petticoat but otherwise it fitted easily enough over my underclothes. The tunic had a disgusting, stale whiff to it and itched against my bare arms. It was not nearly as warm as the jumper.

Holmes appraised me in my new outfit and was not wholly satisfied. He looked about the room, and nosed through a tray of salves and ointments, but nothing quite suited his purpose. Then inspiration struck and he wiped his hands down my sleeves, holding up his fingers to show that they'd picked up some mud. This he now applied to my chin, under my nose and along my jawline. That close to his face, I could see he had not entirely faked his illness: he was drawn and pale, his eyes hooded with exhaustion. Yet he worked on my make-up with delicate care until, still not happy, there was nothing more he could do.

Given that he was meant to be on his deathbed, Holmes could not allow himself to be seen at the window. He lay back in the bed while I ducked between the curtain and the glass. We were on the ground floor of the building, and yet raised up some way above the lane outside. It was a narrow passageway, running between us and the wooden hut opposite, but given it was the dead of night I could see little else. I battled with the latch of the window and it squealed softly open. Then the breeze caught the glass and it almost escaped me, but I held on for dear life and managed to secure the clasp.

The night was very cold, and I had the extraordinary sensation of the breeze on my ears – something I cannot have felt since early childhood. It made me feel almost naked, and I felt a sudden trepidation about the next stage of the plan. Yet Holmes was watching and pride soon overcame fear. I took hold of the window frame and hauled myself up and out.

It was a longer drop than I'd anticipated, onto hard concrete. I landed with quite a bang, and froze, hunched, listening for running footsteps. No one appeared – though I could see little enough in that all-pervading dark. There was no use in hanging about so I hurried on, following the perimeter of the building. I turned a corner and almost ran straight into a whole throng of soldiers.

They should not have been there either; five of them had found this quiet, dark spot for a clandestine smoke and drink. I kept my head down and wove through and round them, and though one of them muttered at me crossly, they did not try to stop me.

A little further and I found a door into the building, and was blinded by the light. I shielded my face with a hand and hurried down the corridor. Holmes had said that I should hurry but not quite run, in the manner of errand boys he had observed. Apart from Dieter, I had barely noticed these youngsters, which Holmes hoped would be to our advantage: they were always overlooked. I passed various soldiers, members of staff and then Captain Weich. He did not even spare me a glance.

Then there were double doors, each one with a square window. The corridor beyond was empty except for the most extraordinary ghost. As I approached, the ghost got closer, but no more distinct. I had to stop in astonishment at the pale, scrawny boy staring back at me. No wonder I'd not been recognised.

I followed the route to the major general's office and skidded to a stop. The door was closed and I had no way of telling if Meyer was inside. I glanced around but there was no one about, so I dared to listen at the door. My ear pressed against the paintwork, but I could make nothing out – and I dared not linger. Head bowed so Meyer would not see my face, I slowly opened the door.

The room was dark and seemed empty. I crept forward and reached for the light switch – but before I got there something *moved.*

I kept perfectly still, not even breathing. There was something in the dark, a long shape against the wall. As my eyes adjusted, I realised it was Meyer, strewn upon a camp bed. I stared at him in horror, paralysed with fear. He responded with a snore.

The coat stand was a few steps inside the door, tantalisingly just out of my reach. Very carefully, I took a single step forward. Meyer continued to wheeze in his sleep. I took another step and then, slowly, slowly, prised the long, leather coat from its hook. The leather creaked as I eased it upwards and it was a lot more cumbersome than I had expected. I had to lean round to free it from the curl of the hook, but as I drew it towards me, one of its brass buttons struck against the coat stand.

Again, I froze, the sound echoing through me. Across the room, the camp bed creaked and I saw the great silhouette of the major general moving, turning towards me. I braced, ready to run the very moment that he shouted.

But instead, he plumped forward and resumed his snoring.

I succeeded in freeing the coat and then took his hat for good measure. Hefting these out of his office, I quietly closed the door, then folded up the hat and leather coats into a more manageable parcel. Cradling this tight against my chest, I hurried back the way I had come. There were more soldiers to weave through, but they paid me not the least regard. Then I was back out into the freezing night and haring round the side of the building. The gang of soldiers smoking in the dark glowered at me as I passed and one man stepped into my path. I skidded to a halt, looking up at him fearfully. He took a sip from his bottle, belched, and then stepped out of my way. I ran on, fleeing their laughter.

I reached the open window and then didn't know what to do – not wanting to call up to Holmes or make any other sound that might draw the attention of the smoking men. As I dithered about my next move, Holmes appeared above me, scrambling nimbly through the window and dropping silently at my side. To my amazement, he looked very different, not least because of a long, thin moustache, its ends curling upwards in the German style. I marvelled at it, leaning in close for a better look. It was very well done, fashioned from hair he had cut from my head and a sliver of surgical tape. He had also used salve on his cheekbones and temples, making his bone structure less prominent and his features more fleshy. Now Holmes pulled on the leather coat I had brought him, which was large on him and so made him seem rather stocky. The hat and the major general's riding crop – still bearing Holmes's teeth marks – completed the transformation.

Disguises in place, we marched away down the lane, in the opposite direction from the smoking men. We emerged onto a yard, a line of vehicles parked up ahead. Lights strung up on posts meant we were now clearly visible to anyone around. There was no way to conceal ourselves, so Holmes boldly set out straight across the yard. Even his walk was different, hunching forward and slightly bowing his legs.

We had not quite reached the parked cars and trucks when soldiers emerged from the darkness, a group of them hurrying towards the building we'd just left. They caught sight of Holmes, staggered to a halt and saluted. Holmes saluted back and said a few cordial words, even sharing some terrible joke at which they politely laughed. I caught the glance of one of the men and rolled my eyes. Holmes carried on talking and I saw the smiles fade, the men restless to get on. Finally, Holmes let them go and they hurried off, grateful. Not one of them looked back.

We sauntered down the line of cars until Holmes made his selection – an elegant open-topped model right at the end, parked under a canopy. It was the car Dieter had driven when Holmes had given me up. Now, Holmes opened the door to the driving seat – but held it open for me to get in. Of course, it would not do for a general to drive his own car!

While I settled in behind the steering wheel, Holmes cranked the starting handle and with a roar she came to life. I didn't dare look round to see who might have noticed: we had to convey that we had permission to do this. Holmes took his time, standing back to admire the purr of the well-tended engine. Then he nonchalantly took the seat behind me and gestured for me to set off.

I can't tell you what a joy it was to drive that beautiful car. She handled sublimely, responding to my slightest touch. The headlamps were bright and powerful, so I had a good view of the road ahead. In command of that vehicle, I felt powerful and free.

"Where to?" I asked Holmes.

"I'll direct you. Left at this junction."

"But where are we going?"

He didn't answer at once, so I knew it would be bad. "We've exposed the conspiracy here," he said. "The Germans are tracking down those involved. But that means they have the military advantage."

"Yes, sir. So we need to inform our own side what's been happening. But how?" Again, Holmes didn't answer at once.

"We need to get back to General Fitzgerald – and quickly, before the Germans launch their next offensive."

"You mean go back across No Man's Land?" I said, a knot forming deep in my stomach at the very thought. "So we head for the road we came in by, when I was driving the ambulance."

"It's too out of the way, and too easy for them to stop us," said Holmes. "No, we're heading for the trenches and the front line. We're going to go over the top."

Chapter Twenty-one

❧

I almost ran the car off the road. It had been harrowing enough to cross the lines the first time, when I had done so without realising. Now, knowing full well what we faced in No Man's Land and the odds stacked against us, it seemed completely insane. Indeed, the knowledge of what awaited us was almost crippling. My whole body recoiled.

Yet I could hardly stop the car. Our disguises worked only so long as we went on in confidence. German soldiers saluted as we passed them on the road. The moment I conveyed uncertainty, they would notice.

"You can't mean it," I said, hoarsely, when there were no soldiers about.

"I can think of no other option," said Holmes. "We must get word to our people – and see that they understand. A great many lives depend on it, perhaps the whole course of the war."

"And if we're killed, what then? Are you saying the Germans will win?"

"They have the advantage unless we can be sure to even things up. Miss Watson, I share your misgivings about this."

"Misgivings! Holmes, it is suicide."

"I do not think so, but I acknowledge your concerns. You can drop me at the front then return the major general's car, and surrender yourself to his mercy."

I cursed him, calling him every name I could think of – and I had spent years among soldiers. Holmes did not defend himself, sitting there in smug silence as I went on, apart from the occasional direction to turn left or right. I hated him utterly, for making a joke of it and for the very suggestion that I might not do my duty. Of course, now I can see that he played me to perfection: by suggesting that I might excuse myself, he ensured I never would.

"How can we cross the lines safely?" I asked him, with a weary heart.

He smiled. "I have the beginnings of a plan."

This did not inspire confidence and yet, without quite saying so, I had acquiesced and would now apparently follow Holmes into whatever hail of gunfire he dictated. The odd thing was that I was no longer shaking. In fact, I felt almost elated. For such a long time I had lived under the shadow of potential calamity. To have it definitely happening was a kind of liberation.

At a command from Holmes, we turned off the main supply road and buffeted along a lane of pockmarked and worn tarmac. It took us through a network of wooden huts. The bright headlights picked out obstacles ahead – a few soldiers about in the dead of night, their campfires, washing lines and what have you. Most saluted us and Holmes nodded back, every inch the important dignitary.

Then he wanted to stop. As directed, I pulled up outside a larger hut with heavy shutters over the doors. Holmes clambered out of the car and, in his bow-legged way, tottered up the steps, battering on the shutters with his riding crop. He had to batter a second time before he got a response. A cross, red-faced man appeared at the door and swore at Holmes in German. Then he saw the coat and hat, and Holmes's twirled moustache, and immediately altered course. The man hurried out in his nightshirt and bare feet, apologising profusely.

Holmes said nothing, which only made him more terrifying. He was led inside by the little red-faced man and a light went on. From my position in the car, I glimpsed shelves stacked with supplies. There were rolled blankets, tarpaulins, gas lamps...

With the engine off and nothing to do but wait, the cold quickly set in. I huddled behind the steering wheel, watching the red-faced man pass back and forth in front of the open door, as he fetched whatever Holmes asked for. I couldn't imagine what the store might provide that would help us cross No Man's Land, but it made me feel better that Holmes had some scheme in mind.

Then there were voices ahead. Two soldiers ambled out of the darkness, leaning against one another, holding forth on some urgent topic. One held a wooden crate in which rattled a number of bottles, as if on their way to a party.

The two men now saw the car and hobbled over for a closer look. One inspected the bonnet with a wistful air, the other – the one with the crate – loafed round to stand beside me at the wheel, expounding something in German. He positively reeked of drink and continued to talk at me, though I had no idea how to respond. Ironically, if we had been speaking English I could have held my own on the relative merits of the Daimler, its transmission, torque and handling. It would have been a genuine pleasure to discuss mechanics as an equal, and not be dismissed or ignored.

But these two soldiers weren't interested in the car so much as what it represented: the gulf between the brass who enjoyed such extravagance and the ordinary soldiers like them, stuck in the dark and cold. Emboldened by alcohol and the surprise of finding me out on their patch, they did not hide their resentment.

I pointed over to the open door of the hut. "*Herr Generalmajor,*" I said, trying to sound gruff and male. This failed to scare off the men and only increased their disdain. The man at my side leant forward, over the door, to inspect the dashboard controls. That meant leaning right over me, too. I pressed myself flat against the seat behind me, but could not quite get out of his way. The clumsy great brute grabbed my shoulder to stop himself falling into my lap. Almost nose to nose, his was breath quite disgusting.

"*Herr Generalmajor,*" I said again.

"*Herr Generalmajor,*" he said, imitating my girlish voice. Across the bonnet, his friend laughed.

"*Ja,*" said a voice behind them, cutting through the night.

Holmes stood framed in the doorway. The two soldiers jolted up straight but, notably, they did not salute him. The man next to me pushed the crate of bottles into my arms, but I don't think he meant to conceal it – he just wanted his hands free, already spoiling for a fight.

Holmes spoke with menacing authority, his words carrying clearly in the still night air. He was every inch the stern imperial officer, a terrifying presence. Yet the men smirked at him, their expressions dark and threatening.

But Holmes's words weren't only meant for them. Up the road, faces poked from other huts, annoyed to have been woken. Someone called out something harsh and Holmes nodded sternly. Undaunted, he approached the man next to me, who towered over Holmes. In a low growl, Holmes asked him a question, loud enough for everyone to hear. I saw the man flinch.

Soldiers emerged from their huts. Some had guns. There was a mean feeling in the air – there had been ever since I first clapped eyes on these two men. But Holmes now had the authority, and the support of those watching. The two men faltered.

Then, with horror, I saw that Holmes's moustache was a little skew whiff. I put my finger to my own upper lip and tried to catch his eye, but Holmes did not notice.

One side of the moustache now gently peeled away from his lip. It looked ridiculous, evidently fake. The man beside me surely must have noticed – had he not been so drunk.

I tapped my lip again and this time Holmes saw me. He turned from the soldier to address the man by the bonnet, and as he did so he stroked his moustache with thumb and forefinger to set it back in place. Yet, because he'd turned away, I couldn't tell if it had adhered correctly. All I could see was the man at the bonnet staring back in awe.

And then he simply turned and fled. The man beside watched, dumbfounded, but did not want to face Holmes alone, and likewise scurried off into the darkness – leaving me with the crate of bottles.

Holmes seemed pleased. "*Gute Nacht*," he told the fleeing men. "*Gute Nacht*," he repeated, firmly, for the benefit of those watching. The show over, the crowd returned to their beds. Holmes turned to me, insufferably pleased with himself – and I almost shouted in alarm.

"Your moustache," I managed to whisper. It had come off entirely, and he quickly retrieved it from where it lay on the ground. But before he could say anything, there was a shout from the store.

The man in the nightshirt stood there, brandishing a bulging paper bag. Holmes sidled over to me, keeping his back to the man in the store as he tried – and failed – to reattach the moustache. It would do no good, so Holmes called something up to the man in the nightshirt then nodded down at me, meaning for me to move.

I hefted the crate of bottles onto the passenger seat and scrambled out of the car. The man in the nightshirt said something to me as I approached him, but I smiled and nodded and that seemed to suffice. He passed me the heavily laden bag. Through the open door behind him, I could see that this storeroom contained a whole cornucopia, with weapons, flasks and camping supplies of one sort and another. The man said something else to me, a question I think, and I had no idea how to reply. Holmes called something from the car and the man seemed satisfied. I hurried away with the paper bag.

Holmes was now in the back seat of the car, thumb and forefinger to his lip, holding the moustache in place in a way that suggested he was lost in thought. I wedged the paper bag in beside the crate of bottles on the front passenger seat, hoping they wouldn't knock about too much on the uneven roads. I then had to start the car myself – for it wouldn't have done for Holmes-the-general to have been seen to help me. Finally, with a cheerful wave to the man in the nightshirt, we headed off once more.

As soon as we had turned a corner and were out of sight of the store, Holmes laughed delightedly, and rid himself of the moustache, shaking it off over the side of the car. He reached forward for the paper bag, from which he collected a few items. I could not turn to see because I was driving, but there were various small bottles and containers.

"I thought we were in for some trouble," I said. "Whatever did you say to those two men?"

In the rear-view mirror, I saw Holmes open a jar, which let loose a pungent, eggy stink. He began to tap powder from it, into a tin. "I reframed the nature of the confrontation," he told me, "so that it was not about them against me, the officer, but about them against the other men. First, I said it wasn't fair for them to break rules everyone else had to follow. Then I asked where this box of drink had come from. When they didn't want to answer, I suggested it came from the mess tent."

He continued to work as he told me this, closing the jar and opening another, which had that itchy tang of gunpowder.

"I see," I told him. "You accused them of stealing something that should have been shared out."

"I didn't accuse them but that was the implication. Instead, I said – very generously, of course – that I would overlook the incident and return the box to the mess tent. How could they decline without those other men coming to believe they had just been robbed? Wisely, the two men decided not to argue, for they could see they were outnumbered. But you see how things are on a knife-edge between officers and men."

"Then they have not stopped the conspiracy," I said.

"It seems not," agreed Holmes. "The major general has begun rounding up the conspirators, and word will soon spread among the troops about what has been going on. However, much damage has already been done, and I fear the major general will conclude that he must do something to unite his army in common purpose."

I realised with dread what that meant. "By attacking our side," I said.

"They tend to launch assaults at dawn," said Holmes. "Which is now just a few hours hence."

"We have to warn our people," I said, with icy clarity now.

"We must ensure they are every bit as united. That is they only way they will withstand an attack. Oh, Mycroft was right all along! I must say, that is infuriating."

"I don't understand."

"You said it yourself," said Holmes. "A feeling in the air in the hospital, a new sense of disparity between the men and their officers. My brother had some sense of it, too, and as he said to me, we have seen the effect of such feelings in the French army. There were the corporals shot because they would not carry out their orders, and then the suggestion that it was their officers who were really at fault. My brother was concerned that, left unchecked, such sentiments might even turn the tide of the war."

"Then," I said amazed, "he asked you to look into this business."

Holmes laughed. "You sound surprised. No doubt you have heard what my brother said about me, for General Fitzgerald to hear."

I gasped at the audacity. "He didn't mean it?"

"He meant the general to have no idea that I was investigating *him*. The question remains, I think: is Fitzgerald culprit or victim? Take a left at the crossing coming up."

Dumbstruck by this latest revelation, I followed his instructions, and we zigzagged our way through the German camp. With my eyes on the road in front of me, I couldn't make sense of the route he took – except that we did not make directly for the front lines, and headed ever westward. The roads got worse and I had go down to second gear for the last stretch. I hate to think what damage we did to that beautiful car.

Finally, we ran out of road. There was no warning: the mud track simply came to an end in front of a wall of sandbags. A soldier on duty snapped to attention at the sight of Holmes, who saluted smartly back and then collected the paper bag from the front seat. I was left to lug the heavy crate of bottles.

On foot, we followed the narrow lane of the trenches. My feet slid on wet duckboards and I could barely see a thing ahead, but Holmes seemed sure-footed and we pressed on in some haste. He exchanged a few, encouraging words with the men we passed, without pausing. They were surprised to see such a high-ranking officer at such an early hour, but assumed it involved something important and kept out of his way.

Sturdy wooden walls gave way to trenches of earth supported by skeletal structures, and then more crudely dug passages. The duckboards ended and we trudged through cloying mud. I did not have a coat, only my grey woollen uniform, and was bitterly cold. My naked ears felt bruised from exposure. The bottles clinked and rattled in the crate, the edges of the box cutting against my hands and chest.

A soldier called out to us in a whisper, and Holmes stooped but carried on. I followed his lead, keeping low, though no shots were heard. Bent like that, still clutching the crate, I thought my burning limbs could take no further punishment, but somehow we kept going.

Then we turned a corner and were in a wider section, a brazier at each end, around which soldiers huddled for warmth. Holmes beamed at these muddy, unhappy men, and then ushered me forward. I thought he meant that I should get warm at the fire, but he spoke a few words and the grim, dirty faces turned to me as one. They groaned and pawed at me – and helped themselves to the bottles in the crate. Holmes had just made us extremely welcome.

He spoke to them, and though I could not understand his words, the tone was encouraging. I had seen this several times now: his ease with all classes of men, the way he lifted their spirits just by showing interest. He unpacked his paper bag, producing tins of food and a length of German sausage. They were astonished but grateful, and led Holmes up to the nearest brazier, offering him prime position in front of the fire.

After more pleasantries, Holmes said something that made them laugh. One big man turned away, put his hand up to his mouth and shouted, in a voice I had heard before.

"Halloa Tommy! Good morning! Wakey wakey!"

Holmes laughed, and as he made some comment to the Germans he handed me a tin. It was the sort of thing that might ordinarily contain beans, but it bore no label and had no lid, and about two-thirds of it was taken up by a mix of black and red powders. Holmes had another, identical tin in his hands, which he handled casually as if it were of not the least importance. At his encouragement, the big man called out again to the British lines, this time with a rude joke about struggling to rise in the morning. As the Germans laughed, Holmes caught my eye, gestured with his tin towards the flames of the brazier in front of him, then nodded at the brazier at the far end of the section.

There were more shouts to the British, and I laughed along as I sidestepped the soldiers and made my way, ever so casually, to the other brazier. Most of the soldiers had joined Holmes by now, but two men remained, curious as I approached. One said something and I nodded along as if I understood. They let me take a place in front of the fire. I readied the tin and looked over at Holmes, whose eyes were on me as he said something to the men.

The big man didn't understand what he'd been asked to do. "Halloa Tommy!" he called, a little uncertainly. "We have captured friends of yours today. Our guests are Sherlock Holmes and Dr Watson!"

Then Holmes nodded, and I saw him thrust his tin into the fire in front of him. I did the same, chucking it hard into the back of the brazier. Nothing happened. I looked up at Holmes, who was on his feet, still laughing with the men as he plucked a bottle from one soldier's hand and indicated me and the two men beside me – who did not yet have anything to drink. Holmes began to saunter over, brandishing the bottle.

There was suddenly a cry of alarm. Behind Holmes, the men were enveloped in thick scarlet smoke. The cloud ballooned horribly quickly, the men entirely lost from sight. Holmes started running, discarding his hat and coat as he ran towards me. Then there was smoke all around – from the brazier to my right. It stank of eggs and cordite and my eyes were streaming. There were cries of alarm, deadened by the smoke and somehow distant. I really couldn't see anything but red. Then something grabbed my hand.

Holmes dragged me after him and we ran a few steps until we hit the wall of earth. We didn't stop, we were climbing, the mud giving way as we scrambled up and over the side of the trench. The red smoke billowed round and over us, but Holmes took hold of my shoulder, ensuring I kept low. Half crawling, half running, we hared out into No Man's Land, utterly blind in the scarlet fog.

Something fluttered ahead and I realised Holmes had his handkerchief in his other hand, flapping it in front of us as a white flag. I did not believe that the muddy rag would do any good – I could barely see it, and I was right next to him. There was, I knew, no possible way we were going to make it through.

Even so, we had made good distance before the shooting started. Holmes didn't stop running, his hand tight in mine. The shots snapped and whispered, but I had no sense of how close they were, or whether we'd even been seen. There was only fog.

As a result, we ran headlong into the barbed wire. Holmes was ensnared, and my sleeve and side were caught. When I tried to pull free, I only succeeded in hauling more wire towards us. Holmes carefully reached his free hand round the wire and unpicked it from my uniform. Once I was released, he held up the wire so that I could step through – though he was still entangled. There was no time to argue, so I dodged underneath and then turned back to help him. My frozen hands struggled for any purchase, and the barbs cut into my palms.

There were more shots, and something hit the barbed wire so it rattled loudly. That dislodged a length of it from Holmes, but he was still caught up.

"Go," he said. "Don't look back."

"I'm not leaving you," I told him, and unpicked another barb.

When another shot sounded very close, I looked round instinctively – and realised I could now see more than scarlet smoke. Dark shapes lurked in it, the churned-up ground beginning to peek through. The smoke was slowly clearing, and with it our one protection.

I worked faster. Holmes again told me to leave him, but I persisted and the wire gradually came away. There was another volley of shots, and I am sure I heard bullets hit the ground beside us. I battled on but it would never be enough. And then there was another sound – footsteps in the mud.

Holmes now pushed me away, using both hands to propel me backwards, away from him and from the German trenches. He used his body to shield mine from whatever was coming.

But the sound came from behind me – from the British side. I struggled to see in the loosening fog. Then there was a shape, a silhouette, a man, haring towards us out of the gloom.

He was on us, he was grinning – it was Captain Boyce.

"Whose bright idea was this?" he tutted, and set to the wire with a pair of bolt cutters. It took both hands to clip through the wire, which suddenly snapped and whipped back in a lethal coil, almost catching me. We drew Holmes out of it and staggered on, as the last fog melted away.

Bullets at our back, we tore across uneven, ravaged ground. There was something up ahead – faces emerging from the ground, as soldiers looked out over the lip of the trench. We were still a perilous distance away, and the shots behind us were increasing now the Germans could see us more clearly. British soldiers shot back, giving us covering fire as we pelted for our lives.

Then Holmes fell. I hurried over, grabbed his hand to help him to his feet – and he shoved me over, so that I tumbled backwards. By the time I'd scrambled up, Boyce was with Holmes, who was lying flat, jabbing a finger towards the British line. I couldn't understand – but there, poking from our own trenches, was a rifle aimed directly at Holmes. In awful slow-motion, I saw it lifting to fire, and in its path Holmes prone and defenceless. He stared back defiantly at the British soldier who was about to shoot him.

Then Boyce threw himself forward, into the ground directly ahead of Holmes, shielding him. The gunman hesitated – and there came a shout. The rifle vanished from view.

That was all the chance we needed. I scrambled to my feet, grabbed Holmes by the arm, and hauled him forward. With Boyce, we tumbled face first over the side of the trench and into the soft, yielding mud.

Boyce scrambled apart from us and was shouting orders. Jack Walker – the new father we had met before – had a gun pressed to the head of another, kneeling soldier. With a start I recognised the man who had tried to kill us, a conspirator exposed. It was another of the men we had met before: George Ludders, who had proposed to his fiancée in Brighton, and had seemed so nice.

"Good man, Walker," said Boyce.

"Thank you, sir," said Walker. "Thought something was up when George said not to go. We should never had doubted you. It really is Holmes and Watson!"

"Apparently so," said Boyce, marvelling at how different – and peculiar – I looked.

I couldn't answer him back: my focus was on Holmes's leg, a neat hole in the thigh of his trouser leg showing where he'd been wounded. His face was deathly white, his features contorted in pain. I shouted for a medic and the boy, Joe, was on us with a tin box of meagre first aid.

Working quickly, I cut through the fabric of the trousers to get a better look. The bullet had struck the fleshy part of the leg, and luckily gone right through. The wound bled profusely, which I hoped would at least have kept it clean. I bound it tight with bandage, making Holmes seethe in agony. Blood seeped into the bandage and in the poor light of dawn I could not tell how well I had stemmed the flow.

"We need to get him to a doctor," I told Boyce, who called for a stretcher.

"Tell them," winced Holmes. "Tell them... the conspiracy."

So I related everything: the planting of the "betting slips" and all we had discovered. "They've tried to divide you," I said to Boyce and Walker. "And there's going to be an attack. You have to be united."

"We will be," Boyce told me. "Isn't that right, Walker?"

Walker glanced around the men staring in astonishment. "Yes, sir," he said.

They took Ludders away under guard. Soon, there was a buzz of activity around us, everyone keen to see the famous Sherlock Holmes and learn the truth he had uncovered. They were thrilled to see him, and thrilled to learn that he had been fighting on their behalf, the strange red mist hanging over the trenches all part of some brilliant ploy against the Germans. Boyce warned them that the Germans were likely to retaliate, but it did not dampen their resolve, not with Holmes on their side. Even I felt buoyed up by it, bonded to these men, all of us brothers in arms.

Yes, I was one of the men now. As we waited for the stretcher, Walker teased me about my strange, cropped hair and the German uniform. They found a coat for me, a British army jacket, and cheered when I pulled it on. For a moment, I felt I really was one of them.

At last the stretcher bearers arrived and, with skill and delicacy, took Holmes from me. Boyce couldn't leave the trench or his unit, but offered us Walker as escort. I realised they expected further attempts on our lives.

Wan and weak, Holmes beckoned Boyce – but not to thank him for saving us. "Telephone the general," Holmes said, weakly. "Tell him… to join us at the hospital, so we can finish this business."

Then the effort was finally too much, and he passed out.

Chapter Twenty-two

W alker went first, gruffly telling soldiers to get out of our bally way. Behind him, Holmes was borne by the two stretcher bearers, almost at a run. I trailed in their wake, struggling to keep up – but then I'd not had months to practise racing through the trenches. All I could do was keep moving.

The soldiers knew the drill as we charged through, pressing themselves into the walls of the trench or ducking into alcoves so as not to impede us. Of course, it was in their interests to keep back, as sooner or later it might be them on a stretcher. But I realised, with some relief, that this familiar drill made a further attack on Holmes less likely – anyone *not* scrambling out of our way would be all too obvious to Walker, ready with pistol in hand. Besides, any conspirator would surely conclude that there was no need for further attack. Holmes really was at death's door, lolling unconscious on the stretcher, oblivious to the commotion all around.

We hurried on as the cold grey dawned. Daylight seemed to be the cue for the German assault, and behind us came a deafening roar of artillery. Impacts shook the ground underfoot and the very walls of the trenches, and one particularly powerful blast knocked me from my feet. Yet there was nothing to be done but to gather myself up and keep running after the stretcher. I could hardly complain – not with the awful thought of Boyce and his unit, who we'd left bogged down in the thick of it. Other soldiers passed us, all set to join the fray. Their courage, their resolve, was extraordinary to see, as they charged in the direction of the gunfire.

At last, we were out of the mud and running across duckboards. It didn't seem so far as when Holmes and I had last trekked this way, I think because I now recognised bits of it – and because we were running. We dodged round some scaffolding and down Watling Street, and then there was the main dressing station, and some familiar faces.

"Whatever do you look like?" chuckled Gwen Moss, Patch at her side as always. They led us to their ambulance and I climbed into the back with Holmes and Walker. He still had his pistol in his hand and Gwen seemed ready to object, but deferred to me. Between us, we got the stretcher secured in its harness. "Patch, get going!" Gwen hollered, and the ambulance lurched away. It was all so quick, I didn't have a chance to thank the two stretcher bearers and never learned their names. My last sight of them, through the back of the ambulance, was of the two men charging away, back into the trenches to find someone else to help.

Walker looked shaken. "You all right?" I asked him.

"Just a lot to take in," he said. "George Ludders was my mate. One of the lads, you know. Would have trusted him with my life." Then he shivered. "Now I think of it, he was the one most against our captain. And he had us fired up about poor Ogle-Thompson an' all, how he was a coward and a traitor, how that was just like the brass. Thing is, if I'd not seen with my own eyes when he pointed that gun…"

He trailed off, horrified at the betrayal. "But you did see it," I said. "And you stopped him. I'm sure Captain Boyce won't forget that."

Holmes murmured in his sleep, and I settled him as best I could as the ambulance bumped and bucked. Patch was one of the best drivers we had in the VAD but there was only so much she could do on that tattered road. I clung to Holmes's hand and tried to soothe him. Deathly pale, I don't think he even knew I was there.

"Is that really Sherlock Holmes?" said Gwen at one point.

"You'd better believe it," enthused Walker. "Seen his magic straight up. And now here he is, fighting right beside us!"

Gwen and I tended Holmes, sponging the mud from his face and mopping up some of the blood around the bandage on his thigh. I'd known Gwen for more than a year but had never seen her at work like this, doting and tender.

At last we pulled up at the hospital. Gwen and Patch lugged the stretcher out of the ambulance, Walker still keeping close guard. I ran ahead to brief the doctors.

It felt utterly surreal to cross the threshold and be back in the grand entrance hall that I knew so well. Nothing had changed – it all looked exactly as I'd left it, as if caught in aspic. What was different was me. Jill Sullivan, on duty inside the door, stared open-mouthed, and I thought she was going to scream. Then there were other people running. I tried to tell them about Holmes, but Dulcie O'Brien had my hand and was leading me to a chair.

Quite honestly, Dulcie was the last person in the world I wanted to see in that instant. But I was bone tired and in a bit of a daze, and by then Gwen and Patch had brought in Holmes, and doctors swarmed around him. I tried to hand over, explaining to Dulcie how Holmes had been wounded and some of what we'd been through. It was so urgent that I made her understand.

"Gwen has it all in hand," she told me. "We have to see about you."

"We have to speak to General Fitzgerald," I persisted.

"And he wants to see you! Darling, we had word from the Chateau, who had it direct from the front line. That's how we knew to expect you. Honestly, darling, the general will be with us as soon as he can. But you've rather put the cat among the pigeons, haven't you? There's this whole blessed plot going on."

"A conspiracy," I said, amazed and relieved that word had got round so quickly.

"They've pulled out all the stops," said Dulcie. "They've already made some arrests. We even had soldiers here."

"Some rather dishy ones," added one of the nurses as she hurried past. It hurt to laugh, and Dulcie saw me wince. Then her eyes were wet with tears.

"You're lucky to be alive," she told me. "We very nearly lost you."

I could not understand this reaction, from her of all people, who had tormented me for so long. My head was reeling and I felt rather out of it as she dabbed at my face with soft cotton buds that came away sticky with blood. Dulcie apologised but carried on, tears falling down her face the more she tended mine. Slowly it dawned on me why. When people had looked at me strangely before, I thought it was because of the cropped, boyish hair. The longer Dulcie swabbed and tended, the more I realised how much I had been through and what it might have cost. I had to ask for a mirror three times before she would relent.

I knew I would hardly recognise myself with the hair and my naked, batwing ears. The real shock was my sorry face. One whole side glistened pink and wet, a graze that had taken the skin off.

My nose and chin were cross-hatched with scratches, and a livid bruise had begun to form under one eye. That was just my face. Dulcie gently teased off my German army tunic, exposing the sorry ruin of my corset and the worse state of my body, all one enormous bruise. She swore under her breath but did not pause in her ministrations.

Dazed, I let her tend to me. After a while I realised she was speaking, sharing more gossip as a way to cheer me along. Lobelia Darlington had been *shameless*, apparently, volunteering to help the soldiers move the filing cabinets from the ward. The nurses had laughed at this, at first, until they'd seen the soldiers smitten with her. Lobelia had been asked out to dinner every night for the next year, or that's what they all said. This had made her *persona non grata* among the nurses, of course, who wished they'd thought to volunteer first.

I wanted to hear Lobelia's version of this, and to appraise these soldiers. But something else intruded on my foggy senses, a detail that didn't sit right in all that Dulcie had told me.

"What filing cabinets?" I asked her.

Dulcie pointed and, despite the pain, I twisted round in my seat to look. The corner of the ward looked oddly, wrongly bare. The line of cabinets where we kept our records and the register – all of it had gone.

"The soldiers cleared them out yesterday," said Dulcie. "No, before that. It was pretty soon after you left us."

"But why?" I said.

"To give us more space, they said. They're hoping to squeeze in another couple of beds."

I stared at the space where the cabinets had been. "But you couldn't fit a single bed there."

"Well I know that, don't I? And anyway, we could have made room by squeezing up the beds we've already got. But that's not the issue, is it? If we're to take on more patients, what we need is more staff. I say, after all this is over they could do worse than promote you to nurse!"

I waved the compliment away, my mind reeling, and in no state to puzzle out exactly what made it feel so wrong. Instead, I got unsteadily to my feet.

"Hello," said Dulcie in surprise. "Where do you think you're off to?"

"I need to see Holmes," I told her, pushing her away. "It's important."

Dulcie could probably have knocked me back into the chair with a single finger. Bless her, she took my arm and guided me further on to the ward. "All right, darling," she told me. "We'll see how he's doing and then find you your own bed."

Together we tottered down the ward, under the gaze of patients and staff, who fell silent as we passed. Of course, I looked a state, but they also had some inkling of what I'd been through over the past few days.

Doctors buzzed round the bed next to Sergeant Oberman. Walker stood back, still on guard duty – though he had holstered his gun. There were other soldiers, too, keeping out of the way but watching everything carefully. It all seemed very serious, except for Laurence Oberman, propped up in bed and waving the stump of his arm at me in greeting.

"En't you pretty now," he grinned. "Jus' be glad you're both in one piece. S'what I been tellin' yer man."

It seemed he had taken Holmes under his wing. I didn't feel I should remind Oberman that the last time we'd spoken he had threatened to punch Holmes – all that had been forgotten now Holmes was a hero. In the next bed, fussed over by the doctors, Holmes was at least sitting up. They'd got him into some striped pyjamas and had cleaned up his leg.

"Bullet went clean through," he told me, as if I didn't already know. "They tell me it could have been a lot worse, but the first aid on the scene was top class. Thank you, Augusta. I have spent the last few days putting your life in danger, and you respond by saving mine."

The doctors also wanted to tell me how well I'd done – as much, I think, to concur with the famous Holmes as because they thought I deserved it. I shook their good wishes aside. Holmes saw my concern and shooed some of the doctors away so I could come close.

"The soldiers took the filing cabinets," I told him. He didn't understand. "The register I showed you. The files on everyone here. They took them just after I left."

"And?"

"They say it was to make room for more beds, but there isn't enough room there. And also… well, I don't know. It feels wrong but I'm not sure why."

It sounded hopeless, even to my own ears, and I thought he would dismiss my concerns as foolish. How mortifying to be brushed off in front of all those people! Yet Holmes smiled up at me proudly.

"That's often the thing with observation," he said. "The telling, incongruous detail that begins the train of thought. Let us see where it might take us." He turned to the soldiers stood with Walker. "You took the files?" he asked them.

The soldiers glanced at one another uncertainly. "Yes, sir," said one. "Orders from the general."

Holmes's nostrils flared in disdain. "Directly from the general himself? He spoke to you in person?"

The soldier again glanced at his fellows. "Yes, sir," he said. A chill ran through me at the thought the general had been part of the conspiracy, too. And yet he had been the one to send Holmes and I into No Man's Land... Holmes, of course, was not so ready to leap to conclusions when there were further clues to be gleaned.

"Did he say why?" he asked.

"No, sir." Then the soldier shrugged. "We never get told why."

"Where did you take the cabinets?"

"Where he told us, sir. Round the back of the building."

"Can you show me?"

"Certainly not," said one of the doctors. The others agreed that there was no possible way Holmes might leave his bed, whatever the urgency might be.

"Miss Watson says it's important," Holmes told them. "I hardly need remind you of what she has already done in the service of His Majesty. Or would one of you care to dispute that?"

This had quite the effect. After some muttered deliberation, the doctors consented to allow us to lift Holmes down into a wheelchair, so long as we didn't go far, weren't outside for too long, and came straight back to the ward. Holmes rolled his eyes but agreed to these conditions. Dulcie helped me wrap him up in a blanket, and we put his shoes – without socks – onto his bare, bony feet. I wanted to push the wheelchair myself but Dulcie said, kindly, that we could get one of the pretty soldiers to do it. She took my arm and guided me after them. No one dared suggest that I stay behind.

So, our small party headed off the ward. Walker and the soldiers led, then the wheelchair, then Dulcie and me. As we passed, Holmes looked over at the space in the corner where the files had been – the spot where I had shown him the ward register on that first night we met. I could see his quick, eager faculties pick over the empty space, no doubt observing details I missed.

Without stopping, we crossed the entrance hall and went out into the cold, bright morning, following the house round to the right as the soldier directed. We passed the walled kitchen garden and went through a gate into an avenue lined by tall hedges. Holmes looked small and ancient, wrapped up in his blanket, and I can't imagine the pain he must have been in as we rattled along. I felt awful, too, exhausted and sore but also with a deep foreboding that his trust in me might not be warranted, and we would find nothing very unusual.

Then we saw the smoke. It curled above the hedge ahead of us, merging with the grey and wintry sky. Holmes glanced up at me, his expression grim. We went on, through a neat arch in the hedge, and out onto a muddy, untended lawn. At one side stood a bonfire, flames flickering bright even in the daylight. The plume of smoke shrouded a grey, diminutive figure, prodding at the bonfire with a stick. Her focus was entirely on the fire, so she didn't hear our party approach until we were almost on her. Then she turned to us, a welcoming smile on her lined, wizened features.

"Good morning," said Matron, quite agreeably. "I'm glad to see you back with us, Augusta. Mr Holmes, I hope you are not unwell."

"I have been better," said Holmes, bundled up in his blanket. "But I thank you for your concern. Are all the records destroyed?"

"The paperwork burns quickly," nodded Matron. "It's the cabinets themselves that take some time. I'm sure there's very little left."

"Then you don't deny it."

Matron's smile faltered. "Is something amiss?"

"You are burning official documents," said Holmes. "I should say that was a crime."

Matron blanched. "I am following orders that come direct from the general. All non-essential documents, he said."

"But you've taken everything from the ward," I protested. Matron's eyes flashed up at me, indignant that I would dare speak to her in such a fashion. Then, with visible effort, she calmed herself.

"Indeed," she told us. "To make space for more beds."

Holmes leant a little forward with interest. He had, I felt sure, made the same assessment as Dulcie and me – that the liberated space was not wide enough to accommodate a bed.

"I haven't burned everything," Matron told us. "The important records have all been retained. I can show you if you insist."

"If that would not be too much trouble," Holmes told her.

"Of course," she said, gritting her teeth.

We followed her back to the building. There were figures at the windows, a few staff and patients watching with mild interest. We retraced our steps past the ornamental garden and round to the front. An elegant staff car now stood in the driveway. At the sight of it, Matron quickened her pace.

"The general," she said. "He must be inside."

"I am not quite ready to receive him," said Holmes. "Could someone go in and tell the general I shall be with him presently. I should like first to see these files, to set my mind at rest."

Matron and the soldiers immediately turned to me, and I started to protest that – despite appearances – I was not some errand boy. Dulcie, however, patted my arm. "I'll do it," she said, "if you're sure you'll be all right."

Holmes seemed rather taken by this gesture, reaching an arm from under his blanket so that he could clasp Dulcie's hand.

"Your kindness is much appreciated," he told her. "I should be quite lost without Augusta."

She was just as baffled by this uncharacteristic display as I was, and had to pull her hand from his grip before hurrying inside. I wrapped Holmes back up in the blanket and he looked even more pale and sickly, his eyes flicking with that same fearfulness I'd seen before, when he thought his powers had failed him.

"You're sure you're feeling all right?" I said, aware of the others watching.

"We are almost at the end," he told me, breathlessly. "I should like to see it through if I can. Please, Sister Gloria, let us continue."

Matron looked to me for confirmation but I would not have contradicted Holmes for all the world. With a nod from me, Matron led us further along, round the side of the building, following the gravel driveway. The soldier pushing the wheelchair went as carefully as he could, flanked by me on one side, Walker on the other, the other soldiers trailing us.

Once round the side of the building, the drive sloped steeply, leading down to the underground garage that had been converted into the morgue. With some trepidation, having never liked the place, I followed the others down the slope. A second soldier helped with the wheelchair.

Matron had a key for the lock, but struggled with the heavy door. One of the soldiers hurried over to help and it creaked slowly open towards us. We stepped into that dark, awful catacomb, the smell quite overpowering.

Unlike before, there were no bodies on the rows of tables now, just the ominous dark stains where they had rested. A bespectacled mortician got up quickly from the desk in the corner that Holmes had searched through a few nights before. Matron told the man to take a tea break, and he scurried away up the back stairs.

"The files are there," Matron told us, indicating the line of cabinets by the desk – the very ones Holmes had looked through that first night. "We co-ordinated the morgue records with those of the ward, and anything we had two of has gone on the fire. It seemed rather sensible when the general suggested the idea."

The tables blocked the path of the wheelchair, so Holmes gestured to me and I wended my way through to look.

"Mr Holmes, you're not well," said Matron suddenly. I turned to see her hauling the blanket away from him. Walker hurried over to assist, and Matron dumped the heaped blanket into his arms. He couldn't see anything over the top of it, but Matron put her hand to his hip to guide him…

And slipped the pistol from his holster.

I shouted a warning and Walker dropped the blankets. But by then the other soldiers all had their guns on us. I glanced back towards the stairs at the back of the room, but there was no chance I would make such a distance before I had been shot – and I would never abandon Holmes.

Matron held Walker's pistol on Holmes, a cruel smile on her face. "You were right," she taunted him. "We are now at the end."

It looked as though she would shoot him there and then. But, in his pyjamas, one leg bound tight in bandages, Holmes sat back in the wheelchair, his eyes shining bright.

"It's not too late, Sister Gloria," he told her, his old wily, infuriating self. "I might yet save your life."

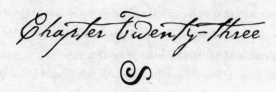

Chapter Twenty-three

Matron laughed at him. I don't think I'd ever heard her laugh before, an unlikely, throaty roar from that small, wiry nun. But then she evidently wasn't at all who I had thought her to be. She brandished the gun in Holmes's face.

"I suppose," she said, "you deduced everything hours ago and know every part of the business."

"There may be one or two small details you can elucidate," said Holmes, agreeably. "Otherwise, you are correct."

Matron hit him savagely across the face with the gun. "Rubbish! You know nothing! If you had even suspected, you would not have delivered yourself, Miss Watson and this poor, loyal soldier to their doom. No, Mr Holmes, you have got it wrong. The mistake will now prove fatal."

The blow to the head had left a bloody gash on his temple but Holmes gazed up at her, smiling pleasantly.

"If you surrender, you and your associates will face court martial, where you can at least make your case. If you shoot us, the general will shoot all of you. That would be a waste of everyone's lives. Don't you think, perhaps, that enough blood has been shed?"

Matron scowled at him. "I'll tell the general that Walker turned on you and Miss Watson, that he must have been part of the plot. We stopped him, of course, but too late for you."

"Somehow, I don't think he'll believe you," said Holmes, then tilted his head to call out. "Will you, general?"

There was no answer. Matron started to smile. And then, quite distinctly, from the slope leading up to the drive, came a familiar growl. "Not bloody likely! Sister Gloria, I have a squad here and men on the stairs. There is no way out of this for you. We've also raked through the fire and salvaged a fair chunk of those files. Very interesting reading, damn you."

Sure enough, soldiers were now creeping down the slope and into view, rifles raised at Matron and the men with their guns on Walker and me. Those men looked to Matron for guidance, but she stared furiously down at Holmes.

"How?" she asked him.

"Simplicity itself," he said. "I passed a note to Nurse O'Brien when I took her hand. It was easy enough to write it, concealed by the blanket."

Matron shook her head. "But how did you know it was me?"

"The bonfire clinched it," he said. "You have the ward to run and who knows what other duties, yet you made time to tend the fire yourself, alone and just out of view of the building. Surely that could only be because no one else might be trusted to destroy incriminating evidence."

"They're just files," she said. "Nothing out of the ordinary." Yet her tone was flat, defeated.

"Once we were onto the betting slips, you knew those files could betray you," said Holmes. "You invented orders from the general to have them moved off the ward. I admit I was a little slow in putting it together. You did not have access to the general's secret tallies at the Chateau, but the slips you secreted into officers' pockets had to be convincing if they were to drive those poor men mad. A random list of numbers would not suffice, and the most effective lies have some basis in truth. Well then, the hospital records each day's intake of new patients, which you then multiplied by some factor. That way, the figures on the slips would accord with what the officers already knew – their first-hand experience of which days had seen greater or fewer losses. It would seem only too credible, for all you made it seem to them that the losses were very much worse."

The gun in Matron's hand wavered, but still pointed in Holmes's face. "You really think that would be enough to drive a man mad?"

Holmes sighed. "I think men have already been going mad. They have been weighed down by pressures unique in the history of war. Of course, you've been in a position to observe the effects of shell shock at first hand. You did not recoil from such an appalling malady; you saw a way to exploit it."

"Ridiculous," she said. "Such a thing would never be possible."

"We have arrested George Ludders," Holmes told her – and despite herself, she flinched. "He wasn't merely secreting these slips into officers' pockets," Holmes went on. "Walker here tells me Ludders ran a whispering campaign against officers on the front line." I saw Walker's look of surprise – but then we had both thought Holmes unconscious in the ambulance when Walker had shared this detail. "Augusta," Holmes continued, "told me on my first night here about a soldier-made newspaper that had to be banned."

"That played into our hands," said Matron, icily. "It showed the ordinary soldiers were not trusted with the truth."

"The truth," said Holmes, with scorn.

"Yes!" snapped Matron. "You of all people should be able to see the evidence. The treatment of the ordinary man! The scale of loss, the sacrifice expected!"

"But then look at what you've done," I said, outraged. "You've only made it worse!"

"To bring about revolution," said Matron, regarding me with malevolence. "You're a great disappointment, Augusta Watson. You seemed to grasp the idea of liberation, for man and woman alike. You embraced honest toil and yet burned with injustice that all things are not equal."

"It was easy enough to kindle such passion," said Holmes. "You thwarted all her ambitions to progress in medicine."

Matron actually looked sorry as she held my gaze. "I thought you would be with us in spirit. Instead, you had your head turned by the very man who made your childhood so intolerable."

I stared at her. "You knew."

"Mention was made of it in the reference I had from your school. The curious detail that you would never allow yourself to achieve anything of note because a few girls once called you names. I, at least, saw your true potential."

"You thought you could mould me, as you have everyone else."

"I hoped," said Matron, "that we might make a better future. One where we could all live on equal terms. What I have done has all been to that end. I am sorry to discover that you do not want the same."

"That's not fair," I told her, but in truth I was shaking.

"Does he treat you as an equal?" Matron asked me. "Do you really think he will?"

Holmes gazed back at me levelly, blood dripping down his face and onto his pyjamas. What an ordeal we had been through, I thought. How much we had suffered together.

"Yes," I told Matron, and meant it.

I saw the fight go out of her then. She still held the gun on Holmes, but her whole body sagged. Her soldiers saw it too, as did General Fitzgerald. The great walrus of a man had made his way down the ramp and now stepped inside the morgue, hands raised in front of him to show he was not armed – though the soldiers flanking him were.

Matron now turned the gun on him. The general raised his hands a little higher, but he did not back down. Holmes, in the wheelchair just to Matron's side, shook his head sadly.

"You cannot kill the general," he said. "That would not do at all. Not if, as I instructed, he is unarmed." He didn't look round to see. "That takes courage, doesn't it? The sort of thing to impress the common soldier. Your own men here feel it, I am sure. It is not the thing to shoot an unarmed man. It would be the same if you shot Walker or Miss Watson – or, for that matter, me. To do so would be calamitous for your cause. Word would soon spread, inviting the scorn of the very men you seek to set free. Of course, you could do it anyway. Or, just this once, you might act with honour."

He said it mildly enough, but it was twisting the knife. He had ensnared her, defeated her, and she knew it all too well.

"If I surrender," Matron said to the general, "I expect you to treat my men fairly."

"You have my word," he said.

She handed him her gun.

* * *

Things after that are a bit of a blur. They led Matron and her soldiers away, and I had started to tend to the cut on Holmes's temple when more nurses arrived and shooed me out of the way. He was wheeled back up to the ward and I followed after him in something of a daze until Dulcie found me. Then I was in her and Lobelia Darlington's care. I remember Dulcie tucking me into bed and thinking I could never, ever sleep after all that I had witnessed. Then I slept for an entire day.

The nurses took turns to watch over me, apparently. When I eventually woke, they vied with one another to help me wash and bathe, changing my dressings and generally fussing round. All I wanted was to pull some clothes on and get down to the ward so that I could check on Holmes. They insisted that first I eat something, and I wolfed down two servings of full English breakfast – a rare treat given our privations.

The staff and patients applauded when I at last arrived on the ward, and I hobbled down the aisle, blushing scarlet. Holmes looked thin and frail in his bed, and they'd given him something for the pain that made our first conversation slightly dreamy. I sat with him and held his hand while Lieutenant Dale read us poetry, all "silver dusk" and "thick goldcup flowers", to which Oberman in the next bed pulled agonised faces.

Later, perhaps another day, General Fitzgerald looked in on us. Holmes was more alert by then and quizzed the general on all that we had missed. The general remained guarded, I thought because we were on the open ward. I didn't learn the half of it until much later, after Holmes returned to London.

I well remember our last afternoon together, the memories suffused with the smell of the Christmas tree they had put up on the ward. Holmes was back in his dark, old-fashioned suit, the bullet holes in the leg having been expertly stitched by one of the nurses. He could get about quite well with a walking stick by then, but he was irritable and restless. I tried to entertain him with some small observations about Mrs Lloyd, the new Matron who had been imposed on us. Holmes rather snapped at me that he did not care. There were more sharp words, I do not remember what, and I took myself off to make some tea rather than say something I would later regret.

When I returned, he had gone. It transpired that he had that morning ordered a car to Calais, where he had passage on a ship. He had not thought to mention it to me and he did not say goodbye.

I shall not claim I was not crushed by that, but I do not think Holmes could cope with parting in any other way. Besides, I threw myself into work and the new regime. There was plenty to do, not least because Mrs Lloyd decided that I could make myself more useful by qualifying as a nurse. Dulcie had led a campaign on my behalf; it turned out that she and the other nurses had all believed, via Sister Gloria, that I had no aptitude for nursing but thought I was entitled to a position on the staff due to my family and background. Now, they supported and encouraged me to get on, and that kept me occupied through the early months of 1918, as did piecing together the last details of the conspiracy.

The general would not tell me anything directly. He now visited the hospital at least once each week, as well as touring the trenches in a renewed effort to share the burdens of the men. But I only ever saw him in passing, both of us too caught up in our duties. The army authorities did not see the need to inform a lowly woman like me what had transpired, either. Most of it I squirrelled out of Lieutenant Dale, who took an admin job at the Chateau but still called in to see us because of ongoing grief from his leg. Poor lamb:

the more he asked what I had seen and done in the company of the great Sherlock Holmes, the more I said I didn't know – and the more he tried to prompt me by sharing further crumbs. I deduced a few other things, too, and built up my picture.

Sister Gloria and the other conspirators were all shot by firing squad. That came as a shock, not least because the general had promised to treat them fairly. I think he would have answered that the court martial had indeed been conducted without prejudice. He was particularly aggrieved because the inquiry revealed that his own secretary, the oleaginous Monty, had been in on the plot. He and at least a dozen others were rooted out and shot. I suppose it is fair that Matron died as an equal, on the same terms as the men.

Captain Boyce died, too, leading a charge on the enemy lines in August 1918. Sergeant Oberman died suddenly of complications from his wounds a little after that, which was a blow to all of us on the ward. A lot of men died before the war was finally over. Jack Walker, at least, went home to meet his son.

Lobelia Darlington and Jill Sullivan both married men they met as patients. Dulcie teases that either one of us might yet do the same. I tell her I should first have to grow out my hair – but she prefers the boyish look, batwing ears and all.

The only other person I know about is Generalmajor Meyer, who wrote a report of his dealings with Holmes for a German 'paper. You'll see from my own account of what transpired that his version is good as far as it goes, but it misses much of the context. He mentions, too, that Captain Weich was wounded before the end of hostilities, but provides no further detail.

Then, of course, there is Holmes. I assumed he went home to his bees, or whatever it was they said in the stories. When Dulcie and I enrolled at Guy's to begin our training as doctors, I felt a sudden compulsion that Holmes should know. I did not expect a reply, let alone for the great detective to cross the river and turn up on St Thomas's Street.

"Miss Watson, we are needed!" he announced from his cab.

Well, you know all that followed, Dr Watson, as it was then that I first made your acquaintance. Nonetheless, do write and say if, for the sake of your archive, you should also care for my own account of those remarkable events.

Acknowledgements

Thanks to Cat Camacho, George Sandison, Dan Coxon, Natasha Qureshi and everyone at Titan. I discussed aspects of this story, or of Sherlock Holmes more generally, with Samira Ahmed, Scott K. Andrews, Dr Niall Boyce of the *Lancet Psychiatry*, Dr Debbie Challis, Subhadra Das, Mark Gatiss, Tom Guerrier, Bryn Morgan, Dr Philip Purser-Hallard, Dr Matthew Sweet and Ben Woodhams, thieving their ideas like some Napoleon of Typing. All errors are, of course, mine. The Institute of English Studies' 2019 symposium "Conan Doyle and London" prompted useful thoughts, especially about the influence of Doyle's medical training on Holmes's methods and outlook, and I'm grateful to Professor Roger Luckhurst for directing me to Doyle's collection of medical stories, *Round The Red Lamp*. I bought a battered first edition for my Dad for what turned out to be his last Christmas and talked through with him some of what I intended here. This novel is dedicated to Dad's memory with love.

About the Author

Simon Guerrier is the author of a great many *Doctor Who* books, audio plays and comics and has written some sixty audio plays for Big Finish Productions, including his original series *Graceless*, broadcast on BBC Radio 4 Extra. He is also lead writer on an animated TV series being developed by Visionality. He tweets @0tralala